*W*hat the critics are saying…

❧

"Storytelling that flows this effortlessly makes a pleasant and satisfying read. *A Certain Want of Reason* is truly exhilarating, one of the best regency romances I have ever read." ~ *Coffee Time Romance*

"a merry romp…truly delightful." ~*Romance Reviews Today*

A Certain Want of Reason

Kate Dolan

Cerridwen Cotillion

Hope you enjoy it!

A Cerridwen Press Publication

www.cerridwenpress.com

A Certain Want of Reason

ISBN 9781419950551
ALL RIGHTS RESERVED.
A Certain Want of Reason Copyright © 2007 Kate Dolan
Edited by Mary Altman
Cover art by Lissa Waitley

Electronic book Publication February 2007
Trade paperback Publication April 2007

Excerpt from *Captain's Lady* Copyright © Sharon Milburn, 2007

Cerridwen Press is an imprint of Ellora's Cave Publishing, Inc.®

About the Author

හ

After coming from Chicago to attend college at the Catholic University of America in Washington, DC, Kate Dolan grew attached to the mid-Atlantic region and never moved back. She holds an interdisciplinary degree in English, history and drama and a law degree from the University of Richmond School of Law, and has written professionally in a variety of fields since 1992. Currently living in a suburb of Baltimore, she is ideally positioned to drag her husband and two children to visit an endless array of historical sites. She also volunteers as a living historian in order to teach-and learn-more about the past. In addition to historical romance, Kate also writes history, historical fiction and mysteries.

Kate welcomes comments from readers. You can find her website and email address on her author bio page at www.cerridwenpress.com.

A CERTAIN WANT OF REASON

Dedication

∞

To my mother, Betty Dolan, who had the good sense to give me my first Jane Austen book and even better sense to let me wait until I was ready to read it. Thanks, Mom!

Chapter One

London 1816

"We've done it!"

Lucia Wright looked around for the source of the exclamation, knocked her knife off her plate and made a futile grab for the implement as it skittered across her lap and down the front of the tablecloth, leaving a trail of butter grease and orange marmalade in its wake. It came to rest against the table leg just out of her reach. With an apologetic glance at her friend Eugenie, she returned her attention to the informal, bustling breakfast table at the Bayles' home—a much livelier meal than she could ever imagine having at home in the country with her brother and sister.

Eugenie's sister Sophie waved a buff-colored card with a triumphant flourish before setting it in front of her father. "An invitation to the Adrington soirée."

"Congratulations, my dear." Mr. Bayles smiled as he spoke to his daughter but kept his attention focused on a slice of toast as he succeeded in spreading marmalade just to the very edge without running over the sides. Only then did he look up to speak to Sophie directly. "You've worked with exceeding diligence to make the acquaintance in time."

"And put in a fair bit of unwarranted flattery," Eugenie added with grin.

"What was that about flattery?" Mrs. Bayles asked, her hand poised in midair as she prepared to strike the lethal blow to the shell of her boiled egg.

"Nothing directed at you, Mother," Eugenie assured her. She winked at Lucia, then turned her gaze toward the door. "Ah, morning mail. I thought I heard the bell a moment ago. You'll forgive us if we read at the breakfast table? It is rude with a guest in the house, but you see, we shall all behave as if you were one of the family."

As if waiting for his cue, a footman entered and began circling the breakfast table, depositing a few cards in front of diners who received them with varying degrees of interest. To Lucia's surprise, a letter appeared in front of her plate as well—a letter addressed in Helen's faint, half-inked scrawl. She reached out to take the folded paper into her hands but could not bring herself to open it.

"I see that my sister already usurped your role as the bearer of good tidings, Allen," Eugenie offered sympathetically to the footman as he turned away.

Allen nodded, a hurt expression barely visible in his eyes.

"Do you see what I must contend with here?" Eugenie asked Lucia. "Sophie, you are the cruelest sister imaginable. The one joy that man gets is to be the conduit of communication, and you have to go and wrest the letter from his hand."

"He never took hold of it, actually." Sophie sucked at a paper cut on her finger. "I saw the postman from the window and managed to reach the—"

"You did *what?*" Mrs. Bayles demanded, pointing her spoon accusingly at her daughter.

"Nothing, Mother." Sophie suppressed a giggle, casting a guilty glance at both her sister and Lucia before resolutely focusing her gaze on her plate.

"I heard something about the door," Mrs. Bayles insisted.

"No, I was, um, pacing the *floor*. Waiting for the post."

"Oh." Mrs. Bayles' expression faded from disbelief to disinterest.

Lucia glanced at the letter in her hand, then tucked it under her plate. Why would Helen have written so soon? Lucia had only reached London the previous evening, so her sister would have had to have posted the letter less than a day after Lucia's departure. Could something disastrous have transpired in such a short interval? It seemed unlikely, and yet...

"Look, look at this one!" Sophie hoisted another card to wave about the table, this one the hue of dried pea soup.

"That is truly a hideous color," Eugenie pronounced. "Nothing that color should be permitted to exist."

"Not the color, you cake. The crest. The Earl of Rathley. An invitation to his ball, as well."

Lucia kept her gaze focused on Eugenie and Sophie so that she would not look at her sister's letter.

"No more than we expected, of course." Mr. Bayles eyed his toast from another angle. "Since his cousin—"

"Yes, yes, I know," Sophie interrupted. "But it's a relief to have the invitation in hand. And then Tulliver has secured tickets for the opera for tomorrow." She stuffed a piece of cold partridge into her mouth.

Mrs. Bayles slammed her cup of chocolate onto the table, setting all the dishes clattering as she glared at Sophie. "You really must not do that, dear!"

"'oo 'at?" Sophie appeared stunned at her mother's outburst.

Eugenie leaned in toward her. "Talk with your mouth full, dear sister."

Sophie swallowed. "What did I do, Mother?"

"You should not refer to the baronet as 'Tulliver'. It is most unseemly."

"He does not mind it."

"Does that mean it is acceptable for her to speak with her mouth full?" Eugenie demanded.

Lucia smothered a laugh, thoroughly enjoying the feminine repartee she had not experienced since her days in school.

Mrs. Bayles ignored Eugenie and kept her gaze riveted on her other daughter. "Have you actually addressed the baronet in such an informal fashion?"

Sophie shrugged. "On occasion."

"Oh, dear." Mrs. Bayles shuddered.

"And with your mouth full of bacon, too, no doubt." Eugenie affected a shudder that would have been sufficient for both herself and her mother.

"We shall discuss this later," Mrs. Bayles announced with a meaningful look at Sophie.

"Ahem." Mr. Bayles looked up. "Would you please stop shuddering? You've set the dishes to rattle again."

"Sorry, Papa."

Mr. Bayles then turned his gaze to Lucia for the first time that morning. "What is our guest to think? You two girls prattling on about bacon and earls while the poor girl is trying to read a letter."

Silence hung almost palpably over the table for exactly three seconds.

"I am sorry, dear. Do not mind us a bit." Eugenie patted Lucia's hand. "Is that a letter from one of the twins?"

"It…it is." Lucia looked down at the paper under her plate with some reluctance. It was far more fun to observe the Bayles family antics than to contemplate those of her own family.

"I hope all is well at home?"

"I hope so too. I've not had time to read as much yet."

"You mean you've not had the opportunity." Eugenie smiled. "We have been nattering on too much. I promise to keep as silent as the grave while you read your letter. You must as well, Sophie."

"I must what?"

"Must promise to keep silent as the grave."

"The grave?" Sophie grimaced. "Can we not pick something a little less morbid for the breakfast table?"

"Very well. As silent as…for the life of me, I cannot think of something silent."

"I wonder why?" Mr. Bayles sighed.

"Never mind. Silent as the grave." Eugenie nodded at Lucia. "I promise."

Lucia picked up the letter warily. "Perhaps I should read it later."

"Nonsense. It is from your family. You must read it now. We will keep silence." Eugenie looked around the table with a ferocious gaze. Then her expression abruptly changed. "Oh—is that the card from the Adringtons?"

"I must say, Eugenie, if ever I came across a grave as noisy as yours, I would send for an occultist straightaway." Sophie handed the card to her sister.

Eugenie's eyes widened. "I am so sorry, Lucia."

"Lucia, I think you may as well learn to ignore your dear school chum and go ahead and read while she is talking," Sophie offered.

Lucia forced a smile. "If you must know, my sister's writing is rather...difficult to decipher. It takes a bit of concentration to read one of her letters."

"I comprehend you perfectly," Eugenie replied with a conspiratorial nod. "My sister also writes with a dreadful hand."

Lucia smiled again. Would that handwriting were the only difficulty! The inanity of her sister Helen's prose, interspersed as it was with miscellaneous measured observations, made it virtually impossible to discern the actual news of the letter. Yet with Geoffrey in the house, Helen was sure to have news of some sort, the only question being whether her news was slightly bad, amusingly bad or terribly bad.

Due to some miracle—or perhaps the fresh rack of toast Allen had just placed on the table—the room fell silent long enough for Lucia to plunge into her sister's narrative with grim determination.

After a few horrendous minutes, Lucia pulled herself free from her sister's words when she realized someone was speaking to her. "I'm sorry. What did you say?" She could not even have told who had called her.

"I said, you've picked a most fortuitous time for a visit, Miss Wright." Mr. Bayles waved his toast, which was still unmarred by any signs of consumption. "What with the earl's ball, the opera and now the Adrington soirée, your visit could not get off to a more splendid start. What say you?"

"I must go home." Lucia set down the letter with determination.

"What?" Mrs. Bayles' empty chocolate cup clattered to the table.

"Surely you jest, Miss Wright." The toast faltered in Mr. Bayles' hand.

Eugenie leaned over to Lucia and patted her arm with reassurance. "I know you worry about your brother and sister. And after a good visit, you will—"

Lucia shook her head. "I must go home now. Today."

Eugenie abandoned her toast with only the faintest hint of reluctance. "Perhaps we'd better excuse ourselves from the company."

"Yes, thank you." Lucia stood, faltering a bit as she stepped on the knife she had knocked off the table earlier. "I need to…but, Eugenie, you need not—"

"Oh yes, I need to." Eugenie had bounded to her feet and pulled Lucia halfway to the door before she could protest.

"Do you not want to finish your—"

"No. Let us go. A pleasant morning to you all!" Eugenie waved cheerily as she pushed Lucia out the door and into the hall. Once outside the room, her grin vanished. "We will discuss the matter upstairs."

"Eugenie, this is not for—"

"I will not let you leave this time." Eugenie dragged her toward the stairs.

"But you do not understand." Lucia wrenched her arm free. "Geoffrey —"

"I will not stand by and let Geoffrey ruin your life."

"Well." Lucia smiled weakly. "I am afraid it's rather a bit too late for that."

* * * * *

"So you see," Lucia stared at the chest of drawers in Eugenie's bedroom as she concluded her narrative, "I have to go home now."

"No, I do not see. I think it is wonderful that Geoffrey's taken a pastime."

Lucia snorted in derision, her embarrassment at the rude sound eroded by her disgust at the contemplation of her brother's habits. "Geoffrey does not take up pastimes. He takes on occupations."

"So? Whatever he chooses to call it, it will keep him busy and it will keep him out of the house."

"If any of the house remains," Lucia muttered.

"What?"

"Listen, Eugenie. You don't understand about Geoffrey. He…proceeds with rather more zeal than sense. When Geoffrey took up the practice of law, he stole our neighbor's horse so he could then offer representation in a conversion action. He was most distressed when Mrs. MacGill refused his offer to represent her in her suit against himself. When he wanted to be a blacksmith, he decided he could get the hottest fire from the fireplace in the main drawing room. He started building a forge — we've never come up with a good way to cover the scorch marks on the floor. In preparation for his planned life as a naval officer, he sank the tea chest and two chests of flatware in a mock battle in Blackridge pond. Last month, he decided he was going to be a chimney sweep, despite the fact that he's nearly eighteen years of age and taller than many full-grown men. He got stuck somewhere between the flue to the dining room and the one leading to his bedroom. It took three local men the better part of an afternoon to free him—and he was still occasionally coughing up wads of black phlegm when I left." She smacked her hands together with a sigh, wishing that once, just once, her family could manage without her having to oversee every minute detail of daily life. "I never should have gone off. He simply cannot be trusted on his own."

"But he's not on his own. Your sister, Helen, is with him and she can take care of him for a few weeks. Or your stepfather—surely he might help."

"Helen is not much better, I'm afraid."

"What? I knew Geoffrey was always a bit of a difficult cracker, but you've never let on that Helen, that dear young thing, was… Well, how bad is she?"

"Not as bad as Geoffrey, of course. Not yet, at least. And her…eccentricities aren't so dangerous. Of course, one day she did fall into the river while collecting her daily sample, but on the whole—"

"Her sample?"

"She collects samples of river water at certain times of the day."

"Oh. That sounds rather…scientific of her."

"Yes, she catalogs her samples in a very studious manner, and some of her findings have even piqued interest at the Royal Society." Lucia sighed. "I just wish she wouldn't insist on keeping all of her collections."

"So she cannot keep an eye on your brother."

"No. Not unless he decides to take up a career as a gill of river water or a measure of garden soil."

"But your stepfather, now, surely he can help."

Lucia shook her head sadly. "I am the only one who can take care of them. My stepfather rarely comes near the house. Or the county, for that matter. I think he cannot bear to see how they are. Or perhaps they remind him too much of Mother. Who knows? He has his solicitor ensure that we've adequate funds to keep the estate, but not enough to run away. And so there we shall all stay, as he says, 'perfectly comfortable together for all our days'."

This time it was Eugenie who snorted. "Perfectly dreadful together, I'd say."

Lucia smiled. "It's not dreadful at all. I love Helen, and Geoffrey too. He really is the sweetest boy. And I know they love me. We've enough money to meet our needs. And so we *shall* all be 'perfectly comfortable' for—"

"Rubbish. If you were perfectly happy, you would not have come here."

"But that was a mistake, I told you. I simply wanted to see your family again. And to see London as—"

"As a grown lady. The places we were not allowed before."

Lucia let a small giggle escape her lips. "Yes, exactly."

"You cannot see those places if you leave now."

"I know," Lucia sighed, "but Geoffrey—"

"How is it that Geoffrey controls your life even when he is miles away?"

Lucia sighed again. "I've told you of his previous forays into the working world. Now Helen tells me he intends to take up hunting."

"Good. The exercise will be splendid, and it is only dangerous for the fox, you know."

"No, not hunting for sport. Geoffrey intends to 'put meat on the table', as she phrased it. He's secured a rifle and has been shooting at targets in the garden. Helen said he takes the occasional shot at the chickens in the Johnson's yard. Apparently Geoffrey's next intended occupation is to work as a poacher. Mr. Johnson has never had much patience with Geoffrey. And *he's* said to be an excellent shot." Lucia shook her head, resignation already pushing aside all thoughts of the exciting visit she had anticipated for nearly a year. "So you see, I must return home."

Eugenie nodded as if in agreement, but something in her eyes indicated that she did not agree at all.

* * * * *

"Would you like to have Peggy arrange your hair?"

"No." Lucia could barely conceal her frustration as she paced in front of the chest of drawers in Eugenie's room for the third day in a row. "What good would that do?"

"It would save the wear on the carpet from you pacing back and forth."

Lucia sank into the nearest chair. "I am sorry. I just do not see any point to all this fuss. I should be packing to leave, not primping for somebody's soirée." It was unfair for her to take out her aggravation on her friend, but the constant worry for Geoffrey and Helen's safety had worn her nerves to shreds. Never before had she felt so helpless.

"You cannot leave until Father is ready to escort you. Unless you've brought money to hire a private carriage?"

Lucia looked down at the floor, twisting her slipper around the leg of her chair. "No, I have not."

"That was not fair of me and I am sorry. You should not travel on your own in any case. And while you wait for Father, you may as well enjoy the attractions of the city you came to visit."

"I came to visit you and your family, not a city."

"You came for both, and I perfectly understand. But to use your own argument, it would be poor manners indeed for you to leave without a proper visit. You've not had full benefit of our company yet."

"Very well, you know I've agreed to stay on until Saturday. But I do not see why I must accompany you out tonight."

"You must accompany me because any unattached *femme* in her right mind would sell her soul for an opportunity to meet the gentlemen of Adrington's acquaintance."

"I'm not in the market, Eugenie."

"We'll see about that."

Chapter Two

ॐ

"You realize that you are not truly obligated to marry her."

Edmund Rutherford turned at the sound of his friend Adrington's low voice. "Oh, but I am," he answered softly as they watched a small circle of ladies and gentlemen flirt with one another across the room.

"No court in the land would hold that promise enforceable. And a breach of marriage suit may be paid off like any other," Adrington insisted.

One of the ladies in the group they watched, dressed in a sheer yellow gown that glowed almost translucent under the bright light of the chandelier, tipped her head back too far and uttered a coarse laugh that echoed off the polished marble floor.

Edmund closed his eyes for a moment but did not allow himself to turn away. "The promise was made on her mother's deathbed. Her family relies upon the connection, the acquisition of the title. My mother promised hers that our families would be joined forever by the match." He shook his head. "Such a promise cannot be set aside like an inconvenient contract for the sale of a horse."

"So you would have yourself bound to the purchase of that animal, whether or not you want it, regardless of the fact that it might perhaps have been ridden before?"

Edmund sighed. "Choose your words with care, sir, for though you are my closest friend and we stand in your house, I will not let you cast aspersions on my intended bride."

"Who said anything about Miss Newman?" Lord James Adrington smiled. "I thought we spoke of horses. Come, I do not believe you have yet paid your respects to Mother and Aunt Darlet."

Edmund allowed himself to be turned away toward the back of the room where older ladies and gentlemen not inclined to dance or speculate on the matches to be made during the season had already begun to size up potential whist opponents. The same annoying laugh echoed across the floor behind him, but now he no longer had to watch Jeanne.

He only had to listen. Every so often, as he exchanged pleasantries with Adrington's older relations, he could discern Jeanne's voice above that of the others, followed by that almost ribald laughter. He could imagine the flirtatious flip of her eyelashes, her pouting lips, a playful slap on a companion's arm—all gestures of which he had long since tired but other gentlemen seemed to still find intriguing.

Why, then, could one of them not be engaged to marry her instead?

"Rutherford, I do hope you will excuse me. I must see to some other guests. I suggest you try some of the Madeira—it is good enough to enable you to forget your troubles with remarkable speed."

Edmund nodded. "And everything else as well, I imagine. Very well, I shall endeavor to obtain a healthy glass of your remedy."

But once Adrington had left his side, Edmund decided to seek solace not in drink but in solitude. Because he had to think.

For the past two years, he had tried every imaginable means of discouraging Jeanne Newman from sustaining the betrothal arranged for them at her birth. But she would not be discouraged. Nor would she keep her flirtatious behavior in check. Any words from him seemed only to encourage her to greater indiscretions. Or else it would lead to a tearful scene where she begged him to set a date, accusing him of breaking the promise and failing his obligation.

For some time now, he had used his mother's poor health as an excuse, but such justification could not be used forever, and indeed his mother's condition had improved to the point where she herself encouraged him to set a date.

He knew, of course, that he should simply accept the arrangement—a very common circumstance to which other men, and ladies, too, resigned themselves as a matter of course. Heaven knew there were enough examples even in his own family. Loveless marriage was the rule rather than the exception.

But Edmund wanted to be the exception. He at least wanted to live out his days in a home with a woman for whom he bore some respect, if not outright affection. For Jeanne, he felt only a mild loathing mingled with pity. She deserved better than that. He wanted better than that. And Jeanne possessed sufficient beauty and fortune to secure a better suitor once she let go of her attachment to him.

So he would force her to let go.

In his deliberations, he wandered down the hall from the ballroom into a small, unoccupied parlor where he paced back and forth like a great caged animal. Two hideous chairs with ridiculous clawed feet took up nearly one entire side of the parlor, so he could cross to the fireplace at the other end of the room in only three steps.

Two, if he lengthened his stride.

The gilt framed mirror above the mantel reflected dark creases on his forehead as his scowl deepened with each turn about the room. What else could he possibly do? He had tried asking her, tried reasoning with her, warned her of the pitfalls of an unhappy marriage. He had tried to discourage her by being inattentive. When that failed, he attempted the opposite extreme, hoping to frighten the girl. Unfortunately, his forward behavior only served to encourage her further.

And now, he had little time left.

He had to somehow make himself so undesirable that Jeanne would not be able to bear the thought of marrying him. If she ended the engagement, then he could not be faulted for breaking the promise.

So what would make him so very undesirable? He could threaten her with violence. Lord knows he had been tempted to often enough over the years. But he might well end up in Newgate or the criminal wing at Bedlam. Even the prospect of spending the rest of his life with a shrew was not enough to tempt him to risk that fate.

But what if he were sent away someplace only temporarily? Perhaps he could act irrational—not dangerous, but simply mad, as if he'd entirely lost his sense of reason. They would hide him away in a private madhouse for a time, Jeanne could continue her season in London and she might well have secured a good husband before summer. Then he could "recover" and quietly return home. His friends would eventually forgive the deception. And while his own chances of making a decent match would be none too great after such an episode, the chances with such an experiment still exceeded the chances without it, which appeared to be zero.

Tonight would be the perfect time to begin. With so many in attendance to witness his behavior, Jeanne would be mortified.

Edmund stopped pacing and stared at his reflection from across the room. The dark scowl had been replaced by a look of fierce determination. He crossed the small room with one great leap, his reflection drawing closer and larger and even more determined.

And that's how it would start. He would make a ridiculous leaping entrance back into the ballroom.

He took a deep breath and marched toward the door, anxious to begin before he could give any attention to the nagging thought that perhaps there were aspects of this plan he had not considered.

This was a time for action, not consideration.

The buzz of voices as he approached the ballroom indicated an even greater number of guests in attendance than earlier. A full audience to view his performance. Withers, the Adringtons' butler, smiled as Edmund approached, but the smile evaporated as Edmund pushed him aside and leaped into the room.

Just as he had done in the tiny red parlor, he leaped across the floor, covering as many of the colored tiles as possible with each stride. In no time at all, he had crossed the room, so that he had to stop abruptly to keep from crashing into the punch bowl. He turned and began to traverse the floor in the opposite direction, deliberately ignoring all comments voiced by other guests. In the middle of his third leap, he was pinned under the arms and dragged unceremoniously from the floor by none other than Adrington himself, with some assistance from the Viscount Mountdale.

"The musicians have not prepared us for this one, yet, old boy." Adrington pulled him to his feet as they reached the perimeter of the room.

Mountdale sniffed his breath. "What have you been drinking?"

"Get away, Candlesnuffer!" Edmund pushed them both aside, leaped into the middle of the floor, then began counting out tiny steps. His friends soon tackled him again, but he twisted away, rolled, then jumped to his feet with a laugh and capered over to the side of the room where a bevy of comfortable chairs invited matrons past their prime to sit and watch the proceedings.

He collapsed into a chair bedecked with cushions. "Pillows love me," he sighed. His contented reverie lasted until Adrington and Mountdale caught up with him. Before they had him in their grasp, Edmund writhed between them and dashed over to the nearest window. "I'll jump off this ship!" he announced. But the window wouldn't open without more of a struggle than he had time to offer. So he made his exit through the more convenient, albeit less dramatic, doorway with Adrington and Mountdale in close pursuit.

* * * * *

"Lucia, you cannot remain behind that plant all evening." Eugenie reached out as if to scold an errant child.

Lucia tried to plead with her eyes, apparently to no avail. "I really thought this the best solution, under the circumstances."

"Well, you thought incorrectly. You'll attract all sorts of the wrong attention back there, with just enough of yourself visible through the leaves that you look like some sort of tropical plant display in Kew Gardens."

Lucia brushed away a large leaf that kept inserting itself in her ear. "That is rather what I feel like at the moment."

"Then come away, for goodness sake. We were scarcely in the ballroom three minutes when you disappeared, and I finally find you out in the hallway hiding behind a potted palm."

"I'm afraid I opened a rather large gash in the back of my gown," Lucia whispered. "And you insisted that I—"

"Take off your petticoat. I remember. I still think that's the best way to show the dress—and your figure—to the best advantage."

"Only now I'm displaying more of my figure than is considered appropriate in these circles." Lucia pushed the leaf out of her ear again.

"We can fix the gown, dear girl, never fear." Eugenie frowned. "However, we cannot fix it while you remain embedded in greenery. I suggest you stand in front of me and we'll walk together to an empty room where we can have the gown mended in private."

"I suppose that does make more sense." Lucia slid carefully from her leafy bower, planting herself firmly in front of her friend. The two of them shuffled slowly down the hallway, away from the ballroom.

"You can take bigger steps, you know. I can keep up."

"I just don't want to get too far—ouch. You stepped on my heel."

"Sorry. Let's try this room." Together, they shuffled to the first available door, but as Lucia reached for the knob, the sound of laughter made her reconsider. "Next room, I think."

"Yes. Wait, now you are getting ahead of me. How on earth did you—"

Lucia waved for her to be quiet. "I'll tell you when we get inside." She reached for the handle of the next door, pausing to listen before she opened it. This door opened into a small parlor decorated in a garish combination of red and gold, completely devoid of human company. "This should work. Hopefully this room will not be wanted for a few minutes. Does your maid carry needle and thread with her?"

"Of course! Do you suppose yourself to be the first ever to stand in need of an emergency seamstress? Though I confess, I've not known anyone to be in such dire need." Eugenie cast an appraising gaze at Lucia's gown. "How did you...?"

"I backed into the knight."

"What?"

"That suit of armor near the punchbowl. I stepped back to allow Mrs. Bracegirdle to pass before me."

"Thoughtless old biddy."

"She did not realize, I'm sure. In any case, I stepped back too far and felt cold metal on my back. I immediately jumped away, but the back of my gown had grown rather attached— caught on a gauntlet or something. And so, we—my gown and I—separated." Her lips puckered in a giggle. "I suppose you could say we had a falling out."

"Yes, I'd definitely say that!" Eugenie snickered. "So before you fall out any further, I shall go fetch Peggy." She flounced out the door, still giggling but taking care not to open the door any wider than necessary. Just before closing it, however, she stuck her head back inside. "Do not go away."

Lucia grimaced. That obviously wasn't an option. In fact, the only option was to either sit in one of the ugly clawfooted, red upholstered chairs or stand and gaze at her wavy reflection in the hideously ornate, gilt framed mirror. Since this latter option would leave her exposed backside open to view from any who might open the door, Lucia chose the former and seated herself in one of the creaking old chairs.

The Adringtons seemed to keep a lot of ancient furnishings about, though the larger rooms she had seen certainly contained enough modern furniture and décor to indicate the family's ability to maintain the latest fashions when they so chose. That suit of armor in the ballroom, though, was purely gothic. Very odd. Now that she remembered, it had been arranged to look as though the knight was reaching to grasp a cup of punch.

Lucia started to giggle again.

The door burst open and a young man hurtled into the room, slamming the door closed behind him. He took a deep breath, leaned against the door, then started when he caught sight of Lucia in the chair.

Neither of them said anything for a moment.

"Good evening," Lucia said at last. Though she had never made this young man's acquaintance, it seemed rude not to say anything under the circumstances.

He brushed an unruly shock of dark hair from his face and bowed. "Good evening."

"I think he went in here!" The door burst open again, this time admitting two more gentlemen, one of whom she recognized as the host, Lord Adrington.

The young man who'd first entered immediately dropped down on all fours and howled.

"He's barking mad," Lord Adrington's companion whispered.

The howling ceased, and the young man looked at the occupants of the room with sad puppy eyes for a moment, his gaze resting at last on Lucia.

Then he started barking.

Lord Adrington and his companion looked from the barking gentleman on the floor to Lucia, nodding. "We must get him out of here."

"But we cannot very well take him back out among company."

"Hmm. Excuse me, Miss…"

"Wright," Lucia replied, after she tore her attention away from the barking gentleman and realized that Lord Adrington was speaking to her.

"Miss Wright, this is most unseemly, but perhaps under the circumstances we might ask you to move to another room?"

Lucia felt her face flush to the roots of her hair. "I-I am afraid I cannot."

The young man on the floor stopped barking.

"I see." Lord Adrington nodded slowly. "Hmm. Then we will have to find another place to secrete him. I'll check for a room upstairs. Mountdale, you try to clear the hallway of any guests until we can get him up the back stairs."

Mountdale scratched the side of his head. "Do you think it safe to leave him here?" He nodded toward Lucia.

The young man on the floor scampered over to the chair opposite Lucia's and wrapped his paws—that is, his hands—around a chair leg.

"I am not sure we have much choice at the moment. Get a servant to stay in the room with Miss Wright. I'd better bring some strong-arm assistance."

"Excellent idea." Mountdale leaned out into the hallway. "You, there! Set down that tray and come in here at once."

"*Comment, Monsieur? Je ne parle —*"

"What? Never mind. Just come *in* here." Mountdale dragged an older servant in by the arm and planted him next to Lucia's chair. "Stay with her, do you understand? Do not leave this room."

The servant looked uncertainly from one face to the other, then nodded.

"Good."

"We shall return in a moment, Miss Wright."

Adrington and Mountdale quit the room in haste, leaving Lucia alone with the nervous servant and the unusual young man, who was now scratching his leg against his elbow. Within a few seconds, he ceased this odd movement and began to sniff at the servant's legs. Then he growled.

"*Mon Dieu!*" The servant looked helplessly at Lucia.

"Arf!"

One bark was sufficient to send the servant scurrying for the door.

"Wait!" Lucia started to stand, but remembered why she had to remain in the chair. Her reticule tumbled to the floor. "I believe Lord Adrington wished you to remain here."

The servant shook his head as he reached for the doorknob with trembling hands.

"I do not think he will hurt you," she said.

Without looking back, the servant wrenched open the door, flung himself into the hallway and yanked the door closed behind him.

Chapter Three

ഌ

The young man on the floor next to her remained still, once again watching Lucia with the sad-eyed gaze that reminded her of a lost puppy.

And they were gorgeous eyes. Bright, rich blue framed by thick, dark lashes that fanned the air when he closed them briefly to take another deep breath.

What a horrid, ghastly shame. This beautiful young man—a gentleman of substance, from the look of his dress and his manners when he first addressed her—had less of his wits about him even than Geoffrey. For Geoffrey had not yet taken up an occupation in the animal kingdom.

"I'm so sorry," she murmured softly, barely aware that she'd spoken aloud.

"Why?" The young man sat up, looking now much more human.

"Why?" Lucia sat up straighter herself, wondering how to answer. If this gentleman was anything like Geoffrey, he would not be aware that his behavior was anything beyond ordinary. "Because…because your friends have left you." This was a lame answer indeed, but one that at least should not put the gentleman on the defensive.

Far from it, in fact. He smiled. It was a friendly, confident smile that warmed the space between them. "I expect they'll be back rather soon."

"Yes, I suppose so." And then hopefully they'd leave again so that Peggy could repair her gown in privacy. Although, for the moment, it was strangely pleasant, things being just exactly as they were.

That made no sense at all. Why should it be pleasant to be trapped in a room with a madman, handsome or no?

He reached over to pick up her reticule. Then, with admirable agility, he leapt to his feet and handed it to her with a slight bow. "Yours, I believe?"

"Yes, thank you." Her gloved hands felt enormously clumsy as she accepted the bag from him.

"A nice party, is it not?" The young man seated himself in the other chair and looked about the room as if gazing on a large assembled company.

"Err, yes." Lucia had actually seen very little of the party, but she supposed the festivities carried on well enough in her absence.

"I do believe, though, that it is about time for Adrington to bring his decor into the nineteenth century."

"What do you mean?"

"Look at this ghastly collection! Kept on display only to remind the rest of us how long the family has held its estates."

"That seems a rather uncharitable judgment." She sat back with a frown. "I wonder, would you voice such opinion in front of the family?"

"I have done, on many occasions." He grinned. "To no avail, obviously."

She felt her eyes widen with surprise. "Oh. And you were not concerned that you might offend the sensibilities of your friends?"

"No. After all, 'He that departs with his own honesty for vulgar praise doth it too dearly buy'."

"Yes, I do agree with that, but there are times…" Where had she heard those words before? From a book of plays? Sermons? Poetry? The quotation seemed so familiar.

"Would you care to dance, then?"

She blinked. "No. No, thank you. I-I promised that I'd remain in this room."

"We can dance here." He bowed. "I'd be honored."

"No." The gentleman was mad, however engaging his appearance. Moreover, had the Prince himself asked her dance, she could rise only if the chair somehow remained miraculously attached to her backside.

"Why not? I see you are not engaged to dance with anyone else."

Lucia struggled to think of an excuse that would not offend him. "I... There's no music in here."

"Music? You require music. Very well, I shall sing for us. 'A bonny lass one day went walking,'" he began in a fine baritone, "'met with a gent and set to talking—'"

He stopped abruptly, and she had the sickening sensation that he was going to drop to the floor and howl again.

But he did not. "This will never do for a dance. Not at all." He tossed back the unruly lock of hair that had descended across his forehead again. "A string quartet, I think, don't you?" Without waiting for a reply, he began to hum a low, steady cadence. "There's the cello." Then he started humming again in a slightly higher pitch, a tune that seemed to echo the first. "And the viola. Now for the violins." He hummed a melody that started very slow and sweet but soon swelled to an intricate pattern. "I wish I had another mouth. It's not easy to hum two parts, you know."

Lucia laughed aloud, not caring if the sound should call attention to the strange *tête-à-tête*.

"And now, for the dance." Still humming, the young gentleman began to step in time to the music. "This is about the right tempo, I believe."

Lucia sat forward, tapping her heels lightly to the tune as he danced.

"And now for the partner." He leaped over in front of her chair and pulled Lucia to her feet. "I believe I've requested the honor—"

She squealed as she jerked away, landing back in her chair with a most unladylike thud.

The gentleman looked at his hands, which had clasped hers only a second before. He smiled sadly at her. "Ah, well, *ma chère*, 'twas not to be, I suppose."

Lucia made no answer because there was none to make. He spoke the truth, but it was a regrettable truth and one that did not bear repeating. Though handsome and engaging and, wonder of wonders, attentive to her, he was clearly removed from the better portion of his senses. Perhaps that was why he was so attentive.

It was not a pleasant thought.

The door swung open with no warning this time. The gentleman in front of her dissolved to the floor, barking as he scampered over to the corner behind the vacant chair.

"Grab him!"

Adrington, Mountdale and two men dressed in livery followed the barking man into the corner, one of them carefully shutting the door with a glance into the hallway.

Lucia began to propel her chair in the opposite direction. With four men blocking her view, she could no longer see her erstwhile dance partner, but a snarling sound issued from the corner that indicated he was still back there somewhere.

"Ouch! He bit me!"

The door opened again. "I think this was the room, but…" Eugenie peered inside, squealing at the sight of the men scuffling in the corner. "Most definitely not!"

"I'm here. Over here." Lucia waved forlornly.

"Oh, dear." Eugenie grimaced. "What are they—never mind. We've got to get you out of here!"

"Yes. I quite agree. But…"

"I have an idea. Wait in here, Peggy." Eugenie shoved the confused maid into the room. "I'll be right back."

"Eugenie!" Lucia begged. "Don't leave me like this!"

But the door shut again.

Both Lucia and Peggy turned their attention to the cursing mess of masculinity not six feet away. Somehow, the snarling, barking gentleman managed to crawl through the tangle of his pursuers to scamper over to the opposite corner. Though he was panting from exertion and sporting a number of scratches and torn clothing, his eyes danced with laughter as if he thoroughly enjoyed eluding his captors.

They rapidly followed him, of course, so that Lucia and Peggy now enjoyed a bit more breathing space on their side of the room.

"Lucia." Eugenie's head appeared at the door again. "Oh, good. You're still here."

"Where else would I be?"

"I've brought some help." Eugenie entered, followed by Sophie and another lady who was clearly amused by the spectacle that met her eyes. "Lucia, may I present Miss Caroline Glaisher. Miss Glaisher, this is Miss Wright."

"Very pleased to make your acquaintance, Miss Wright." Miss Glaisher exhibited a graceful curtsy, rising with the ghost of a smile on her face.

"Yes, yes." Lucia waved them over. "I'm pleased as well. This is a most fortuitous time to make new acquaintances. Now, Eugenie—"

"It's quite simple, really. The four of us will surround you, and walking close together, we'll make our way down to another room. You can hide behind the curtains or—"

"I understand. Peggy, if you would be so good as to step behind me back here." Lucia indicated the space next to the chair. "And Eugenie, you take the other side." Lucia cast a glance toward the men in the room, but they were so engrossed in their efforts to capture the elusive barking gentleman that they seemed unlikely to notice the deficiencies in her gown. She stood and took a step away from the chair, and the other ladies immediately closed in to surround her, with Eugenie standing so close it was as if she was affixed by glue. Sophie and Miss Glaisher led the way as the fivesome shuffled slowly toward the door.

Which then opened again, admitting two more gentlemen, these decidedly older than the others already in the room. "We heard odd noises coming from this room and wished to—oh, excuse me, ladies." The first older gentleman bowed. He and his companion attempted to move aside so the ladies could make their egress, but bunched together as they were, the feat was simply impossible.

"Oh, just hit him with something and have done with it."

The latecomers turned their attention from the ladies to the other men in the room. "I say."

"It's a wonder we didn't hear more."

"Hardly." He tapped his ear. "It's a wonder we ever hear anything, these days."

A particularly loud howl cut short all attempts at conversation in the well-populated room.

The howl itself was in turn cut short by an angry thud.

"I believe that was sufficient." Mountdale nodded with satisfaction.

"More than," one of the footmen commented *sotto voce*.

"I do not believe he will be up to trouble us for some time." Mountdale replaced a hefty crystal vase on the mantel beneath the mirror.

"If he's ever up again at all," the other footman muttered.

"Perhaps it would be better if he is not." Mountdale eyed the insolent footman crossly as he stuffed a collection of red silk flowers back into their crystal enclosure.

"Are you saying you hit him that hard deliberately?" Adrington asked.

"I am simply stating the obvious. Edmund Rutherford has clearly lost all sense of reason." Mountdale sniffed. "If it were me, I'd rather be dead."

After the moment of silence that followed this morbid pronouncement, the ladies' procession suddenly set in motion at double speed. Adrington, Mountdale and the footmen prepared to remove Lord Rutherford from the room. The two most recent arrivals, however, desired to lay eyes on the young gentleman who had caused all the commotion. And so began an impossible snarl of human traffic, as the men sought to squeeze past the women, the women struggled to exit *en masse* and everyone tried desperately to avoid touching one another.

By the time Lucia and her party finally reached another room and completed emergency mending procedures on her gown, the soirée was more than half over and Lucia had missed most it.

But she'd seen enough.

* * * * *

As pain gradually forced Edmund into a conscious state, he became aware that he must have grown an extra head during the night. The throbbing ache was more than could be contained in one head alone. Or perhaps his skull had simply been cleaved in two—he could now feel a definite split along the back of his head.

He groped his hands around on the pillow, wondering if his brains might have spilt out onto the bed.

It was not his bed.

Behind the pillow in his own bed, he would have felt a gap before the wall, enabling him to stretch out his full length without hitting anything.

Here when he reached up, he touched hard, cold wood just beyond the pillow. Carved wood. His fingers traced up several inches of engraved design. He could not detect the pattern, but he was willing to bet it was an ugly one.

He was somewhere in Adrington's house. In one of the heirloom rooms, stuffed full of furniture that had in been in the family since the reign of Charlemagne or some such. Though the family would not part with these dubious treasures, they generally hid them to a certain degree.

He must be upstairs in one of the less fashionable guest bedrooms used by distant family members.

He sighed. He could not remember coming up to bed last night. He must have drunk himself into a stupor to avoid speaking with Jeanne so that one of the servants had to see him up to bed.

But he had not taken a single drink the previous night. The memories now flooded back with painful intensity. Images swept over him in waves, as if he watched excerpts from the life of another. Leaping through the ballroom, growling and barking at Adrington and the others. And speaking with a shy young lady he'd never met before.

And would never meet again, no doubt, after she witnessed last night's performance.

He had put on quite a show. An odd sense of pride welled up as he reflected on his feat. With but a few minutes' work, he had convinced everyone that he had lost his wits. He had not planned in advance how to act crazed. He simply started and…everything seemed to just happen.

Did that mean he really was crazy, or close to it?

After all, it had been rather enjoyable, up to a point. It had been quite fun to push past somber, self-important cliques in the ballroom, fun to scramble around on the floor barking like a dog and fun to speak with an unknown lady without giving any thought to propriety or common sense.

In a sense, he was free. Free to behave however he chose, without regard to whether it was the right thing to do. No one could hold him responsible now. After all, he was crazy.

Now if he could just figure out a way to end an evening without being chased, collared, and pummeled on the head, he could be in for a rather entertaining season. And by the end—no, much sooner than that—Jeanne would realize that she could not possibly marry him.

Then he would be truly free.

Chapter Four

"Well, if you do have to leave so early in the season, at least you have the satisfaction of knowing you've witnessed the biggest debacle of the year." Sophie munched thoughtfully on a piece of toast.

"Debacle?" Lucia paused, her spoon held in midair above her teacup. "I thought the Adringtons threw a lovely party."

"Certainly they did. For the first quarter of an hour. Then Lord Rutherford turned it into a rout. He was quite funny, though. 'Get away, Candlesnuffer!'" she mimicked. "Depend on it. No other event will match the excitement of the Adrington soirée."

"What if the gentleman," Lucia knocked her spoon off the saucer as she reached for the teacup, "Lord Rutherford, that is, puts in an appearance elsewhere during the season? Might that not be just as 'exciting' as you say?"

Sophie chewed on that thought, as well as her toast, for a moment. "I do not believe his family will let him out in company anytime soon."

Visions of the scenes her own brother might cause in a crowded ballroom swam before Lucia's eyes. "Yes," she agreed readily. "I can believe that."

"So you leave tomorrow, then?"

"Yes." *Thank goodness.* The events of last evening made Lucia realize how truly urgent it was for her to return to her home and her place caring for Geoffrey and Helen. What if they should get into a crowd and take fright? Either might behave just as the unfortunate Lord Rutherford had done. Or worse. If she were home with them, she could ensure such disasters did not have the chance to develop.

She wondered whether Lord Rutherford had someone to keep similar watch over him.

"Where is Eugenie? I would think with this being your last day in London, she would be affixed to your side."

Lucia smiled. "One might think. But I have not seen her this morning. Peggy said she was dressed and out at an unusually early hour." She winced when she noticed a tea stain spreading across the tablecloth near her cup and wiped at it with a napkin.

"You know," Sophie reached for another slice of toast, "you missed the biggest scene last night. At least I think you did. How long were you hiding in the hall before Eugenie dragged you into that little parlor?"

"I don't know." Lucia couldn't imagine that she had missed much.

"Were you in the ballroom when Lord Rutherford—and it does indeed sound odd to refer to him by that title under the circumstances—started to dance?"

"No." But he had asked her to dance. Was rather persistent about it, in fact. "With whom did he dance?"

"Oh, he did not dance *with* anybody. That is, he actually did not dance at all. He took great leaps about the room," she demonstrated with the butter knife, "like the dancers in the opera. It was quite funny. He knocked the Earl of Osterbridge into the Dowager Countess Fortescue and her turban fell right into his punch. She was quite mortified, for she is grown nearly bald and now everyone knows it. I'm glad, after the nasty things she said about our neighbor, Sir Reginald last year."

"Indeed?" Lucia wanted to ask what the Countess had said, but she also wanted to hear more about the young man's leaping dance. The more she thought about it, the more the latter topic interested her.

Sophie looked at her freshly buttered piece of toast as if unsure quite what to do with it. She cut it into quarters. "Yes, quite an entertaining evening. I wonder if I might compose a song about the countess's bristling bald head."

That was one topic Lucia did not care to hear more about. "Did Lord Rutherford do anything else out of the ordinary? I mean, besides what we witnessed in the parlor."

"Let me see. Other than rolling on the floor, shouting nonsense words, barking like a dog and trying to jump out the window — no, nothing out of the ordinary."

"Oh." He did truly sound mad. Why did that notion fill her with such despair? She really did not even know the man.

"Do you suppose he might just have been really in his cups?"

"No," Lucia answered with a catch in her voice. She could not be absolutely certain, of course, but the young man who spoke to her in the intimate parlor did not have the demeanor of one who had been drinking, and there was no aroma of wine or spirits on his breath.

"Were you and Peggy in that parlor with him for very long?" Without waiting for an answer, Sophie rushed on. "I do think it was rather splendid the way Lord Adrington and Viscount Mountdale took control of the matter, don't you? Both handsome gentlemen, but I think the Viscount carries himself better. Eugenie prefers Lord Adrington, but says that both of them are spoiled fops. I must disagree with that." She picked up a square of toast, considered it for a moment, then set it down and cut it into triangles. "I don't think even Eugenie believes that herself. I believe she rather fancies Lord Adrington and doesn't want to let on. In fact, I shall tell Lady Georgiana Adrington so the next time I see her."

"You wouldn't!"

Sophie looked up with a wicked grin. "Wouldn't I?"

"That is terribly cruel. If Eugenie has no interest in the gentleman, you've spread false rumors. And if she does, it is even worse, for you've put her in an embarrassing position indeed."

"No worse than when she threw a fox at me last year at Vauxhall Gardens. In front of my whole party."

"She threw a fox at you?"

"Well, she did not actually do the throwing, as she was a member of the party at the time. I believe she had one of the footmen lie in wait." She popped a tiny toast triangle into her mouth.

Lucia shook her head. "I still don't understand."

"For my birthday last year, we made up a party of friends and took a trip to the gardens. While we were walking about, we passed a small grove of trees. Then a fox jumped out—or rather, was thrown out—in front of me. It was quite a shock, as you can imagine. I'm afraid I screamed rather indecently. And I hiked up my dress and cowered against one of the gentlemen of the party. Only for a moment, mind you, until I recovered. But the damage was done. For the rest of the season, I was known as the 'Screamy Mimi'."

"What makes you think Eugenie was responsible? Why on earth would she—"

"Oh, she confessed. We had a bet, you see. We'd had a discussion about hunting, and I said foxes were rather sweet, meek creatures and it was a shame to set great dogs and men on horseback to hunt them down. Eugenie said they were vermin that would bite you as soon as look at you and that I would be afraid of one if I saw it face-to-face."

"And so she—"

"She had to have someone throw it at eye level in order for me to see it 'face-to-face'. That's how she explained it, anyway. I believe she did it just to make sure I really screamed in front of all those people."

"Ah. So you desire revenge."

"Naturally. I've only been waiting for a good chance. And this seems it. For I believe Eugenie really does have an interest in Lord Adrington."

Lucia looked over the remains of her breakfast. She had eaten little of her toast and bacon, and while she disliked waste, she had been unable to persuade herself to take another bite for the last quarter of an hour. It seemed unlikely she would do so now. "Sophie, I understand your desire for revenge—"

"Do you? I do not see that quality in you. I'm sorry, I should not interrupt."

Lucia leaned closer, hoping to impress on Sophie the need for restraint and some sense of familial loyalty. "This is much more serious that being embarrassed in front of a party of friends."

"First of all, I was not merely embarrassed before a party of friends—it was a slow week for gossip, so everyone in the *ton* knew of the event within two days. Second, the matter of Eugenie's interest in Lord Adrington is not a serious matter because it will not signify. The Adringtons are so far beyond us they would never consider a match with anyone in our family. We were extraordinarily fortunate even to be invited as one of the lowest guests at their enormous gathering. We can only hope to clutch at one of the other guests on the lower rung of the ladder. To aspire to the top is ludicrous."

Hearing the matter set forth so bluntly was a bit of a shock. But it made sense. Lucia supposed that had she spent more time in society, she would become as pragmatic about marriage matches as Sophie.

"I will see Lady Adrington at a small party in a few days' time. That should be just the place to enlighten her."

Poor Eugenie. Though Lucia could well believe her capable of setting up the fox episode for a bit of fun, she knew her friend would never stoop to the meddling machinations her sister Sophie now outlined. Eugenie had far too much respect for others to even think of such a thing.

* * * * *

He would have to tell someone. Edmund had spent the better part of the morning playing scenarios in his mind in between bouts of blissful slumber. Now, finally, he felt a little more himself. He could even sit up in the bed without too much difficulty, so long as he moved very slowly.

Bright light filtered through the cracks in the window shutters. It might be late into the afternoon, for all he knew. A tray sitting on the table in the corner offered an unappetizing array of breakfast food, however, so he assumed his initial assessment was correct—he had spent only the entire morning in bed.

And no one wanted to talk to him this morning.

But he had to talk to someone. If he were to keep up this ruse, he needed to ensure that at least one person knew that underneath the façade, he was still himself. One person to whom he might occasionally confide. And one person who could help him prove, when it was all over and Jeanne safely married to someone else, that he was indeed quite sane.

He would be ruined in society, but his friends might one day forgive him.

Who could he choose for a confidant? Who would be able to keep this secret until events played out as he planned?

Edmund looked longingly at the pot of coffee on the table. Certain to be cold as the Thames, and probably as cloudy. Was it worth the effort to drag himself over to pour a cup anyway? He could ring for a servant, if any were brave enough to enter while he was awake.

Curiosity suddenly overcame the headache. He slid off the bed, padded gently across the floor and reached for the door handle. It turned, but the door did not open. They had locked him inside.

So his choice of confidants might be severely limited, if he needed to divulge the secret any time soon.

His sudden burst of energy now drained away, Edmund sank into a chair near the table with the untouched breakfast tray.

Adrington would be sure to stop in sometime during the day. It was, after all, his house. And he would dearly love to enlighten his friend. The look of anguish on Adrington's face last night, which Edmund had so blithely ignored at the time, now came back to haunt him. His friend thought him lost entirely. And unfortunately, for the time being, he would have to let him continue to think so. After his performance last evening, essentially ruining the party, he could hardly saunter into Adrington's study and admit he had engaged in a calculated ruse.

For that reason, there was no one in the house in whom he could confide.

Who else?

Mountdale was not clever enough to keep the secret. In fact, he probably wouldn't even understand the need for secrecy.

But perhaps one of the other members of his club...

He could tell his valet, if he had one. It had seemed disloyal to interview replacement candidates right after Mayer's death, but the days soon turned to many weeks. He had been without a valet for longer than he realized.

It looked as though his best option would be to find a suitable confidant at White's. If he hurried to dress now, he should have plenty of time.

But not if he remained locked in his room.

He stood and looked about for a bell pull, but could see none. Perhaps the less elegant guest rooms had not been outfitted with such devices. So on the rare occasion when a guest found himself locked in his room, presumably to prevent him from biting another member of the household during the night, he would simply have to stay put until someone thought to check on him.

But how long would that be?

Edmund walked back to the door and pounded on it three times. "Open up!" He pounded several more times. "Is anyone about?"

No answer. No sound at all, in fact. It was as if all occupants had deserted this section of the house, like rats fleeing a ship in a storm.

Perhaps they had. After all, he had provided a storm last night.

He smashed his fist against door in a careless, sloppy blow that nearly broke his knuckles. He would have to use more sense than that. Hit hard and straight on.

Or quit banging on the door altogether.

If Adrington and his guests heard frantic hammering and pounding on the door, they might not be terribly anxious to let him out. He would have to wait, perhaps act as though the episode had never occurred. Once he'd found someone to confide in, then he could act the crazy man again.

* * * * *

"Lucia?" Eugenie rapped on her door. "Are you within?"

"Yes." Lucia pulled the bedroom door open and beckoned for her friend to step inside. "Come in."

Eugenie remained in the doorway. "No, no, I want you to come downstairs."

"I will soon. I need to finish packing my trunk."

"Just for a moment. Please?"

Lucia smiled. "You are as impatient as a child. But I really do need to finish. I promised your father my belongings would be ready to be delivered this evening, since we leave so early in the morning."

"You no longer need to concern yourself about that." Eugenie grabbed her arm.

"But I promised your father —"

"He will not mind. Trust me." Eugenie pulled her into the hallway.

"Eugenie!" Lucia laughed. "You are behaving in a ridiculous fashion."

"I have something to show you. A surprise."

Lucia allowed herself to be propelled down the stairs where Eugenie parked her in front of the door to the first parlor.

"Now, close your eyes."

"Eugenie!" Lucia found her friend's enthusiasm contagious—she could barely contain a fit of giggles.

"Close both eyes, if you please!"

"I am. I am!"

"Very well," Eugenie intoned with mock solemnity. "I shall now say the magic incantation—words that will keep you in London so you can enjoy the season."

"What in the—"

"You cannot interrupt the magic! It could prove most dangerous." Now Eugenie apparently had trouble maintaining her serious demeanor, for a sound very much like a giggle escaped her lips as well. "If you mess up the incantation, who knows what might happen?" She mumbled something about eating toads and remaining in town for an impossible length of time. When Lucia began to laugh, Eugenie put a hand over her eyes. "Keep them closed!" She turned the squeaky knob and opened the door with a tremendous yank. "You may open your eyes now."

Chapter Five

ℰℴ

Lucia was still laughing when light began to flutter through her opening eyelids. But the sound died away as the room came fully into focus. "Geoffrey! And Helen! How...however did you get here?"

"I brought them down." Eugenie beamed with pride.

"You did?" Lucia stared at her brother and sister incredulously.

They, in turn, stared shyly at her, standing almost so still as to appear as if they had been carved of wood.

"Well," Eugenie confessed, "I had them brought by hired coach as far as Roxeth. Then I went to collect them with our carriage. Is this not a wonderful surprise?"

"It's a wonder, certainly." It was a wonder that they survived the trip without Geoffrey insisting that he take the reins and driving them all into a ditch. Lucia reached out to take their hands to assure herself that they were really here, in the flesh and safe. "Are you quite well, Helen?"

Her sister nodded, her big eyes solemn, her mouth drawn closed in a prim bow.

"And you, Geoffrey? Did you stand the journey well? Does Nicholas accompany you?"

Her brother waved her questions away as if brushing falling leaves from his cloak. "Yes, the journey was quite satisfactory. And of course Nicholas accompanies me. You did not think I would leave Helen alone in the coach while I drove, do you?"

Lucia groaned. "You drove?"

"Of course. Is that not what a driver does?"

"But I thought—Helen said you'd taken up shooting as a profession."

Helen grabbed her wrist and shook her head emphatically.

"Ah, no," Geoffrey scoffed. "A beggar's sport, that's all it is. But to drive, to drive a team of fine horses over hill, through dale...now that is a fine undertaking indeed."

Lucia nearly held her breath. "Through the country, then. You did not try to—that is, care to—drive in London traffic?"

"Certainly not." Geoffrey sniffed.

Lucia allowed herself to relax ever-so slightly.

"I was a guest in the Bayles' carriage," Geoffrey continued, "under the guidance of the most excellent skills of Christopher Smith. I would not presume to put a fellow driver out of his place."

"Well..." Lucia felt her spine stiffen as she prepared to be on guard once again. "I think you'll find here in London that all the drivers take their role seriously, just as you do. You, of course, will not want to put any of them out their place, either."

"Of course not," Geoffrey agreed. "Unless their driving stands in need of improvement. Then it would be incumbent on me to demonstrate—"

"Oh, look, Geoff!" Lucia dashed over to a glass-enclosed bookcase in the corner. "I believe I see a copy of Cosin's Devotions. Does it not make you long for the blissful days you spent studying with Reverend Cadwallader?"

"Tedious in the extreme," Geoffrey drawled as he strolled over to join Lucia. "I never did understand all that fuss made over a piece of bread." He leaned over and peered through the glass. "And that is a book on horticulture, in any case." He turned back to face his other sister. "Helen, you might find it of interest. Perhaps it might inspire a new collection?"

Lucia stifled another groan. What might Helen try to collect in London? And where? "Remember, Helen, that in town ladies never venture in public on their own. Never. In fact, you are not out, yet, so you may not go anywhere without a proper chaperone. And that means me."

Helen's eyes widened to an even greater degree, giving the appearance that they might jump free from her face were she given just the merest jolt from behind. "Lucia, does that mean I may not go out on walks with your maid in the mornings?"

"Err, no. I've not had the opportunity to hire a maid as of yet." It seemed a futile exercise, really. After a month or two, the personal servants always gave notice. All except Nicholas, and his service was so diluted as to be of dubious value. With the aid of neighboring villagers they hired to care for the house, gardens and stables, they had been able to get along well enough. In the country. Here, however, they would need at least one personal maid to dress their hair and keep their clothing in shape. Lucia had already infringed upon Peggy's services more than she would have liked. She would need to hire a maid if they were to stay.

Which was absolutely out of the question.

"But you needn't worry, Helen." Lucia squeezed her sister's hand to reassure her. "Our stay in London will not be a long one and I shall make my company available for frequent walks during that time."

Eugenie, who had been speaking with the butler about dinner or some such arrangement, now entered back into the conversation. "Whatever do you mean, Lucia?"

"I shall take Helen out every morning—"

"No, not that. You said your stay in town would not be long."

"Of course. We'll take rooms for a few days and then—"

"You shall do no such thing! You shall all stay right here, in this house, and finish the season. And you will enjoy it." It almost seemed that Eugenie stamped her foot at this last pronouncement.

"But how can we? To do so would impose upon you too much."

"Nonsense. We have plenty of room, so long as you don't object to sharing a bedroom with your sister."

"No, but…" Lucia nodded toward her brother and sister, then leaned in to whisper to her friend. "I believe I explained to you earlier why this would not be a good idea!"

"I think," Eugenie pronounced, "that you are much mistaken. You have all simply lived too long in isolation. The company of town and the pleasures of society are what you all need to restore a sense of balance to your lives. And I shall see that you all get a full measure."

"You do not know what you are proposing, Eugenie."

"Oh yes I do. And believe me, Lucia, one day you shall thank me for this." Eugenie patted her on the hand before turning to lead them out to dinner.

"I wouldn't stake my dowry on it," Lucia muttered as she followed her friend from the room. "Not a single farthing."

* * * * *

Edmund was not certain how long he had been asleep this time. The room was dark with little evidence of light at the window, but darkness came early enough at this time of year that it was difficult to ascertain the time — it could have been five o'clock or well past midnight.

The rapping at the door that awakened him, however, indicated that it was more likely to be the former than the latter. Flickering light framed the edge of the doorway. "Rutherford, are you awake?"

"Getting there." Edmund yawned, pleased that the two split pieces of his skull now seemed to be fusing back together once more. He sat up, grateful that he had not bothered to undress earlier so that he was decently clothed to meet whoever chose to visit him in exile.

A key turned in the lock and the door soon opened. Adrington stepped forward, the candle in his hand illuminating a handsome face creased with concern. "You look well enough," he said uncertainly. "How do you feel?"

"I feel quite well, apart from having the impression that my head was cleaved into two pieces last night." Edmund looked toward the shuttered window. "It's almost the next night now, isn't it?"

"Yes. We thought it best to let you rest after…after…"

Edmund grinned and tried to lighten the mood. "I suppose I must have had rather too much to drink last night. New recipe of Kennedy's. Potent stuff, that." He slid off the bed. "Did you happen to bring a candle? The maid seems to have missed this room on her rounds to fill the candle-boxes this afternoon."

Adrington watched him as if in a trance. "Yes, of course." He shook himself into motion, removing two candles from his coat pocket. Handing one to Edmund, he fixed the other into the empty candlestand near at hand.

Edmund stepped over to retrieve a candlestick from the mantel. "I don't even remember how I earned this bump on the head. Must have been a terrific brawl."

"Uh, well, I suppose you could say that."

"Don't tell me—it wasn't a fight at all." He grinned. "I banged my head against something and knocked myself out cold in front of the whole company. Was that it?"

"W-well…"

"Have you a knife with you?" Edmund held up the candlestick with the remains of a candle stub embedded in the base. "My pocket knife seems to have gone missing."

Adrington took out a knife but seemed reluctant to hand it over.

Edmund had to turn away to hide the smile that threatened to burst into a laugh. He could not very well blame the man for his hesitancy in handing over a dangerous implement—after all, Edmund had tried to bite him the previous night.

"Here, allow me." Adrington reached for the candlestick, then dug in the knife blade to pry out the embedded wax. After he handed the empty candlestick back, he folded and pocketed the knife. Then he waited, watching Edmund closely.

Edmund decided to drop the subject of the head wound. He had made his point—that he didn't "remember" how it had happened—and it was better just now not to remind Adrington how it actually had. "I hope I've not slept through dinner?"

"No. The ladies will be coming up to dress shortly."

"Then I had better get a start." Edmund rubbed his unshaved chin. "I don't want to frighten them."

"Yes, um, do you not think you might prefer to dine in your room tonight?"

"I don't believe so. I'm feeling much better, and I do think I would enjoy some company."

"Are you certain? I could dine up here with you, so you would not be alone."

"No, no, I don't want to put you to any trouble. I am quite up to it, I assure you. Of course, I won't be sampling any of Kennedy's handiwork tonight." He touched the back of head and winced. "Or ever again, for that matter."

"Do you really think that's what it was?" Adrington asked softly.

"What *what* was?"

Adrington turned and paced several steps away. "You behaved rather oddly last night, Rutherford."

"Oh. I suppose I ought to dock Kennedy for sending me out in public under the influence of his distilled evil spirits." Edmund paused. "Of course, last night I think I gave him a raise in salary." He shrugged. "It seemed good stuff, at the time."

Adrington turned back to face him. "If that was indeed the cause of your behavior, I'd suggest you destroy any remaining stock as well as the recipe."

"Ha!" Edmund wagged a finger at him jokingly. "You wouldn't be so quick to say that if you'd tasted it."

"This is not a laughing matter, Rutherford. I don't know how to say this, but somehow I must tell you."

"Tell me what?"

"Your behavior last night was not that of a drunken man. You behaved as if you'd gone insane. Everyone saw you and heard your lunatic ranting. By this afternoon, all of London will have known of it."

"Oh. I see. What about Jeanne? Was she a witness to my...madness?"

"She had not yet come into the ballroom at the time of your...ill-mannered display. But of course, everyone told her of it soon afterward. We removed you to an empty room as quickly as possible. You exhibited your worst behavior there, but only a few people know of it."

"Only a few?"

"Mountdale, of course. And my footmen."

"No one else?" He was curious to know if Adrington knew the identity of the ladies in the room.

"A few others came into the room by accident. There was a lady, who, uh, refused to leave for some reason."

"Who?"

"I don't know. A friend of Georgiana's, I suppose."

"Did I frighten them?"

"I don't know. I kept my attention focused on you, not the others." Adrington stopped and raked his fingers through his hair. "Oh, you'll hear of it soon enough, so I must tell you—you were acting like a dog."

"I was? Barking and everything?"

"Yes, yes. Barking, crawling about on the floor. You even tried to bite people."

"I think I understand now why you wish me to remain in my room tonight. No one wants a dinner companion who might try to bite them during the soup course."

"So you understand?"

"Yes, and I will remain up here for tonight, if you desire. Or I can go home."

"No, I don't think you should leave so soon after your...injury."

"Fine. I'll concede for tonight. But tomorrow, I will come down and will mix with company, and I won't so much as growl at anyone. I promise."

Adrington looked as if he was trying to smile. "You really believe it was simply the drink?"

"I do. I feel well. Does my behavior seem at all odd now?"

"No."

"You see? Whatever may have happened last night, you can depend on it — it will never happen again."

Chapter Six

ഔ

"Lucia, will you come into my room for a moment? I've something to show you." Eugenie nodded toward her room with a conspiratorial wink and a glance back at Helen who followed them along the upstairs hallway.

Lucia shook her head, but it was too late.

"Why may I not see it too? Why did she not invite me?" Helen hurried on without giving anyone time to respond to her indignant outburst. "You can't expect me to go down a strange hallway by myself. I won't do it."

"No, no, dear," Lucia soothed her younger sister, gently taking her arm. "I shall walk you down the hall."

"I want to see what's in her room."

"You know it's not polite to insist when you've not been invited."

"She invited you. Why did she not invite me? We are sisters of the same blood and family. I am as good as you. If you're good enough to be invited, then I am as well. So it was wrong for her to—"

"Yes, yes, it was wrong," Lucia narrowed her eyes at Eugenie, "for her to issue such an invitation, and I won't be going, rest assured." She moved her hands to Helen's elbow and slowly guided her down the hall. "Our room is just down here, directly across from...this mousehole, see." She pointed to a miniscule opening in the baseboard.

"Lucia!" Eugenie huffed down the hall after them. "That is not—"

Lucia waved her objection away. "Now, I shall open the door first, very slowly, and you can see that—"

"You've been sleeping on my side of the bed!" Helen rushed into the room, pointing accusingly at the pillow on the right side of the bed which looked, to the untrained eye, exactly like the pillow on the left.

Lucia made a quick mental calculation, then breathed a sigh of relief. "Last night you would have been sleeping on the other side, so I slept on this side. Tonight is Tuesday," she ushered Eugenie inside and closed the door, "so naturally, Helen, you will be on this side."

"Ha, that was silly of me, wasn't it? I forgot that it would be a different side last night." Helen laughed, a bright sound almost desperate with relief. "That *was* so silly of me, wasn't it, Lu? I say, wasn't it, Lu?"

"It was indeed. You are a very silly girl sometimes." Lucia kissed her on the top of the head. "Would you like to fix the pillow now or do you want to wait," she leaned in to whisper "until after you've changed into your night rail?"

Helen giggled as she looked at Eugenie.

"It really is not improper to speak about undergarments in front of a lady, Helen, particularly a close friend."

"I know," Helen snickered. "But it still sounds so funny."

From the expressions crossing her face, Eugenie seemed to have recovered from her initial shock and had now settled into a general sense of confusion.

"Shall I help you," Lucia leaned in again to her sister, "undress?"

"No! I *said* I was going to fix the pillows first. I always fix the pillows first. I have to fix the pillow first. I can't very well—"

"I am indeed sorry, Helen. I did not hear you." Lucia waved toward the bed. "Please, do go ahead."

Helen shot a resentful glance at Eugenie. "I don't want her to watch. Does she have to be here?"

"Helen! That is very rude. And it is Eugenie's house, after all. She has perfect right to go wherever she chooses."

"No, no that's just as well." Eugenie retreated to the door. "I think I had better start settling in for the night myself. You will come and say goodnight to, uh…"

"Sophie! I don't believe I said goodnight to Sophie before we came up." Lucia smiled. "Her room is down next to yours, is it not?"

"Yes." Eugenie nodded, relief evident on her features. "Goodnight, Helen," she called.

Helen's only answer was an impatient scowl before she returned to her silent contemplation of the pillows.

Lucia offered an apologetic smile before she closed the door. Then she turned around to face her sister. "You showed very little consideration for our hostess' feelings just now."

"She's not our hostess. Mrs. Bayles is our hostess." Helen tucked under one corner of the pillow on the right side of the bed. "She's just a younger daughter, the same as me. Why do I owe her any special courtesy?" She eyed the pillow critically.

"It is by her invitation that we stay in this house at all. And all I ask is the same courtesy you should show toward anyone. Why do you need a reason to behave decently toward someone?"

"I don't think she showed much consideration for my feelings this evening." She patted down a perceived lump just past the midpoint in the pillow.

"She did not know you would want to visit her room and so—"

"There is that as well," Helen cut her off, "but I was thinking of earlier, at dinner. She did not invite me into the kitchen to collect a sample of the wash water."

Lucia winced. Here was another of Helen's habits gone out of control. "In London, ladies do not frequent the kitchen, and a guest would never be invited into such a working environment. She meant you no discourtesy—the opposite, in fact."

"Well, she could have had a sample brought up from the kitchen."

"I do not believe she is aware of your collection. Nor was I aware that you now routinely collect water samples from inside the house as well as out of doors."

Helen looked at Lucia as if she had lost her mind. "How else can I possibly make comparisons?"

"Indeed. How else? And now how does your comparison of the pillows fare?"

"They are about as even as can be expected under the circumstances." Helen sighed. "It is so hard to get the adjustment right by candlelight."

"Well, tomorrow you may arrange the pillows right after breakfast, in full daylight, and then —"

"I can't do it that early, silly. They sink during the day."

"And I suppose they do not sink at the same rate?"

"Of course not."

"Very well, you may come up to arrange the pillows in the last possible moments of daylight tomorrow."

"I want you to leave now so I can undress."

"I shall go say goodnight to Sophie, then." Lucia stepped toward the door, hoping Helen would not suddenly change her mind.

"Do not come back in until I am under the covers!"

"I won't," Lucia promised, grateful at least that this was one promise she could keep with no difficulty whatsoever.

* * * * *

As Lucia knocked on the door to Eugenie's room, she checked the passage behind her to see whether Helen, or, God forbid, Geoffrey had followed her.

"Is it you, Lucia?" Eugenie called out in a rather desperate whisper.

"Yes."

"Are you alone?"

"Quite."

The door sprang open. "Come in quickly!"

Lucia complied, taking a seat in a chair near the fire. "I believe Helen will stay put now. And Geoffrey has Nicholas to watch over him, so we should be set for the night. You have arranged for someone to keep an eye on Nicholas?"

Eugenie nodded as she joined Lucia by the hearth. "Allen has been ordered to offer him watered spirits only."

"Good." Lucia exhaled as she looked into the fire. "I could use some watered spirits myself."

"Without the water," Eugenie agreed. She paused for a moment. "I had no idea about Helen. She appeared the perfect angel at dinner."

"Well, that's because she did not say anything during dinner. She didn't actually eat anything, either, but she usually will not on the first night in a strange place."

"Do I want to know why?"

Lucia grinned. "In case the food's poisoned, I believe. Geoffrey has offered to serve as official taster at past dinners."

Eugenie began to laugh.

"Fortunately," Lucia continued, fighting to keep her own laughter in check, "he did not repeat that performance again tonight. The other diners find it rather disconcerting to have him insist on taking a bite of all their food. And it slows down the meal considerably."

"Yes, I imagine it does!" Eugenie burst into a new fit of laughter, then took a deep breath in an obvious effort to resume the conversation. "But Geoffrey, too, gave no sign of trouble at dinner."

"Other than asking whether Mr. Smith would be joining us."

"Who?"

"Your coachman."

"Oh." Eugenie looked lost for a moment. "But as I said, the dinner went quite well. I really do think you should take the twins out in society more."

"Well," Lucia looked down her nose at Eugenie in jest, "that is where our opinions differ."

Eugenie made a face. "I do think your stepfather would agree with me, though."

Lucia sighed. "If he did, do you not think he would take them out himself?"

"I thought he was too ill."

"Hmm." Lucia tapped her cheek with her finger. "I should not speak unfavorably of my stepfather, but I must confess that I really do not believe there is anything wrong with the man's health. He seems as fit as you or I."

"Then why does he live like a hermit in Bath? I thought he was ordered to take the waters every day."

"Oh, I am sure some doctor has ordered him to do just that." Lucia smiled. "But I could get a doctor to order the same prescription for you, my dear, if I paid him enough."

"That is terrible, then." Eugenie leaned closer and lowered her voice. "Is he keeping all of your money down there?"

"No, not at all. He has placed the money in trust for the twins and myself, and we receive ample allowance." Lucia picked at a loose thread hanging from the cushion on her chair. She was so grateful for that allowance, for the continuous supply of money ensured that she would not have to seek a husband for support. She would never find a man able to understand and tolerate the twins, let alone love them the way that she did. Even their own stepfather seemed not to care for them. When she thought of men or marriage, she always pictured herself protecting the twins from a dark, menacing male form. The husband she ought never to take.

But for some reason, she now thought of Lord Rutherford, remembering the moment he handed her reticule to her. A gesture of kindness, and not menacing at all. There, now, was a man who would understand Geoffrey and Helen.

And it was indeed frightening that she would find such a man attractive. He was just as detached from reason as they.

"I think you should talk to him about it."

"What? Who?" For a moment, Lucia had forgotten she was still in Eugenie's room. Was it obvious that she was thinking of Lord Rutherford?

"Your stepfather."

"Oh." It took her a moment to turn her consideration from a gentleman handsome and young to one prone to baldness, age spots and melancholy. She sighed. "I do wish my stepfather would come to see us, or ask us to visit on occasion. But he seems rather anxious to avoid our company altogether."

"Well, perhaps you should surprise him with a visit without waiting for an invitation. Perhaps the waters might prove beneficial for Helen's constitution."

"I do not think surprise is a good thing for anyone in my family."

"But if he will not visit on his own..."

"Promise me, Eugenie." Lucia looked up into her friend's eyes. "No more surprises."

"Oh, very well." Eugenie folded her hands in her lap. "I promise I will not undertake any more surprises."

For some reason, the promise did not provide the sense of relief Lucia would have liked.

Chapter Seven

ॐ

Edmund felt the tension drain from his limbs as he climbed the familiar steps to 18 Hanover Square. His home. His mother would be napping, more likely than not, at this time of day. He would have to speak with no one other than Franklin, unless he so chose. After this morning's ordeal, where family and staff alike stared at him in apprehensive silence, an afternoon of merely *unpopulated* silence would be most welcome.

But it was not to be. He realized that as soon as he opened the door—and should have thought of it long before, so that he could have detoured to the club instead. Some clue would surely have given it away, had he only paid more attention. Footprints in the thin layer of dust on the marble steps, the hint of perfume in the air or merely the sensation that the door had been opened too many times that morning.

They were here. The Samaritan's Club. A weekly gathering of ladies from the neighborhood who met to drink tea, eat sweets and plot to save the world from the excesses of its own evil desires. After just one more cup of tea, of course.

And they were all here, right now. For all he knew, they were at this moment planning to undertake his restoration as their next project. The sound of many women talking at once, generously peppered with laughter, streamed down the stairs from the drawing room. He expected the door of the room to fling wide open and the women to cascade down right behind their voices, all eager for a glimpse of the man who ruined the Adrington soirée.

But the drawing room door remained very much closed.

"Good morning, sir." Franklin materialized to take Edmund's cloak and hat. "I am sorry I did not see you approach."

"Not to worry, old man. You know I prefer to open the door for myself."

"Yes, sir." The butler nodded with a frown. "But Lady Rutherford, sir, has expressed a distinctly different preference."

"On numerous occasions. Yes, I am well aware." Edmund glanced up the stairs. "But I am sure she did not see the violation this time."

"No, sir, I believe not."

"I suppose you had better tell her of my arrival." Edmund sighed, dreading the interview ahead.

"I suppose so, sir." Franklin echoed the sigh as much as his sense of propriety would allow. "Will you wait here, or shall I tell her you've removed to your study?"

Edmund paused, at first tempted by the thought of taking the escape Franklin offered. Then he envisioned his mother descending the stairs in haste to see him while the "Samaritans" trailed behind her and proceeded *en masse* to invade his sanctum. "I'll follow you up," he decided.

"Very good, sir." Franklin disappeared for a moment before returning *sans* hat and cloak. His absence at such times was of such a brief duration that Edmund often wondered whether the butler simply dropped the garments on the floor in the next room. They always reappeared in exemplary condition when needed, however, so he saw no reason to worry the point excessively.

Edmund followed Franklin up the stairs, several paces behind, of course, heartily wishing he could simply keep going up the next flight and disappear into a bedroom. His head had started to hurt again. He probably should rest, or he would never be able to think clearly. And he needed to think clearly because he still had not chosen a confidant.

Franklin rasped on a door with his knuckles so softly it sounded as if a tiny lapdog was unsuccessfully scratching against the door to gain admittance.

"Surely you do not actually expect them to hear that, do you? The volume of inane chatter within would drown the sound of a highland brigade's entrance. Go on, give it a real knock," Edmund urged.

Franklin scraped his knuckles against the door once more, then grasped the handle and turned it slowly. He bowed to Mrs. Rutherford. "Your son, madam, wishes to inform you of his return."

Edmund reached the doorway a few seconds later and offered a bland smile of greeting.

"Oh, look, Miss Newman." His mother turned to a tall young lady who chatted with two older matrons near the fire. "Edmund has arrived. Will you not come in and pay your respects to the club, my dear? Many of our friends have not seen you in some time."

Edmund could hear a certain amount of whispering as he made his way around the room with his mother, but he met no more than a few incredulous or disapproving stares. Impossible as it seemed, many of these older ladies, who never stirred from the house past sunset, had either not heard the tales of his behavior two nights ago or had not believed them.

The ones who did obviously had enough manners, or at least enough sense, to keep quiet in the presence of his mother. Had anyone said anything outright, his mother would probably have no qualms about asking the offender to choose a weapon and name her second.

Jeanne, of course, was another matter entirely.

And why was she here? She stood out like a thistle among violets, a head taller and a generation younger than any other lady in the room. And she alone among his mother's guests showed no compunction against staring at him outright. Every time he glanced in her direction, she was staring. Somehow, she managed to move about so that, as he and his mother circled the room, she remained on the opposite side.

Actually, he didn't mind that at all.

He noticed with pleasure that they now approached the sofa that had been the starting point on their social circuit. He would be able to make his escape shortly. And, apparently, he would not even have to exchange words with his betrothed.

He would have to explain things to his mother later, of course. But for now, he would be free to rest.

"Good afternoon, ladies." He bowed before stepping out into the hall, where Franklin waited to close the door behind him.

* * * * *

Someone was knocking on his head again.

No, that was not it. The knocking in his head reverberated with a low, steady pulse. This other knocking was harsh, uneven and coming from somewhere over his left shoulder.

"Edmund, open this door," a feminine voice hissed. "I know you're in there."

Edmund sat up and pried open his eyes. He was sitting at his desk, his arms folded over a sheaf of papers as a makeshift pillow. He had been fast asleep.

But a bad dream woke him up.

And she was standing outside, demanding entrance.

With eyes still half shut, he pushed his chair away from the desk and made his way over to the door by touch as much as by sight. He fumbled with the lock for moment, then realized the door had never been locked to begin with.

He heard an impatient huff from the other side. "Pray hurry. I do not wish anyone to see me."

Edmund opened the door wide enough so that he could see Jeanne, but not wide enough for her to gain admittance. "Why did you not simply enter, then?"

Jeanne pushed past him into the room. "Don't be ridiculous. I could never be so rude."

"Indeed not," Edmund offered as he closed the door behind her. "I am sorry that I did not answer your summons right away. I had a headache and must have fallen asleep."

"Why did you not go up to your bedroom?"

"I thought I'd better attend to some correspondence first."

"And did you?"

"Well, let us say that I put a few matters to rest. Now," he said as he motioned for her to take a seat on the sofa near the window. "Whatever can have drawn your attention from the riveting activities of the Samaritan's Club?"

"I cannot believe you would even dare to ask me that." She made no move to sit.

Edmund closed his eyes, waiting for her to continue.

"You scampered across the floor on your knees and tried to bite Lord Mountdale."

I did bite him actually, Edmund wanted to say. But that would not fit with his pretense of having forgotten the whole affair. Instead, he simply nodded. "So I've been told."

"Is that all you are going to say?"

"I do not exactly know what I can say. What does one say after making a *faux pas* of this magnitude?"

"Well," she tossed her head, "you could apologize, for a start."

"I apologize."

"For making a fool of me in front of the *ton*."

It seemed to Edmund that *he* was the one who had appeared the fool, but he said nothing.

"Well?"

"I apologize."

Jeanne stalked over to the fireplace, then whirled around to face him. "Why on earth would you do such a thing? Whatever could have induced such behavior?"

"Honestly, Jeanne, I don't know. I believe I was drugged, in a sense."

"Drugged?"

"In a sense. A bad batch of homebrew." He smiled apologetically.

"*Humph.* If that is the case, it is nearly as embarrassing as the rumors."

"Rumors?" He hoped his voice betrayed none of the hope he felt.

"That you have gone mad. Surely you've heard?"

"Yes." Edmund forced a large sigh. "I have."

"Aunt Morris tells me there is no history of insanity in your family." She took a few steps closer to him. "I'm not quite sure whether to believe her."

"How could you doubt the word of your aunt? She raised you from an infant."

"But in the matter of this..." Jeanne waved a grotesque flourish with her arm "With all evidence to the contrary..."

"What evidence?" Edmund held up his hand to fend off her objection. She did indeed have evidence—he had made certain of that. "Never mind." Then he slowed, made his voice hesitant and uncertain. "This was but one episode, one evening of, I will admit, less than exemplary behavior. It is not likely to happen again." He did not promise, and was grateful that she did not ask him to.

She walked closer to him, and he looked to the floor, stifling the urge to back away.

"Edmund." She leaned down to catch his gaze. "Please."

With reluctance, he looked into her eyes.

"I am worried for you."

Worried about your reputation, you mean, he answered silently.

"Aunt Morris has said she's ready for us to set a date now."

"She is?" Edmund took a step back, fearing he might lose his balance.

"Yes." Jeanne followed him forward, a vapid tenderness oozing from her voice. "She thinks this is a temporary malady brought on by an absence of…well, I cannot explain fully, of course, but I did understand her meaning."

"Oh." *What can one say to that? And from one's own bride-to-be, moreover.*

She somehow moved in even closer so that there was scarcely any space between them at all anymore. "I think I agree," she said in a soft, husky voice that should have sent shivers of desire racing down his spine.

Instead, the shivers were more closely aligned with revulsion.

"Yes, well…" He inched away.

"Shall I have her speak with your mother?"

"Err, yes, I suppose. If you are certain that you are really ready."

"I am." She inched closer still, her clear gray eyes staring deeply into his own. "And I do believe you are too."

Despite his revulsion, a part of Edmund wanted to reach out, fold Jeanne in the embrace that she so desperately seemed to want and ultimately fulfill the desire that Aunt Morris so brazenly hinted about.

But then he'd be stuck with Jeanne through all eternity.

That thought enabled him to continue his retreat across the room.

"Yes, well, that's…I suppose we're all set, then." He had never more fervently wished to be caught in a lie in his life. Something would have to prevent this wedding.

"We are." Jeanne grinned. "I believe there is nothing wrong with you, Lord Rutherford, that I cannot cure in a fortnight."

"I'm glad you think so."

"Or less." She winked as she moved toward the door. "I am going to make my farewells to the club so I can go speak with Aunt Morris right now."

"Oh, do not be, uh, too hasty. We wouldn't want to put your aunt to any worry."

"Edmund!" Jeanne shook her head. "You really are too naughty. Now I had better make my escape before someone sees me."

"Yes, absolutely. Don't let me stop you."

But he wished someone would. He offered a little wave as she shut the door, then fought the urge to collapse onto the floor in a heap.

Once she started scheming with her aunt, they'd have a date set before he could draw his next breath. And his mother would very likely agree, since she'd been mentioning "poor Katherine's dying wish" with alarming frequency of late.

Only his mother's earlier illness had enabled him to put off the wedding this long. She'd had an attack of apoplexy the night Jeanne and her aunt were expected over for an intimate dinner. Details no doubt would have been fixed that very evening. Instead, he'd been able to keep them all away for months to assure his mother a quiet recovery. She now showed no effect from the attack, so it had almost seemed a miracle of sorts.

And the miracles kept coming. For not ten minutes after Jeanne quit the room, Edmund could hear the unmistakable sounds of a flock of ladies descending the stairs, signaling the end of the Samaritan's Club meeting a full hour earlier than usual.

Which meant his mother would be down to speak with him very soon.

A knock sounded at the door.

Now, for instance.

"Do come in!" he called out with more enthusiasm than he felt.

"Edmund, I must have a word with you," his mother announced while crossing over to sit on the sofa which Jeanne had ignored a few minutes ago. She nodded at Franklin to close the door.

"Of course, Mother." Edmund joined her.

She closed her eyes and put her hand to her forehead. "Oh, I did not think they would ever leave."

"Actually, did they not leave earlier than the usual custom?"

"I suppose so. I cut short a conversation on the advisability of giving Christmas baskets to Methodists, hoping they might take the hint."

"I see that they did."

"Yes, although I'm not sure Jane Watling will ever speak to me again."

"Would that be so great a loss?"

"Edmund!" his mother admonished. "It is particularly wicked of you to point out a truth when it is an evil one. You are no help to me at all."

"I try."

"Yes," his mother grew pensive, "but what are you trying? That's what I wonder."

"I'm afraid you've lost me, Mother."

"What were you trying to do two nights ago, at the Adrington's?"

Edmund forced a laugh. "What do you mean? I wasn't trying to do anything."

"You must have had some reason for feigning insanity in such a public forum."

"Mrs. Adrington would not be pleased to hear you refer to her ballroom as a public forum."

"You know what I mean, and as usual, you're trying to steer the subject off course. What were you about the other night?"

"I was not 'about' anything. I merely had too much to drink."

"Then what on earth were you drinking? You forget, I am your mother. I've known you for twenty-seven years. I have seen you drink wine, too much of it, on numerous occasions. I have, however, never seen you display the sort of behavior that was described to me by Mrs. Delacroix."

"What did she tell you?"

"She said you hopped about the room like a large toad…"

I rather thought I was more graceful than that.

"And then you spouted nonsense, rolled on the floor and tried to cut your head off by jumping out a window…"

I did not even attempt to jump out by the window. The very idea.

"And there was something about behaving like a dog, growling, biting and so forth."

Edmund shook his head. "Can you believe I would really do all that?"

"If you had reason enough, yes." His mother narrowed her eyes as she peered closely at him. "Did you place a bet with Mountdale or one of those other rapscallions at the club?"

"No." Absolute truth there.

She sat back slightly. "I didn't think so. I would not believe you could be that foolish."

Edmund smiled.

"But I do not believe you were merely suffering the effect of too much drink, either." She shook her head. "I know of no mental weakness in our family, but that does not mean such does not exist. And if you insist that you did not affect this behavior deliberately, I know not what to think." Tears sparkled in the corners of her eyes.

For the first time, Edmund began to feel misgivings prick at his conscience. It would indeed feel awful to believe that your only son was going mad.

But she would not have to suffer for long.

And there was absolutely no way he could explain that he planned to feign insanity in order to avoid the marriage she had promised her best friend on her deathbed. He sighed. If only Jeanne hadn't grown up to be...herself.

He turned his attention back to his mother, who was watching him in silence while tears streamed down her face. Opening his arms, he gave her a hug as if he were the parent and she the disappointed child. "Don't worry, Mother. Everything will come out well."

"I am sure it will, dear boy. I'm sure it will." But she did not look convinced.

Chapter Eight

ഇ

"How long of a drive will it require?" Geoffrey asked as he speared a large chunk of ham from the dish on the buffet.

"Geoffrey," Lucia whispered to him, "it is customary to use a *fork* to serve your meat. So put away the dagger. Besides, it is really not appropriate to appear at the breakfast table with a sidearm."

He sheathed the weapon after wiping it carefully on his handkerchief. "Nonsense, you silly woman. One can never be too careful in questionable company. We are in London, after all."

"Yes, we are in London, but we are at the home of one of my dearest friends from school. Her family can hardly be called questionable company. In fact, that description might better apply to us."

"Certainly not. Our reputation is well known—ask anyone in Hertfordshire."

He was right in one sense, at least. The family reputation was indeed well known back home.

"By contrast, you have only seen Miss Eugenia Bayles and her family on one other occasion since leaving school. Who knows what could have happened to them in the interim?"

Geoffrey was starting to sound as though he were preparing for a career in criminal prosecution. With a shudder at the memory of how he had sought to shortcut his start into the legal profession, Lucia decided it would be best to steer him away from this path and back onto the subject of driving a coach. After all, how much harm could he cause in the dense

London traffic? She raised her voice. "Does anyone know how far we shall have to drive to get to the theater this evening?"

Mr. Bayles looked up from his newspaper. "I believe it is no more than a mile, all told."

Geoffrey seated himself at the table and swept a napkin into his lap. "How long does it customarily take you to make the journey?"

Mr. Bayles looked up for a moment, as if the answer were spelled out on the ceiling. "Half an hour? It depends on the traffic, of course."

"What is the shortest amount of time in which you've traveled the route?" Geoffrey pressed him.

Mr. Bayles pursed his lips. "Perhaps twenty minutes?"

Geoffrey rubbed his hands together with anticipation.

"Do not even entertain the thought," Lucia warned him in a low voice. "You will sit beside Helen in the carriage tonight."

"I do not believe that's strictly necessary." Geoffrey dumped copious amounts of salt on his egg.

"It is, in fact." Lucia replied. "You are the tallest among us and best able to block her view of the street."

"But," Geoffrey waved his fork for emphasis, "she was able to travel the way here perfectly well with the road in sight the better part of the time."

"Was she?" Lucia smiled at her sister. "That's wonderful. I'm so pleased to see you making progress." It seemed as though Helen had outgrown her fear of traveling by coach. Perhaps she might yet outgrow some of her other eccentricities.

Helen wrinkled her nose as she looked up from her meticulous dissection of the egg on her plate. "What do you mean, 'progress'?"

"Never mind." Lucia seated herself at the table, then tasted a bite of her poached egg. "Mmm. This egg is delicious."

Geoffrey eyed her disdainfully. "They're stone cold."

"Whst." Lucia waved toward Mr. Bayles, who had once again buried his nose in the newspaper. "It is still good. Even cold."

Helen burst into tears.

Lucia turned to her with concern. "Why, Helen, whatever is the matter?"

"It's ruined, totally ruined. I'll never be able to get it right, now." Head bowed, Helen appeared the picture of total dejection.

Mr. Bayles laid down his paper and focused a kindly smile on the sobbing young lady. "What is ruined, my dear?"

"Her egg," Geoffrey replied without looking up from his own plate. "It usually takes her at least three attempts to get it separated correctly."

Lucia smothered a laugh so that it came out as a muffled gagging noise, which no one appeared to notice.

"Indeed?" Mr. Bayles peered across the table. "How does one properly separate an egg with a runny center?"

"You see the difficulty, then?" Geoffrey nodded in a rare display of commiseration with his sister. "Lu, you're the closest. Why don't you fetch her another egg?"

Glancing around, Lucia saw no sign of Allen or any other servants. "Yes, very well." Still working to keep a straight face, she took a clean plate, ladled an egg into what she hoped was the geometric midpoint of the circular surface and took it to her sister, whose sobs had quickly subsided into a case of hiccupping sniffles. The other plate, splattered with rivers of egg yolk, she removed, looking around for a place where it could be secreted out of sight.

On her way back to her seat, she leaned over to whisper to Geoffrey. "When did she form this obsession with eggs?"

"Three mornings ago."

Lucia nodded. She had been away from the twins for less than four days. In that time, Geoffrey had flirted with one new profession — poaching — and started on a second. Helen had apparently lost her fear of viewing the street while riding in a moving vehicle but had taken up the habit of dissecting eggs at breakfast.

And it could have been worse.

She could never leave them for that long again. Ever.

* * * * *

Lady Rutherford stepped in front of her son to prevent his progress toward the door. "Do you really think you are well enough go out tonight?" She peered up intently into his eyes.

"Stop that, Mother. It is very disconcerting to have you stare in my face all day as if I were a museum exhibit."

"I'm sorry. I *am* worried about you, that is all."

"You are welcome to accompany me tonight, if you wish."

"Would you mind?"

"Not at all." As soon as the words were out of his mouth, he regretted them.

"You shall have to wait while I dress."

"That will be fine. The opera does not start until eight o'clock. I believe you have sufficient time yet." But now he would not have time to stop in at the club beforehand as he had planned.

"Thank you." His mother smiled as she whirled away toward the stairs.

Edmund removed his hat and cloak with a sigh. If he did not have time to visit Whites in search of a confidant, he would have to seek one out during the opera — a dicey proposition at best.

His mother descended the stairs after a reasonable interval, which time Edmund had consumed primarily by pacing back and forth in his study considering possible confidants.

It would really all depend on who was in attendance tonight anyway, unless he waited for a future opportunity.

After settling into the carriage, Edmund and Lady Rutherford exchanged smiles, nervous at first, but gradually growing more relaxed.

"I'm so glad you are well tonight, Edmund. I know Mercet is one of your favorite composers."

"Indeed, a most charming and witty fellow. His music may not be the most original, but he always chooses a very entertaining libretto."

"And it is early enough in the season that there won't be too much conversation to drown the sound of the performers."

"One hopes, anyway."

"And I believe we shall be in fine company tonight. The Ponsons are to attend, and I believe Miss Newman said she and her aunt planned to go as well."

"Really. That is...splendid."

Had Jeanne known that he planned to go to the opera tonight or was this merely one of those horrid coincidences that made life so deuced unpleasant at times?

Edmund could think of nothing else to say and so they rode the rest of the way in silence, with his mother peering in close from time to time, apparently to make sure he had not transmogrified into some hideous beast.

Outside the theater, the interminable wait began as carriages queued up in front of the building to dislodge their occupants with maddening sluggishness.

Despite the chill in the air, Edmund opened the window to watch the disembarkation, hoping for some entertainment from the experience.

He was not disappointed.

The sound of distant shrieks called his attention to a carriage that had just rounded the corner behind them. The cries subsided somewhat as the horses drew to a stop. A tall, gangly young fellow hopped down off the box and opened the door.

"Now I shall sit next to Helen as you wanted, Lu!" he announced before squeezing his frame inside.

The horses in the line of waiting carriages began to plod forward again as space cleared in front of the theater.

Shrieks issued forth from the carriage behind him again. Edmund ignored them this time.

The horses stopped.

The shrieks stopped.

The horses started forward.

The shrieks grew even louder. Edmund turned back to look again and saw that this time the carriage behind remained stopped. The door was open and the gangly young gentleman hoisted out a young lady. Gradually her shrieks became audible as words. "Put me down, Geoffrey! Put me down this instant!" She hit him with an umbrella.

He obediently started to lower her into a large mud puddle at the edge of the street.

"No, no, pick me up! Pick me up!"

Edmund chuckled.

"Set her on the sidewalk, Geoffrey, please," called a voice from inside the carriage.

The said Geoffrey complied, then assisted two other young ladies to step down from the carriage without landing in the mud. An older gentleman followed, offering his arm to help a silver-haired lady, presumably his wife. After much straightening of gowns and cloaks (they must have been packed exceedingly close in the carriage), the party set forth toward the theater. Since they were still some way from the building, they walked alone, all other carriages not depositing their occupants until at least within the scant glow of the lanterns at the entrance.

Edmund's carriage moved forward again so that it took another minute or so for the party to walk close enough that he could see them in detail. The young gentleman strode out well ahead of the others in an exceptionally rude display of physical prowess. One of the young ladies strolled in the company of the older lady and gentleman. At the rear of the party, somewhat lagging, was the young lady who had been dragged shrieking from the carriage at the start. Like the gangly young gentleman, she was also somewhat tall and awkward, though she hunched forward as she walked so that her height did not make much of an impression. After a moment, he realized the reason for her stooped posture—she was counting the paving stones as she walked.

At her side was another young lady who seemed to urge her to move faster and frequently gestured toward the other members of the party, now a great many feet ahead. He could not see her as clearly as her counting companion until they drew quite close to his carriage.

Then he recognized the dark eyes and sad countenance of the young lady he had encountered in the small parlor at the Adrington soirée. At this moment, she looked rather more impatient than sad, and he could well understand why. Her companion's odd behavior, walking with mincing steps while banging out counts with a gentleman's umbrella, was starting to attract unfavorable attention.

"Helen, please," she urged, "you will have to stop counting now and take bigger steps."

"Three hundred and seventy-eight…"

The young lady from Adrington's grabbed Helen's elbow and propelled her forward.

"You've ruined it!" Helen wrenched herself away. "I've lost count now."

Her companion closed her eyes in a long, exasperated sigh.

Edmund admired her patience. He himself would have given up and heaved Helen back into the mud puddle long ago.

His carriage pulled several paces forward and he lost sight of both young ladies and their party amid the crowd flooding into the theater building.

What was her name?

She had given her name to Adrington during the soirée, in that ghastly little room where they had cornered him. He had only half paid attention at the time. After all, though pleasant enough, the young lady was shy, unassuming and not really the sort to attract attention or remain in the memory.

Though apparently she had remained in his.

And he had heard her name. It galled him to think he could not recall it now. The name was there, certainly, in the recesses of his mind. All he would have to do was resolve not to think of it, and the name would spring to mind while he was fully occupied with something else.

"Mother?" He turned away from the window. "Do you know any of the players for tonight's…"

He saw that his mother had fallen asleep.

* * * * *

Mr. Bayles' face suddenly loomed large in front of her in the dim light. "Are you enjoying the opera so far, Miss Wright?"

"Yes, very much, thank you," Lucia answered. *Though I would enjoy it a great deal more if Helen would stop poking me.*

"I find the pace rather too slow," Geoffrey opined. "The entire first act is at an end, and they have done no more than talk to each other. Or rather, sing."

Helen leaned in across Lucia to address her brother. "This is the opera, Geoff. That's all they're *supposed* to do. Though I do believe there has been entirely too much hand wringing."

"Hand wringing?"

"Yes. The heroine has wrung her hands thirty-seven times so far."

"Perhaps it is a nervous habit she affects to help her reach the high notes?"

"Perhaps." Helen sat back.

"So there's to be no swordplay, then?"

"In 'The Virtuous Vicar'?" Lucia shook her head. "I'm sorry, Geoff. Some operas do indeed have a more active theme and fights of some sort. But even those you would probably find a bit droll. I believe they rather more sing about fights than actually engage in them."

Geoffrey stood. "All this talk has made me restless. I need to take some exercise. If you will excuse me, ladies, Mr. Bayles?"

Lucia stood to join him. She absolutely could not allow Geoffrey to roam the theater by himself. "I would like to join you, if I may."

One eyebrow arched, giving Geoffrey the look of a distinguished older gentleman questioning the propriety of a young relative's proposed venture. "Are you sure that would be appropriate, Lucia? I may go in for a smoke, you know."

"You don't smoke, Geoffrey."

The eyebrow arched even higher, if that were possible. "How do you know?"

Lucia smiled. "You are right, of course. It is no business of mine what you do in the company of gentlemen after dinner." Though she knew for a fact that Geoffrey had never smoked at home, at least. Nicholas always provided her with a summary of her brother's activities during the interval after dinner, which he usually spent alone because they so seldom entertained guests.

"Nevertheless, I will accompany you as far as practicable." It was indeed unfortunate that they had not room to accommodate Nicholas in the carriage—he could have at least kept watch over Geoffrey during the intermissions. As always, the duty now fell to her. She placed a hand on her brother's arm.

"I shall go with you," Eugenie announced from her seat behind them. "Mother, will you come sit with Helen so that she will not be lonely?"

"I am never lonely," Helen objected sullenly.

"Nevertheless, I would appreciate the opportunity to visit with you, Miss Wright." Mrs. Bayles stepped around to take the chair vacated by Lucia.

"Thank you!" Lucia whispered with a smile. Then she followed Geoffrey and Eugenie out into the mêlée.

It was all a little overwhelming. People clustered close together in a series of small spaces, all trying to get past one another yet avoid touching or making eye contact with those not of their acquaintance. Lucia found it easier to simply keep her eyes focused on the floor, following Geoffrey wherever he might lead.

After a few moments, Eugenie put a hand on her arm. "You cannot go in there, Lucia."

With a start, Lucia looked up to see that they stood outside the gentleman's smoking room, just as Geoffrey portended. She grinned with embarrassment. "You are right about that. I hope he does not stay too long."

Eugenie spread her fan and fanned her face a few times. "It has grown rather warm in here."

"We could step outside for a few moments."

"It is not *that* warm. Why do we not look for a space that is not so crowded?"

The two strolled for a moment, then soon found a great deal of said space. The crowd parted like the Red Sea under the staff of Moses. In the center of the dry seabed was not the chariot of the Egyptians, however, but the young gentleman who demonstrated such odd behavior at the Adrington soirée.

How could she forget his name when his face and voice and manners reappeared so often in her memory?

"Lord Rutherford," Eugenie whispered.

Lucia wondered if she had voiced her question aloud.

"We'd better keep back." Eugenie pulled her arm.

Lucia resisted. "Why?"

"He's dangerous."

"He is not dangerous," Lucia scoffed.

"You *saw* how he behaved at the Adrington's. You probably saw more than anyone else, now that I think of it. He was in that parlor with you when I came back with Peggy."

"Yes, and his behavior posed no danger to me at all. It was only when Lord Adrington and the others arrived that he started to behave unsoundly." As if he were putting on an act for them, but not for her.

Nonsense. His words and actions when in the room alone with her were just as unorthodox, albeit rather more appealing. He was the first gentleman to ask her to dance, and certainly the most enthusiastic.

In any case, his behavior now, as he stood speaking with an older lady who appeared to be his mother or another close relation, was beyond reproach. If the two of them realized the rest of the company avoided them like the plague, they gave no sign. Instead, the two smiled as they carried on their quiet conversation, occasionally gesturing or looking briefly about the room.

"We can have nothing to fear from this man. Come, step a few steps from the crowd and give yourself some breathing room." Lucia walked a few steps toward the isolated couple, then turned and invited Eugenie to follow suit.

Which she did with considerable reluctance.

"You are really quite funny, Eugenie. You are afraid to step within twenty feet of a gentleman who stands quietly speaking with his mother, yet you purposefully set out yourself to bring Helen and Geoffrey to stay under your own roof."

"I do not understand what your sister and brother have to do with this crazy man."

"Eugenie, they are very likely as imbalanced as he. If not more so."

"How could you say such a thing about your own brother? He has never tried to bite anyone."

"Not yet, anyway." Lucia had to agree with that assessment. "But I may have given him ample opportunity, leaving him alone for this long. And we did not bring Nicholas, either. Take a final breath of air, Eugenie. It is time to dive back into the crowd." As she turned to head off in search of her brother, Lucia's gaze landed squarely on Lord Rutherford. He had been watching her, and the realization sent a warm, tingling sensation spreading from her head to her toes. His mother followed his gaze to look at her also, and Lucia smiled, acknowledging their previous, if unusual, acquaintance.

Then he turned away as if he had not seen her at all.

Chapter Nine

ഇ

Edmund wanted to howl — not as a canine, but merely as a gentleman suffering extreme frustration. He could not find anyone who would come close enough to give him the time of day, let alone allow him to confide his plan. Why had he not thought of this beforehand?

From the moment he and his mother disembarked from their carriage, the assembled company had parted before him like...

He disliked biblical analogies. People stayed away. They scurried from his presence as if he were the village tanner.

And while he enjoyed his mother's company, he would not accomplish his objective by speaking to her all evening.

For a brief moment, it looked as though someone would, finally, end the isolation. Two figures emerged from the throng in the lobby, but his hopes faded quickly as he realized that they were ladies — moreover, ladies not of his acquaintance.

Then he looked again. Though he had not formally been introduced and knew neither of their names, he did feel as if he knew *them*, at least a little. Watching them from the carriage window had given him a sense of familiarity, as if he were closely acquainted and knew something of their lives.

One of the women he'd seen very little of at all. The shorter of the two, she had a round face with a bowed mouth, much given to dimpled smiles earlier when walking into the theater. Now, however, the bow was drawn up into a pout, as if she were worried or displeased.

The taller young lady he recognized better. Her dark eyes, fringed by black lashes, did not exhibit the sadness they had earlier, nor the concern of her companion. In fact, they danced with light, as though she were laughing privately at some joke. Her eyes had looked that way for a time, when he had tried to get her to dance.

"Do you know that young lady?" his mother asked.

He was supposed to have no memory of his time at the Adrington soirée. "No, I do not know her." He turned away in time to receive a faint smile from one of the members of the Samaritan's Club, Lady Silthwaite. For a brief moment, he even considered her as possible confidante, but she was so hard of hearing that any secret he might confide with her would have to be made audible to the whole room.

Intermission would soon end. Even now much of the crowd, including the young lady and her companion, began to move back toward the theater.

The young lady he had met at the Adrington's might be his only hope. He steered his mother toward Lady Silthwaite and then hurried over to catch up with the young lady. "Excuse me, Miss…"

She paid him no attention, but her companion turned to face him with a horrorstricken gaze as if he'd approached from the grave instead of the other side of the room. She moved her mouth to speak, but no sound came forth as she clutched the arm of her friend.

"Ouch, Eugenie! You are as bad as Helen. Stop squeezing my arm so." The young lady from the Adrington's grabbed her companion's hand, turning so that she could now see him.

And he could see her. Up close, for the first time since their meeting at the fateful soirée. Such expressive eyes. Filled with mirth when she had first turned to him, they now reflected the fear and concern that he was growing used to, and something more.

She waited for a moment for him to speak.

What on earth could he say to her?

"I thought we were looking for Geoffrey." Her companion had edged around to be as far from Edmund as possible, and she now attempted to steer the pair of them back into the crowd, away from him.

How could he confess his plan to someone he did not know, someone being physically pulled from his presence by a terrified companion, someone whose sincere gaze apparently caused him to lose the power of speech?

Still she waved her companion to be silent and waited with patience for him to speak.

"Ahem." He hoped an attempt to bring sound to his throat might bring words to his mind. "It is said that fortune favors fools."

"Yes, I have heard that." Her forehead creased in a thoughtful frown. "I cannot recollect where."

"Well…" He could not believe that she continued to listen to him when all he seemed capable of was poor recitation of dramatic prologues. "What I mean to say is that if you can remember that, then I want you to remember also—"

"Ouch!" The young lady whirled around to face her companion.

"There's Geoffrey now. We must be after him, Lucia!" The companion yanked the young lady away with sudden force.

Her face flashed an apologetic smile just before she disappeared into the crowd. Edmund slowly returned to his mother's side.

His last chance to confess to an acquaintance, and he had thoroughly botched the matter. To be sure, the circumstances of the conversation had been less than ideal, and he could hardly consider the lady an acquaintance. He did not even know her name. But he could not shake the sense that he had lost an invaluable opportunity, that her confidence was one he could trust.

Surely there were others.

Perhaps not in the theater, where so many came only to "see and be seen", but London was an immense city, and beyond this company, where the paste jewels outshined the sparkle of any true wit, there lay street after street filled with industrious, honest-working people. If nothing else, perhaps he could buy the trust of one. Employ the trust of one. He could hire a confidant.

Edmund and his mother slowly made their way back to their box just as the roar of conversation quieted to a mere hum and the singers took the stage. Usually, he savored this moment, anticipating the music and drama to come. But tonight he wished the players on stage might simply give up and leave. He could take no pleasure in other's acting when he had his own to consider.

Coins clinked together. "Thank you, boy."

Edmund turned to see an usher hold the chair next his mother steady while Mrs. Morris, Jeanne's aunt, slowly lowered her substantial frame into it. "Good evening, Lord Rutherford," she whispered.

Jeanne took the seat next to her, fortunately at the other end of the row in their box. Before sitting down, she flashed him a lascivious grin, showing that she had not forgotten their earlier conversation. Or, at least, her part in that earlier conversation. He hoped he had done nothing to encourage the thoughts she apparently still entertained.

He could hear his mother and Mrs. Morris exchange a few whispered words before a sudden loud interval in the music rendered all conversation momentarily inaudible. Then they started again. He could catch few of their words. However, he had a pretty good idea, from the looks cast in his and Jeanne's direction, about the subject of the conversation.

He had failed, then. His plan to make Jeanne break the engagement had somehow only encouraged her to speed it to conclusion.

Unless...

Unless he acted right away.

If he could find no one to listen to his words, he would commit them to paper. That would prove — later — that his actions had been the calculated moves of a rational thinker. More or less. He stood, offered whispered excuses to his mother and made his way to the back of the theater.

As he walked, he puzzled his next move. Who would bring paper, pen and a traveling inkwell to the opera?

No one of his acquaintance, certainly. He could send the carriage back to fetch them from home, but that would take too much time.

He gently pried open the doors leading to the lobby, heartily wishing that it were later in the season so that conversation would drown out any noise he might make. The lobby was empty, save for a young man sweeping up broken glass in a far corner. He didn't look to be the sort to be able to write, let alone one to carry writing implements on his person.

Or paper. But as his eyes scanned the lobby, he realized that a source of paper surrounded him in the form of the playbills nailed to the walls, memorializing past productions and advertising new ones.

It seemed unfair to remove the publicity for an upcoming program, so he focused his attention on the older playbills, quickly spotting one that was perfect for his purposes — low enough so that its absence would not be terribly noticeable and from a production that had been so awful he was doing the theater a service by removing the evidence of its existence.

He gently ripped the playbill free from the nail attaching it to the wall and rolled it up. What could he use to write? There was probably some sort of office on the premises, but he had no idea where it might be located. He could, perhaps, try looking backstage. As his thoughts wandered in that direction, he remembered something he had seen in the theater itself. A young man sat very near the stage, off to the far right, making sketches of the performers. Perhaps he might borrow one of the man's pencils.

The exercise would have been much simpler had he thought of this before intermission. Now, he had to creep down a side aisle, hoping his mother, Mrs. Morris and Jeanne would not notice and that he would not be too disruptive to the rest of the audience.

Several people turned to glare at him as he passed, but he made his way to the front, borrowed a charcoal pencil and returned to the lobby without incident.

"Boy!" He summoned the lad with the broom. "Half a crown for you if you summon my carriage. The name is Rutherford."

The boy's eyes widened. "'essir!" He tossed his broom aside as he dashed toward the door.

Now Edmund had to write. "*I, Edmund Fairfax Rutherford*," he began, "*am of sound mind and body this day, February 3, 1816. On this page, I set forth my intent to appear as a lunatic for the said purpose of discouraging the attentions of…*"

He could not give his reason. It would leave him liable for a breach of marriage suit. Moreover, it could injure his mother's sensibilities most keenly. So he scratched out the words purporting to give a purpose and instead listed a duration for his feigned lunacy. Three months should be sufficient time for Jeanne to come to her senses, see that he had lost his and end the engagement. With a little luck, she might even become attached to someone else. After all, she was considered quite a beauty and the social events of the season had barely begun.

"*The resumption of normal behavior in three months time, along with this letter, will constitute proof that I am indeed sane and perfectly able to conduct my own affairs. You are charged not to tell anyone of this intent until three months have expired. Then you are to use your best efforts to see that I am released from whatever confinement I may be in at that time. Your silence will be amply rewarded.*"

He signed his name and added the date again, just to make certain.

He had nothing with which to seal the letter. All he could do was fold the stiff paper into quarters and hope for the best.

After another moment, the boy reappeared. "'f'you please, sir," he touched his cap, "your carriage is just outside now."

"Good. Thank you." He handed the boy the promised coin, then stepped out to speak to his coachman. "Deliver this paper to Franklin. Instruct him to set out with it tomorrow morning and bring it to a solicitor of good reputation. It should *not* go to Mr. Stansbury, our family solicitor, but to another. Do you understand?"

"Yessir." The coachman nodded.

Edmund handed him the folded paper. "No matter what happens, he must deliver this letter into the hands of a solicitor tomorrow."

"Yessir."

"You'd better hurry." Edmund waved him on.

"Now, sir?"

"Yes. Deliver the letter to Franklin, then come back for Lady Rutherford and myself."

"Yessir." The coachman snapped the reins and the carriage started forward with a jerk.

Edmund watched him until he turned a corner and faded into the fog at the far end of the street.

Then he returned to wait for the professional performance to end so that his amateur one could begin.

Despite his impatience for the opera to be over, he found the voice of the lead soprano so beautiful that he became mesmerized by the music in the final scene and greeted the closing notes of the performance with reluctance.

With a start, he realized that already people were standing and preparing to leave. If he wanted to demonstrate his insanity in front of an audience of sufficient size, he would have to begin soon.

Somehow.

What had been easy at the Adrington soirée now suddenly became difficult. What should he do? He could climb up on stage and leap across, as he had in the ballroom, or he could drop to the floor, barking and snapping at the heels of patrons, but neither option seemed right, somehow. Whereas it had all come rather easily the first time.

He stood, looking about the theater for inspiration.

"What did you think of the performance, Lord Rutherford?" Jeanne had sidled up beside him while he was unaware.

"What?" He turned his focus to her with some reluctance.

"I thought the soprano uncommonly good, though she looked a perfect sow on the stage."

"Yes, I did enjoy her voice. And for that reason, I paid little attention to her appearance."

"How could you not notice? Draped as she was with fake jewels and pearls, she was a perfectly ridiculous display."

"My mind was not on jewelry."

"Goodness, you are cross this evening...Edmund." She leaned in to whisper this last intimate address. "But I believe I have a solution. Aunt Morris and your mother have fixed the date for the fifteenth of March."

"Beware the ides."

"What?" Jeanne fixed him with a vapid gaze.

"The ides of March. 'Beware the ides of March.' We cannot be married on the day they murdered Caesar."

"Oh, Edmund, I did not realize that one of your friends met with such an awful fate on that day. I shall ask Aunt Morris to select another date. A closer one?" Jeanne glided away, leaving Edmund with his increasingly panicked thoughts.

He could not possibly be expected to marry a woman so stupid she did not recognize one of the most famous lines in the history of literature. Or the history of history, for that matter. She thought Caesar was a personal acquaintance?

And all this, of course, brought him no closer to his objective. Perhaps he should pretend he was Caesar. Go about wearing a bedsheet and a coronet of leaves? He could see no bedsheets in sight here, though, or leaves.

But how about a crown of jewels?

Edmund looked around again, searching for a glimpse of sparkle on someone's head.

Not far away, an older lady stood chatting with the occupants of her box, apparently oblivious to the fact that others were leaving all around them.

Edmund first walked toward the bejeweled lady, then flung off his sense of decorum and ran toward her at full speed. When he was only a few feet away, he jumped up onto a chair and reached out to snatch the glittering prize off her head. It was a turban rather than a coronet, but still bedecked with large and hopefully imitation jewels, he could set off to begin his reign as Caesar or perhaps the sultan of someplace.

Soon after he made his escape, however, he found his new career as sovereign cut rather short as someone tackled him from behind and pulled him to the floor.

"At last, I've caught you," a male voice announced in triumph.

"Unhand me, you peasant!" Edmund rolled free and scrambled to his feet, glancing back just long enough to see that he had been "captured" by Geoffrey, the long-legged young man he watched outside the theater. Who had been somehow connected to the dark-eyed, patient young lady whose companion had called her "Lucia." Edmund ran from him, uncertain what his next move should be. Steps leading up to the stage beckoned from beyond the rows of chairs.

Despite the clusters of people who still remained conversing in the theater, it seemed to take no effort to brush past them and fly up the steps onto the stage. "I am the Sultan of Perkestra" he announced, lifting his hands into the air in a gesture meant to convey regal authority. "And this man," he pointed at Geoffrey, "has offended my person."

"You keep sad company, then, your majesty," Geoffrey called out as he approached the stage. "For I have been tracking you and your collection of guttersnipe thieves through the very sewers of London."

"Geoffrey!" a woman's voice hailed in anguish.

"How dare you accuse my entourage of thievery!" Edmund looked about the stage, wishing the production had involved a fake sword or some other weapon, but grateful at least that Geoffrey had decided to join the entertaining ruse. This was turning out to be as much fun as the Adrington's soirée.

"I accuse no entourage." Geoffrey vaulted onto the stage, stumbling slightly as he scrambled to his feet. "I accuse *you*, known to all of London as 'Redcloak'. It is you who have been stealing the valuables from the helpless and innocent. And now you shall be brought to justice."

"Geoffrey!" The woman's voice drew closer.

It had to be *her* voice. "Nonsense. My cloak is blue." Edmund pointed at his nonexistent cloak, taking the opportunity to turn and look for the woman whose voice he'd heard.

Though she was still some distance from them, the look of worried anguish in her eyes stopped him cold. He might be enjoying himself, but she obviously was not. He started toward her to reassure her that she had nothing to fear.

But in the next instant, he found himself facing the floor instead of the young lady as Geoffrey hurled into his legs and pulled him down.

Chapter Ten

ﮀ

Lucia squeezed back tears as she rushed up onto the stage. Geoffrey had now apparently decided he was a Bow Street Runner or some such thing, which would have been a difficult but manageable proposition at home. But now he brought his delusion to the attention of London society. He had knocked down another gentleman not once, but twice, and appeared ready to do so a third time. Lord Rutherford had regained his footing and raced off toward the wings with Geoffrey in hot pursuit.

"Come back, Geoffrey. Please!"

She turned at the sound of running footsteps behind her and saw that Lord Rutherford had circled behind the stage and reappeared on the other side with two poles made of bamboo. "I insist you stop this unseemly scuffling," he demanded. "If you want to fight me, it must be as a gentleman." He tossed one of the poles to Geoffrey. "*En garde*!" He began to circle Geoffrey as an opponent in a fencing match.

For a moment Geoffrey merely looked at the pole in his hand. Then he tossed it aside with a grin. "You're a bloody fool, Redcloak." He drew his dagger.

"No, Geoffrey! No!" Lucia hurled herself forward, but it seemed her feet were weighted with lead. In her mind's eye, she saw Geoffrey stab the dagger into the slab of meat on the buffet that morning. "Stop, please. This man is not Redcloak. He cannot be." She struggled to think of something, anything to dissuade her brother from acting the part she had unwittingly created for him. "Redcloak was captured and hanged last month."

At the sight of Geoffrey's dagger, Lord Rutherford's expression changed from bemused superiority to terrified realization to grim determination all within moments. He began to back slowly toward the wings.

Geoffrey stalked after him, his pace matching that of his prey. "A ruse. It was all a ruse, Lu. This is the real Redcloak, and I've caught him. Me! And I'm going to do this all without your help this time." He lunged forward, and though Lord Rutherford parried with his pole, it splintered into bits.

Geoffrey drew the dagger back and stabbed Lord Rutherford in the leg. With a grunt, Lord Rutherford struck Geoffrey on the wrist, knocking the dagger free from his grip. Both men collapsed on the floor just as Lucia caught up with them.

She found it increasingly difficult to breathe. A crowd of other men had gathered at the edge of the stage, but they seemed frozen into inaction, so she pressed forward. She alone would have to stop Geoffrey. In vain, she tried to grasp his arm from among the tangled mass of limbs before her. Instead, she grabbed at his hair. Her fingers first slipped through without gaining purchase, but on the second grab, she anchored her hands near his scalp and heaved with all her strength.

Her efforts actually pulled both men up for a moment, entangled as they were, but Lord Rutherford soon slipped back to the floor.

"What the devil?" Geoffrey twisted around to see her. "Let me go, Lu!"

"No!" The word came out as a choked sob, scarcely audible even to her. Her arms felt like they were being pulled from their sockets and she was liable to tumble forward at any moment. But she knew she had to keep hold of Geoffrey to give Lord Rutherford the chance to get away.

He did not run away, however. In fact, he barely moved at all. She stared in horror, not listening to her brother's screams, barely noticing when others pulled Geoffrey away from her so that she stood clutching at empty air.

The space around Lord Rutherford immediately filled with men and their shouts as they ordered one another about. She stepped toward him, not trusting herself to say anything, simply hoping against hope that she would see the same animated light in his countenance, that he would live through this and somehow forgive them.

For though he might blame Geoffrey, she was the one at fault.

* * * * *

Edmund forgot, for a time, that he professed to be the sultan of someplace or other. When the odd young man drew a dagger, the whole charade had become rather more serious, since he had nothing more lethal to defend himself with than a bamboo pole.

Which had shown itself to be a poor weapon indeed.

He cursed himself for relying on instinct, parrying with the pole as if he held a sword, rather than his intellect, which would have instructed him to do something a little more effective. Like run.

Men were talking all around at a furious rate—talking at him, over him, to each other. But not to him.

His leg hurt like hell.

He was propped up only a little, so that he could not really see his leg too well. Something dug against his shoulder blades.

He did not recognize any of the gentlemen around him, and his adversary was nowhere in sight. Now and again, he could hear his voice crying out with exuberance. "I got him. Did you see that? Me! I captured Redcloak!"

Why was that gawky young man calling him "Redcloak"?

"I'm the sultan," Edmund finally protested, just to see if anyone would listen. He tried to load his voice with indignation, but the sound came out a hoarse, mumbled growl instead.

"You'll have to take him too."

"He needs a doctor, first, though."

Someone moved his leg.

"Ow." Edmund slapped at the offender.

"You are right. He will need a surgeon."

"Edmund!" His mother's voice cut through the fog of unfamiliar voices. He had slumped down so far, however, that he could not see her. He tried to scoot himself back upright, but the pain in his leg caused him to abandon the effort immediately.

"Do not try to move," someone above him said. "You're making it bleed more."

"This man is my son," his mother announced imperiously. "Of course you will let me see him."

Edmund tried to reach out to reassure his mother, but his arm now seemed too heavy to raise. He offered a smile instead, hoping it bore none of the weakness he felt.

His mother's face, so stoic as she approached through the crowd of men around him, now collapsed into an expression of pain and sadness far more intense than anything *he* had ever felt in his life. He never intended to cause her such pain. Was it too late to tell her the—

"I've sent for a doctor, Edmund. Then we shall take you home."

"Do you think that wise, madam?" one of the gentleman in attendance asked. "After..." He pointed to the turban lying forgotten on the stage floor.

"I do not believe I have the pleasure of your acquaintance, young man," Lady Rutherford answered with a look that would melt iron at a hundred paces. "You'll forgive me then if I save that *joy* for another occasion?" She turned back to Edmund. "As

I said, as soon as your wound has been tended, I shall take you home."

He tried to answer, but his mouth seemed too dry to form words. Or his tongue was too thick and heavy to move. He could only offer a brief smile.

"Madam?" The gentleman, cut so sharply just a minute ago, appeared reluctant to attempt counsel now. Nevertheless, he pressed on. "Your, ah, slippers, Madam."

Mrs. Rutherford looked down to see a red stain spread up the side of her light gray kid slippers. "One of you, tell that doctor to hurry!" She bent down, then fell to her knees and cradled Edmund's head in her arms. "They assured me it was just a flesh wound," she said in a hoarse whisper, "and yet you look so pale. So very pale."

He wanted to tell her not to worry, not to cry, but his voice would not answer. Above her head, he could see the face of an angel with big, dark, sorrowful eyes framed by waves of dark hair. Angels should never look so sad.

The vision faded. Now all he could see was a pattern on fabric, the colors gradually fading as the room grew darker. It must be getting late. He should say something about leaving. It was time for them to leave.

But it was apparently too late. The colors faded into blackness, and in another instant, he let go, wishing he could see the angel one last time. The roar of voices and the sound of his mother's quiet sobs ebbed into an all-encompassing silence.

* * * * *

Lucia felt a warm arm across her shoulder—Eugenie had come up next to her and was offering words of comfort.

"Do not fret, Lucia. Everything will be fine." She tried to guide Lucia toward the stairs.

Lucia pulled away, turning back so she could see. More men had come onto the stage now, gathered in two throngs, presumably one around each of the two combatants, though she could no longer see either of them.

"There, there, dear." Mrs. Bayles handed her a handkerchief.

Lucia was not aware that she stood in need of a handkerchief, or even that she had been crying. But she pressed the cloth to her face anyway. It was soaked through in an instant.

"Mr. Bayles will see to your brother. Come away, now." Mrs. Bayles and Eugenie succeeded in turning Lucia back toward the stairs, and they had progressed several paces toward them before Lucia froze in place.

Helen was coming up the stairs. Had she seen the fight? What would she do when she saw the men take Geoffrey away? For they would surely take Geoffrey away somewhere. Remembering Helen's earlier shrieks at the sight of the road from the carriage window, Lucia could not begin to imagine the hideous cacophony her sister would unleash at the sight of the commotion on the stage.

Helen kept her eyes focused down as she crossed over toward Lucia. Then she looked up. "Is that Geoffrey over there?"

Lucia nodded, not trusting words.

Helen watched the men for a moment. The gestures and raised voices made it apparent that they were arguing. Then she turned her gaze to the splintered pole lying on the stage. "Somebody's going to have to clean that up soon. Before it congeals." She pointed to an uneven pool of blood on the stage.

Lucia fought off a wave of nausea.

Eugenie cringed. "Please, ladies. I think we should leave now."

"Geoffrey really has gotten into it this time, hasn't he?" Helen asked.

"I am afraid so." Lucia sniffed.

"But Mr. Bayles will take care of him, will he not?" Helen nodded toward him.

"Yes, I believe so."

"Can we leave, then?"

"Yes, we can leave." Lucia sighed. *But we cannot go home.*

Chapter Eleven

ରୁ

Lucia was in no mood to eat breakfast the next morning. But she longed for the warmth of company, for the chatter of friends to chase away the gloom that had settled into her soul. She dressed carelessly, knowing that perhaps they might be able to get out to see Geoffrey but not worried as to whether her appearance met the mark.

"Good morning," she said softly to the company assembled around the breakfast table.

"Lucia!" Eugenie beckoned her toward the empty chair next to her.

"Miss Wright, so good to see you." Mrs. Bayles smiled kindly. "I was about to have Peggy bring up a tray, since I'd rather imagined you would need to rest this morning."

"I have rested, thank you." Lucia sat next to Eugenie. "As much as I was able," she confided in a low voice.

"Mr. Bayles has gone out, but we may expect to hear back from him before the morning is through. Will you take some tea?" Mrs. Bayles asked.

"Yes, thank you."

"Good morning, dears." Sophie sailed into the room like a colorful kite into a circle of rain clouds.

"You are infernally cheerful this morning," Eugenie greeted her. "It's hurting my eyes."

Sophie picked up a plate from the sideboard and began making her selections from the buffet. "I had a splendid time at the Garland's last evening. I've never laughed so much in all my life. We decided the same collection—all eight of us—will meet again next week." She started over to the table. "I hope your evening at the opera was quite enjoyable?"

"In a word, no." Eugenie indicated the open seat at the table with a halfhearted wave of her hand.

"What happened?" Sophie looked around at the sea of gloomy faces above the breakfast plates. Concern creased her brow as she sat down. "Oh, dear. Has somebody died? I do seem to be the last to hear these things."

"No," Eugenie sighed. "Nobody has died."

"Yet," Helen added helpfully.

"Not yet," Eugenie corrected herself.

"What do you mean, 'not yet'?" Sophie demanded. "Is someone gravely ill? I can cancel my plans for this afternoon if we need to visit…"

Eugenie held up her hand. "Yes, someone is ill, but it is no one of our actual acquaintance, so we will not need to pay any visits."

"That is well, then." Sophie sawed the corner off a slice of toast. "I am sorry to hear that anyone is ill on such a fine day."

"It's rainy and cold," Helen announced. "Hardly fine by my definition."

"Yes, well, I am equally sorry to hear that someone is ill on a rainy day. But, really, in London there must be scores—no, hundreds of ill people every day. I cannot very well go about gloomy on their behalf, can I? So why do you?"

"It is rather more than that, I'm afraid." Eugenie glanced at Lucia before continuing. "It's a most awkward situation, really, but I suppose I…*we* had better tell you before you hear of it elsewhere."

Lucia nodded.

Sophie lowered her knife. "Tell me what?"

"The opera was the scene of some rather…unusual events last evening." Eugenie paused as if unwilling to continue. She looked into her cup of chocolate.

"And?" Sophie prompted with her knife.

"Don't do that," Eugenie said crossly.

"Do what?"

"Do what you're...with the...oh, just put the knife down, Sophie."

Sophie looked at the implement and shrugged. "Very well. Now will you continue?"

"Yes. I don't know where to begin, really." Eugenie looked at Lucia.

"Lord Rutherford attended the opera last night," Lucia prompted.

Sophie's eyes widened. "Oh. Did he bite the conductor?"

"No." Eugenie shook her head. "There was no animal behavior last night."

"I beg to differ." Helen looked up from her mutilated egg. "Geoffrey behaved quite like an animal."

"Geoffrey?" Sophie's forehead wrinkled with confusion. "What has he to do with it?"

"I shall—err," Eugenie glanced at Lucia apologetically, "get to that in a moment. At the end of the performance, Lord Rutherford swiped the turban off Lady Greer's head, then ran about the theater announcing that he was the sultan of...someplace."

"Perkestra," Lucia added softly.

"Where is that?" Sophie asked.

Eugenie shot her sister a glance of supreme annoyance. "I haven't the faintest idea. And it does not signify, Sophie, really. The point of the matter is that the man is clearly not the sultan of any place."

"Except, perhaps, Bedlam?" Sophie snickered at her own joke, but quickly stopped when she saw the others exchange despondent glances. "I am sorry. Did they really take him to Bedlam, then?"

"No."

"*Geoffrey* was taken to Bethlehem Hospital," Helen explained. "Lord Rutherford was taken to his home."

"What?" Sophie clamped her fingers together so that the piece of toast in her hands exploded across the table in a spray of crumbs. "Geoffrey is in Bedlam?"

"I think it sounds much nicer when you refer to the hospital by its proper name, Bethlehem. Peaceful, almost." Mrs. Bayles patted her daughter's hand. "And your father will have him out soon, I daresay." She wiped the excess crumbs off her fingers.

"How in the world... I thought Lord Rutherford was the crazy one." Sophie brushed crumbs across the tablecloth with a look of mild distaste.

Eugenie glanced at Lucia again.

This time Lucia felt it incumbent to smile and put her friend's uneasiness to rest. "Geoffrey rather outdid him last night."

"What? How?" Sophie demanded.

"If you'd stop interrupting," Eugenie countered, "we might be able to tell you."

"Yes, well." Sophie waved her knife again. "Go on."

"I told you not to do that!" Eugenie glared at her.

"Who's interrupting now?"

"Girls, enough. Can't you see this is hard enough on your guests," Mrs. Bayles nodded at Lucia and Helen, "without your constant bickering?"

Both Eugenie and Sophie dipped their heads in silence for a brief moment.

"Now then," Sophie snapped her head upright again, "you said Lord Rutherford professed to be a sultan?"

"Yes," Eugenie responded with equal vigor. "But Geoffrey claimed he was really the, uh, a thief, wasn't it? Redbreast or some such?"

"Redcloak," both Lucia and Helen corrected. Lucia immediately looked down at her plate.

"Redcloak?" Sophie swallowed. "Who in heaven's name is that?"

Eugenie shrugged. "A famous thief, I suppose. I don't keep up with these things."

"No, he's not famous." Lucia stared at the floral pattern on the china plate until the tiny leaves blurred into a continuous chain, like a snake winding its way through her toast.

"Well his name would have been in the papers." Eugenie started to gesture with her spoon, then set it down hurriedly. "You told Geoffrey he'd been arrested and hanged."

"Well, he was not." Lucia pushed her toast until it covered most of the leaf-snake. "And his name was never in the papers."

"Why not?"

Lucia looked up. "Because I invented him."

"This gets stranger by the moment." Sophie licked her fingers. "Why did you invent a thief?"

"It was a story I told to entertain Geoffrey and Helen. We often take turns telling one another stories in the evenings."

"I see." Eugenie nodded. "And Geoffrey thought Lord Rutherford was this Redcloak person. Did he not realize such a person does not actually exist?"

Lucia looked down again. "I-I think he does not."

"Why was Lord Rutherford wearing a red cloak? Only grandmothers wear red cloaks," Sophie asked.

"I do not believe he was, in fact, wearing any article of clothing that was red. But that did not deter Geoffrey," Lucia answered.

Sophie leaned forward. "So, Geoffrey confronted 'Redcloak', and then…?"

"He did not merely confront Lord Rutherford. He attacked him."

"Attacked him?" Sophie's features contracted into an expression of disbelief.

"Attacked him." Lucia sighed. "Jumped on him. Then, later, stabbed him."

"With a dagger," Helen added for clarification.

Sophie's hands dropped motionless to the table. "Oh my. Then it is he who is...was he almost killed?"

"I don't know. At the time, they — all the gentlemen — said it was merely a flesh wound But...he was unconscious when they carried him away." Lucia felt a lump rising in her throat and she realized her sadness was by no means on Geoffrey's account alone.

"There was a lot of blood on that stage," Helen noted. "A big mess for someone to clean up."

Sophie waited for them to continue, then prompted, "So then Geoffrey...?"

"The men seemed uncertain what should be done. Since his behavior had become so violent, they felt the need to detain him. We left before it was fully resolved." Traversing the length of the theater and out to the street was the longest walk Lucia could ever remember.

"But we did hear one more thing," Eugenie added. "We were almost out of the theater, so we did not see it happen. But I believe Lady Rutherford — the crazy gentleman's mother — suffered an attack of apoplexy after he was carried out."

"Oh, that is too awful." Sophie smashed the larger of the toast crumbs on her plate, then brushed them together in a pile of toasted powder. "But I suppose seeing someone so close in your family act that way in front of all those people..." She stopped. "I am sorry, Lucia. I did not think—"

"Do not worry about offending me, Sophie. You cannot possibly say anything I have not already heard in my mind countless times over."

"What an evening." Sophie sighed. "That poor lady. And Geoffrey...and Lord Rutherford, and..." She cringed.

"All that mess, remember." Helen twirled her fork in an intricate pattern in the egg yolk. "I do hope someone has cleaned it up by now."

"Helen, I do believe we've heard enough about that aspect of the evening," Lucia said sharply.

"I believe we've heard enough about all of it." Helen pushed her plate forward and herself away from the table. "I'm going for a walk now."

Lucia then had a pretty good idea of how the rest of her morning would proceed.

* * * * *

Why was he still in his own house? Edmund swatted at his bedpost with disgust. After last night's escapades, he should have been sent to a discreet private madhouse somewhere far in the country. Or even to Bedlam. It did not matter, really. He could survive anything for three months if it would buy him a lifetime of freedom.

Edmund sat up in bed, wishing it were not so dark, and then wishing he had not sat up so quickly, since the movement had left him a little lightheaded. He felt at the bandages on his left leg, which pulsed with a constant, throbbing ache. He was no better off than before. Worse, even. Still at home, still engaged to that insufferable girl, and now with a wound that would leave him unable to walk or ride properly for months.

It was time to take drastic measures. Feign an insanity so intolerable they would be forced to send him somewhere. That would scare Jeanne off for good.

The injury to his leg made it pretty impossible to leap around the room or scamper about on all fours. In any case, he had to garner attention first.

He started to sing, but quickly decided the sound of a few bloodcurdling howls would send the servants running in faster.

In fact, he barely had time to count to ten before the door burst open.

"Lord Rutherford. It is good to see you…up." Franklin eyed him warily from the doorway. "Shall I open the shutters?"

"Shutters, clutters, dutters hutters jutters," Edmund sang. Then he dropped into flat prose. "Do what pleases you."

"Very good, sir." Franklin moved to the window closest to the bed.

"*Ahhh!*" Edmund screamed as he buried his face in the pillows. "It burns my eyes! Curse the sun! Close the shutters at once, you beast!"

"V-very good, sir." Franklin slammed the shutters closed.

Edmund sat up and began singing once more. "Shutters, clutters, plutters flutters, flutters flutters flutters." He lowered his voice to a growl. "How do you expect me to see anything with those shutters closed? Open them at once!"

"Are you quite certain, sir?"

"No, I'm not quite certain. I'm quite Edmund. Now, refresh my memory, if you please. Do I pay you and give the orders or is it the other way around?"

"Very good, sir. I'll open them, sir." Franklin stepped toward the shutters as if approaching the gallows. He reached one hand tentatively toward the opening and glanced at his master.

Edmund said nothing.

The butler grasped the bottom of the shutter with shaking fingers, his gaze shifting back and forth between the window and the bed.

Edmund said nothing.

Franklin turned his full attention to the window for a split second, pulling the shutter open the merest sliver of an inch.

Edmund howled, "You beast! You *are* trying to kill me. I know it."

"No, sir! Of course not, sir!"

"You opened the shutters after I told you the sun burns my eyes."

"But sir…"

Edmund waved away his objection. "So you're not trying to kill me, then, but merely to blind me. It would be just as bad. Trapped as I am in this bed by my war wounds, unable to move, unable to see…a horrid life you have left me to."

"Sir, please," the butler was fighting back tears now, "you must believe me. I have the deepest respect for your family. I would never try to hurt you. But you told me to open the shutters…"

"So you always follow my orders, do you? Even when you know it will be harmful to me? Does that show respect for my family?"

"I-I don't know, sir."

"Ha, of course you don't. Bring me some breakfast."

"Yes, sir." Franklin wasted no time but made straight for the door.

"And hurry! I am quite hungry this morning."

"Yes, sir!" The door closed scarcely before he was all the way through it.

Edmund wished he had thrown a fit about too much dark, rather than too much light. It was rather gloomy sitting in the shuttered room, knowing the full light of day shown outside. What would Franklin think if he came in and found Edmund contentedly sitting in a sunlit room after insisting on darkness?

He smiled at the thought. Admittedly, it was a wicked smile, because his behavior obviously put the man to some distress. But it would still be funny to see the look on his face.

Edmund eased himself to the edge of the bed. He placed all his weight on his good leg, then took a tentative step on the other. For a brief second, all seemed well and Edmund had almost moved the right leg forward to take his next step when the throbbing ache flashed into an explosion of pain. Both legs buckled, sending him to the floor. His elbow smacked the bedframe.

"Damn!" He felt around in the dark for the bedpost, gritting his teeth to keep from whimpering at the tearing sensation in his thigh. Finally grasping the bedpost with both hands, he dragged himself along the floor until he was right next to the bed, pulled himself up to sitting position, then shifted all his weight to the right side and heaved himself upright, clinging to the post in desperation. He made it all the way up so quickly that he swung around the bedpost and smashed his backside against the wall.

"Ouch." He'd hit his elbow again, in much the same place as before.

The searing pain in his left leg receded to its former throbbing but tolerable torrent, however, so long as he put no weight upon it. So he would be fine as long as he propped himself against the wall.

And didn't move.

But that was none too comfortable, either. So Edmund gritted his teeth again and hopped on his right foot until he was in position to slide back onto the bed.

It was a great deal of exertion to have accomplished nothing.

So when the door opened and Franklin stepped forward with a heavily laden breakfast tray, it took little effort for Edmund to turn his frustration into a feigned indignation directed at the unfortunate servant.

"What is this? Do you see this?" he demanded, holding up a piece of meat.

"What, sir? No, sir. I-I don't—"

"Someone's taken a bite of my breakfast. *You've* taken a bite of my breakfast!" Edmund felt himself building up to a full-fledged rant.

"No, sir, I would never—"

"I am the sultan. I can have you killed for this!" Edward waved the offensive bit of meat under the butler's nose.

"No, oh no. It's true," he whispered hoarsely. "It's all true." He backed toward the door.

"Where are you going?" Edmund demanded. He threw a muffin at the retreating servant. "Come back here this instant!"

"I-I've forgotten something."

"I said to come back here."

"I've got to...to get you another piece of beef."

"I *ordered* you to come back here."

"I will be right back." He grasped the doorknob as a drowning man might reach for a line. "Sir."

"I can have you killed if you disobey me!" Edmund considered throwing the butter knife but decided on a spoon instead. "My subjects must obey me!" He aimed the spoon at Franklin's backside. "And where is my turban? Bring me my turban!"

The door slammed shut.

Edmund smiled and set about trying to eat what remained of his breakfast in the dark.

Chapter Twelve

୨୦

Lucia cried when she saw Mr. Bayles step out of the carriage alone. Tears of worry and frustration had threatened to spill all day. Now the tears of outright fear and failure poured out in an unrestrained torrent.

Eugenie joined her at the window. "Come, now, Lucia." She produced another in a seemingly endless supply of lace-edged handkerchiefs. "We've not heard what he has to say yet. I'm sure Geoffrey will be home very soon."

"W-why did he not bring him back now?"

"I do not know, of course. But he will be up to tell us in a few minutes. We shall simply wait here for him."

But the wait turned out to be more than the mere matter of minutes Eugenie anticipated. Allen announced dinner, and still they had not had word from Mr. Bayles or anyone else in the family.

They descended the stairs in silence.

Silence continued as they entered the dining room, where Mr. and Mrs. Bayles sat with downcast eyes. Lucia and Eugenie took their seats, Sophie soon followed and they all sat quietly, studiously ignoring the empty chair occupied by Geoffrey only yesterday. Lucia focused her attention on Helen's empty chair. After what seemed an eternity, she decided to excuse herself to see to her sister's whereabouts.

At that moment, however, Allen opened the door and a somewhat disheveled Helen scurried into her seat.

"Where were you, Helen?"

"I was reading."

"What is that in your hair?"

"Hay?" Helen felt around on her head, then detached the offending matter. "Straw," she corrected herself after examining the article closely.

"How on earth did you…" Lucia stopped as she realized it was better to keep Helen's exploits as private as possible. "I want to talk to you right after dinner, Helen. Right after dinner."

"Very well. You usually talk to me right after dinner, do you not?"

Lucia refused to reply.

Mr. Bayles blessed the food, but said nothing else for the remainder of the meal.

Lucia chewed sawdust—or straw—and swallowed over a hillock in her throat.

After dinner, Mrs. Bayles rose and her daughters followed in such rapid succession it seemed a choreographed move. Helen and Lucia got to their feet at a somewhat slower pace. As they were leaving the room, Lucia tried to catch Mr. Bayles' gaze, to plead silently what she could not voice aloud.

He never looked in her direction.

"Ahem." Mrs. Bayles cleared her throat after they had settled in the drawing room with their tea. "I fear all did not go well today for Mr. Bayles. He has had a most trying afternoon."

"What happened?" Lucia fairly exploded. "Why did he not bring Geoffrey home?"

"He tried his best, Miss Wright. But the magistrate would not let your brother out of custody."

"Why?" But she knew the answer to that.

"Oh dear, I do hate to have to tell you this. I believe they fear that Geoffrey is a danger."

"He is not." But even as she said the words, she knew she did not believe them to be true. Geoffrey *was* a danger. Geoffrey had always been a danger—except when kept under control, safely at home under her supervision. She had failed in her duty to supervise him, and now he suffered.

And Lord Rutherford — he had suffered too.

"Well," Sophie ventured, "perhaps Geoffrey *is* better off where he can be looked after."

"Looked after? Who is going to look after him in Bedlam? He's locked up with a herd of lunatics with no one to help him at all." Lucia felt the pressure in her head that indicated more tears held at bay.

Mrs. Bayles winced. "It is perhaps not what we would choose for ourselves. But the magistrates must think of the good —"

"Geoffrey was fine at home, in the country. He will be fine there again. I must see that he gets home." Lucia smacked the back of her hand against her palm in emphasis.

"But he *stabbed* another man," Sophie objected. "You saw it. You told me so yourself. Are you not afraid that he might some night come up and stab you in your bed?"

"No. Geoffrey would never hurt me."

Sophie shook her head. "You cannot be sure of that. I, for one, must confess I really do think it best for him to be looked after somewhere."

"He *was* looked after somewhere. He was looked after at home. My only mistake was in leaving to gratify some…worthless whim. I must now do everything in my power to rectify that mistake." Lucia waved away the teacup proffered by Mrs. Bayles.

"It was not a worthless whim that brought you here, Lucia. It was my urgent entreaty. I so wanted you to enjoy the season with me. We were going to have such fun together, you and I." Eugenie's eyes threatened to spill over and her nose turned red. "I thought the visit would be good for you."

"I know you did, Eugenie." Lucia patted her friend's hand. "You simply did not understand about our family. Not many people do."

"Yes, well." Mrs. Bayles looked desperate to steer the conversation to something more pleasant. "Mr. Bayles will do his best again tomorrow, I am sure. Sophie, tell me more about how the Lowells do, now that they are back in town."

Like her mother, Sophie seemed eager to drop the conversation concerning Geoffrey's unpleasant situation. She launched into an animated description of her meeting with Lady Anna Lowell and the latter's astronomical projections for marriage partners likely to be secured within the first three major events of the season.

Lucia soon lost interest, having no acquaintance with the said Lowell family and after hearing more of them, no desire to enter into an acquaintance. Instead of listening to Sophie and Mrs. Bayles, she began to plan how she might bring about Geoffrey's release and return. It was difficult to know what to do when she did not even know what opposition Mr. Bayles had encountered.

"I know what you're thinking," a voice whispered into her ear.

"What?" Lucia blinked. Sophie and Mrs. Bayles chatted on about the price of tea somewhere.

"I said, 'I know what you're thinking'." The whispered voice belonged to Eugenie, who had circled the room to stand just behind the sofa where Lucia perched uneasily.

"I do not think you do."

"Then I do not think you think I know you as well as I do."

Lucia felt a grin spread across her face despite her worry. "Very well, then." She kept her voice low. "Tell me of my thoughts."'

"You are putting no faith in my father's efforts and are planning instead to find a way to bring Geoffrey home yourself."

"Oh, dear." Lucia cringed. "Am I so very transparent, then?"

"To me, who has known you since you were eleven, yes. Come down to my room after Helen is asleep. I have an idea that might work."

"Eugenie, no. This is none of your concern, and besides, I believe I've had enough of your 'ideas'."

"It is my concern, and my idea is a good one. And if you think it is not, you can take great joy in exposing the flaws."

"Very well." Lucia sighed and waved Eugenie to take a seat near her mother. What harm could there be in hearing Eugenie's plan? After all, she had yet to come up with a plan of her own.

* * * * *

Two days later, Lucia came down the stairs fervently wishing she had come up with a strategy of her own. Because Eugenie's plan could not possibly work. She would never keep the headdress on straight. And she would probably be damned to hell for all eternity.

While it was nice to humor her friend and to allow her to atone for her mistake in bringing Geoffrey to London, eternity *was* a long time.

"Whoops! I stepped on the hem again." Eugenie giggled as she plowed into Lucia from behind. "We really should have waited until we got into the carriage to dress."

"Yes, you're right. Let's go back upstairs now and—"

"Oh, no. We've made it this far without anyone seeing us. Peggy has told Harrison to open the door when I rap on the window at the landing. So then we dash down the last few stairs and out the door."

"Do you not think someone watching from outside might find it a bit odd seeing two nuns fly out of the house and into your family carriage?"

Eugenie giggled again. "That's why we have to move extremely fast. Anyone who sees us will think they've seen a ghost!"

"If your father finds out, then those people will be right—you *will* be a ghost."

Eugenie rapped on the window three times.

After a few seconds, the door downstairs cracked open ever-so slightly.

"Make ready!" Eugenie's eyes sparkled with excitement. "One, two—"

"Oh, let's just go!" Without waiting for a "three," Lucia rushed down the final flight of stairs and pushed out the front door, not daring to look about the entrance hall to see if anyone observed them. Harrison, the most junior of the family footmen, stood at the carriage door, swinging it open just in time for her to climb inside without pausing.

Eugenie scrambled in right behind her. "Ouch. I think you're sitting on my habit."

"No, you're sitting on your habit."

"It feels like every hair on my head is being slowly pulled out by the roots."

"Then I suggest you not make a habit of wearing that long, heavy veil on your head. Wherever did you contrive to find these, in any case?"

"Lucia, you are too funny. Not make a habit!"

"You did not answer my question."

"I do not recall you asking one."

"I asked you where you obtained these costumes."

"Would you believe that I just happened to find them in the old servants' clothes press last week?"

"No."

"Oh. You've found me out then. I was up 'til all hours sewing. I suppose the lack of sleep shows on my face."

"Well, something is evident from your face, but it would appear to have more to do with a lack of truth than a lack of sleep."

"Oh, very well. Yesterday I had Harrison drive Peggy over to St. Helen's, Bishopsgate. We borrowed some of the nuns' clothing that was airing in the yard."

"We?" Lucia stared at her friend. "You mean that you went out to steal—"

"Borrow. We borrowed them. We shall return them, with ample compensation, when this whole mess is concluded."

"I cannot believe you stole clothing from nuns."

"I could not very well ask my servants to do something I was not willing to do myself. And we *borrowed* it."

"Just as you borrowed my gloves when we were at school? I am sure you always meant to return them."

"This *is* like our days at school, is it not? Sneaking off for a bit of fun, hoping not to be caught."

"It does remind me, somewhat," Lucia agreed. "We've rather more at stake now, though, than just a pie or scrap of lace or whatever else it was we used to make such a fuss over."

"Do you remember the— You're right, of course." Eugenie peeked out the window. "This is much more serious and important than anything we ever did at school. And we never could have procured such good costumes."

Lucia smiled but made no answer as she, too, peered out the curtained window into the London streets. They seemed to be moving past at a lightning pace. After a time, she let the curtain fall forward.

Apparently inspired by the mention of school days, Eugenie chattered about their old acquaintances—those who had married, those who ardently sought to make a match this season, those who, in her opinion, ought give up all hope of making a match in any season. She had sighted one of their classmates at the Adringtons' but had not had the opportunity of conversation, due to the crush.

Lucia recalled the odd conversation she had enjoyed that evening, when Lord Rutherford exhibited a few minutes of civility between his bouts of lunacy. Some memory jogged uncomfortably at the back of her mind, however. And strangely enough, it was not either the thought that such a handsome, engaging gentleman suffered a certain lack of reason, or that he had been grievously injured by her own brother, who was now locked up in the criminal wing of Bedlam. These thoughts pained her so that she had steeled herself not to think of them but in small doses, allowing herself to feel the ache for a time but not to wallow in it.

So it was not these great troubles but rather a small, different, puzzling thought that nagged her memory—a question unanswered, a riddle she had yet to work out.

Something to do with the conversation and Lord Rutherford's words to her.

There had been a familiarity, as if she had spoken with him before, or heard his words before.

Or as if they were someone else's words. He had quoted a phrase with which she was familiar.

If she closed her eyes, cleared her mind and allowed Eugenie's chatter to fade to a gentle hum, she could recapture...

"'He that departs with his own honesty for vulgar praise doth it too dearly buy.'" Her eyelids snapped open.

"What? Whatever do you mean by that?" Eugenie sat back in her seat. "This time I swear I am telling the truth."

Lucia grinned. "I believe you always tell the truth, such as you see it to be. No, I was thinking of something said the other night—a quote I was trying to place."

"About honesty?"

"Among other things. It is from one of Jonson's *Epigrams*."

Eugenie wrinkled her nose. "Oh, I knew all this talk of school would be dangerous. Now the conversation has brought forth horrid recollections of Miss Finkle's literature class."

"The class was not so very horrid."

"Well, she was, at any rate. What a memory you have."

"You give me too much credit for scholarship in those days. I do not actually believe we read the *Epigrams* in school."

"Do you mean to say that you read Ben Jonson at home without the threat of exams?"

"I confess, I enjoy his work. Much of it is prodigiously funny."

Eugenie frowned. "Not that I remember. And were he the best dramatist of all time, he could not create a scene half so amusing as looking at you in that ridiculous costume."

Lucia looked down at the expanse of black cloth covering her from neck to foot, then over at Eugenie, her form all but swallowed up with the combination of black gown and headpiece. She sighed. "I still think I might stand a better chance if I simply went in to the institution, properly dressed, and explained that Geoffrey could be safely released into my custody."

"They will not even listen to you. They would not listen to Papa, so why should they listen to you who are younger and, moreover, a woman?"

"I am his sister."

"They do not care about relations. Oh, we've stopped." Eugenie pulled the curtain back again to peer out.

"We've already reached St. George's Fields? What are we going to say? Why are two nuns arriving in a carriage like this?"

"I am not worried about that at all." Eugenie threw the curtain back into place.

"Good." Lucia tried to straighten her headpiece. "What are you worried about?"

Eugenie waved her question away. "There is no need for both of us to worry."

"I believe there is no chance to avoid that now," Lucia muttered.

"Let's go!" Eugenie rapped on the top of the carriage three times. They heard the creaks of Harrison climbing off the box. Then the door to the carriage opened for them to make their assault on the new Hospital of Bethlehem at St. George's Fields, better known simply by the name and reputation it carried through various incarnations over the centuries.

Bedlam.

Chapter Thirteen

Making no attempt at decorum, both Lucia and Eugenie scurried from the street up the silent expanse of walkway, past the marble columns and into a massive entrance hall. Then their pace slowed to a slow shuffle. They passed two bronze statues of men evincing a variety of distress (labeled "Raving" and "Melancholy Madness"), but could see no live habitants except at the back, where a gentleman of sorts sat at a large, ornately carved table spread with papers, ink and an assortment of food that indicated he had been attempting to dine and carry on correspondence at the same time. A man of even less refined appearance stood near the doorway at the back of the room.

"Good afternoon, sisters." The gentleman at the desk chewed through these words and swallowed as he stood to greet them. "I am the superintendent at Bethl'em. How may I be of service to you?"

A large, hairy man scampered up from behind them and leaped onto the table.

Eugenie clutched Lucia's arm but uttered only a mild whimper.

"Shoo, Barclay, shoo, get along there. Johnson, would you be so good?" The superintendent looked at the greasy man standing by the door, then waved toward the hairy man occupying the greater half of the table. Johnson ambled over and fit a hook into the collar around the neck of the hairy table-sitter. Barclay was unceremoniously dragged off the table and pulled to another room.

The superintendent shook his head. "We're still not quite sure how he manages to get down here, but I assure you, he's quite harmless. Now, may I assume that you have not come to visit our resident gymnast, Barclay?"

Lucia felt Eugenie's fingers dig into her arm. "Um, we have come to see a Mr. Geoffrey Wright."

"You're not employed by Mr. Wakefield are you? Or the newspapers?"

Eugenie pointed to her headpiece, knocking it slightly askew. "Dressed like this?"

The superintendent waved them closer and lowered his voice, glancing out toward the street before he responded. "I know it seems difficult to believe anyone could stoop so low as to impersonate a bride of Christ, but some so-called reformers would stoop to means of sheer deviancy to gain access to our galleries."

"How very sad." Eugenie feigned a pious expression. "We shall say a prayer for their poor, misguided souls."

"That's charitable of you. Now," the superintendent frowned at a stack of papers, "I believe Mr. Wright has been placed in our new criminals' wing. Why do you wish to see him?"

"We've been paid to pray for him," Eugenie answered with no hesitation.

Lucia stifled a groan. Catholics may have indeed allowed such a mercenary practice, but they no doubt expressed it in a more dignified way.

The superintendent, however, did not seem put off by her blunt comment. "Do you not customarily pray for the poor, distracted souls of Bethl'em Hospital from the...sanctity of your convent?"

"Well, yes in most cases." Eugenie nodded, then leaned in a little closer. "But, you see, this time the donation was rather large. So enormously large, in fact, that we felt it incumbent to visit the charge in person."

"Oh." The superintendent frowned at the stack of papers again, then transferred his gaze to his guests. "Well, in that event, I suppose I should let you see him."

"Is he delusional?" Lucia asked softly.

The superintendent smiled wearily. "Who among them is not?"

"That is," Lucia clarified, "does he profess to be someone he is not?"

The superintendent shifted his jaw to the side and wrinkled his forehead in thought. "I confess I've not spent any time with him. The keepers have told me he is most insistent about speaking to the constable, though. And he asks if we've some 'Red' fellow in custody."

"Oh, I see." Eugenie nodded again. "The poor man."

"No, I would say he is obviously not poor at all. Rather well-off, to judge by his clothing." The warden laughed at his own joke. "If he were poor, your services would not have been…arranged. So he is most definitely not poor, whatever else you may say about him."

"Yes, well, if you would be so good as to direct us to his whereabouts?"

The superintendent laughed all the harder, the sound echoing off the marble and stone surroundings with a ghostly cadence. "Heavens, no, sisters. I could never send you unescorted through the galleries of Bethl'em. Half the diseased minds of Great Britain reside within these walls. Now," he assumed a serious face, "ask me where to find the other half."

Lucia blinked. "What? Very well. Where may we find the others?"

"In Parliament, mostly. Ha!" The superintendent roared, nearly bringing tears to his eyes. When his laughter subsided, he apologized. "You'll have to excuse me—just a little Bethl'em humor."

"So where do the others live?" Lucia persisted.

"Well," the superintendent tugged at his cravat and cleared his throat, now showing signs of embarrassment at his earlier outburst, "many stay within their families, of course, when they have the means to keep them in control. Those not up to the task send their troubled family members to a private asylum such as Ticehurst or, if they are really wealthy and not too violent, an elegant licensed house such as Shady View. Those without money may be put in county asylums or live on the streets, much as anyone without money would do."

"What is a 'licensed house'?"

"Merely a private asylum." He pulled at his cravat again. "Shady View, for example, is just a home in the country where the distracted souls are given safe harbor but are offered no chance of a cure as they are here."

"May an inmate be moved from Bethlehem to such a home?"

The superintendent pursed his lips. "In many cases, yes, provided the family has the means."

Lucia felt the warmth of hope swell in her chest. "Then perhaps Mr. Wright's family might have him removed to a site closer to their home."

"Err, no. Not Mr. Wright. Those placed in the criminal wing must remain here, on the order of the courts."

"He is a prisoner, then?" The warmth shrank into a cold pit of stone, plummeting through her insides.

"He is an inmate, like all the others. A resident, if you will. Even those in the criminal wing are not restrained, unless they pose a danger to themselves or others. I believe Mr. Wright is under no such restraint."

"But he cannot leave."

"None of them can, until granted a proper release. Now, you speak of questions that may be better brought before the governors, and I am only a lowly superintendent. Shall I have Mr. Wright brought into the visiting room to meet with you?"

"Yes, please." Lucia felt the pit in her stomach sink lower with each passing minute. Though the new Bethlehem hospital appeared stately and beautiful on the outside and in its public rooms, the shrieking sounds echoing from the galleries on either side promised that the atmosphere within the asylum was anything but dignified and serene. She could see but little, however, for their walk from the entrance hall to the room where patients visited with guests was a short one, leaving them some distance from the galleries where the patients lived. And the criminal galleries were the farthest away, set back from the public traffic of the street.

The visiting parlor was empty of human company, although Lucia could well imagine a host of vermin living in the ornate but dirty sofa, daybed and ottoman that graced the room. She chose to remain standing, as did Eugenie.

She would not leave Geoffrey in this place one hour longer. But she could not simply take him back to the Bayles home and she did not have transportation arranged to return to Hertfordshire. And at either place, he could be pursued by the magistrates and returned to Bedlam.

"Let's take him to Shady View," she whispered to Eugenie.

"I thought we were taking him back home."

Lucia shook her head. "No, your family would not care for that. And if someone were to complain, they might send a magistrate to collect Geoffrey and return him here. But the superintendent said the residents at Shady View would be kept 'safe'. Hopefully the magistrates would not object to that."

"I imagine Father would have tried to move him there, if such a move were possible."

"He may not have known of Shady View. We ourselves did not until the superintendent mentioned it just now."

"True. Very well. We shall take—"

Lucia held her finger to her lips, with a look toward the doorway. Johnson entered, followed shortly by a very despondent looking Geoffrey.

"Lu!" His eyes glowed with joy. "You're here!"

Johnson scratched his leg. "You know 'er?"

"Know her?" Geoffrey scoffed. "Of course I know her. She's my sister."

"Oh, yeah, right." Johnson spat into a corner and mashed the spittle into the floor with his foot. "Well, sisters, you've seen 'im. Now I'll put 'im back and you can be on your way."

"What?" Eugenie demanded indignantly. "But we have not even had the chance to—"

"To pray," Lucia cut in. "Mr. Johnson, you must allow us time for a simple prayer over this poor man."

"A'right."

"In private."

"In private? No, I don't think—"

"Are you a Catholic, Mr. Johnson?"

"Lord, no." He took a step back.

"Then I suggest you wait outside."

"And close the door," Eugenie added. She took a vial of perfume from her reticule. "We've brought Holy Water. I would hate for—"

"Right." Johnson wasted no time in putting the closed door between himself and the occupants of the parlor.

"Lu, I do not understand." Geoffrey's forehead creased with worry. "When did you join the papists? Will you go to live in a convent? Will our family lands be confiscated?"

"No, Geoffrey, you needn't worry. This is simply a disguise."

"A disguise? From whom are you disguising yourself?"

"Hurry!" Eugenie hissed.

"I haven't time to explain. Let me simply say that…that you were right about Redcloak and he is set free once more. His henchmen hold you captive here, and we must get you free so that you can capture him again."

"And bring him to justice!"

"Yes, yes. Now, you must act as though you do not know that Redcloak holds you here. You must pretend that we have come to take you to the chapel for worship."

"You're not going to say a Mass over me, are you?"

"Nuns cannot say Mass!" Eugenie objected.

"Can they not?" Geoffrey shifted his weight, his brow wrinkled in thought. "I understood that—"

"Hush!" Lucia waved him to be quiet. "He's coming."

The door handle turned slowly, and within a few seconds, the door cracked open just enough to enable two dark eyes to peer into the room. "Are ye finished now?"

"For the moment, yes." Eugenie bowed.

"Good." Johnson opened the door fully, stepped in and grabbed Geoffrey none too gently by the wrist. "Come along, now. Let's get you back to your room."

Geoffrey pulled his arm free. "I think not. It is time for me to leave this place."

"What do you mean?" Johnson looked suspiciously at each of them.

"I believe what he means, Mr. Johnson, is that it is time for matins. Do you ring the Angelus here?" Eugenie asked.

"Oh, no." He resumed his hold on Geoffrey's wrist and yanked him toward the door. "Ye've 'ad enough of your prayer time in here for the day."

"Quite right, Mr. Johnson," Lucia nodded as she followed him to the door. "We will naturally offer matins in the chapel."

"And the rosary, too, of course," Eugenie added, holding up some beads in her hand. "If you would be so good as to lead us there?" She gestured toward the door.

Johnson backed away from the "rosary" beads as if they had been made of burning coals. "Err, I should be getting back to the superintendent now."

"We shall need for you to take us to the chapel. Surely you know the way?"

"I do, but—"

"Then, lead on, please. Will you be so good as to join us in prayer?"

"No. I can take you to the chapel." He waved toward the central staircase. "Then I'll wait outside."

"Very good, Mr. Johnson. We shall follow you."

Chapter Fourteen

ജ

"Do you think he will be able to hear us through this door?" Lucia listened to see how much noise from the hall leaked into the cold, somber cavern of worship.

"I do not believe it matters." Eugenie opened a window in the back of the chapel. "Oh dear. We're up rather higher than I'd thought."

Lucia joined her at the window. It led to a courtyard where several inmates appeared to be playing a game of blind man's buff, except that all of them seemed to be blindfolded, so they stumbled into one another a good deal. "We cannot escape this way."

Geoffrey opened a window on the other side of the chapel. "This is perfect. Our escape is assured."

"Splendid." Eugenie rushed to look.

"Yes. We jump from here to that ledge—"

"What ledge? I don't see—"

"There, under that window. Then we can climb over to—"

"Over *there*? Are you daft?"

"Eugenie, Geoffrey—look over here!" Lucia called from the altar.

"Oh, sorry, Geoffrey, I didn't mean—"

"Up here, both of you." Lucia put more insistence in her voice.

"You can't stand on the altar!" Eugenie objected.

"This is hardly the time to worry about religious proprieties." Lucia urged her forward. "Now look."

Eugenie crossed her arms in front of her chest. "I will not climb up there."

"Very well, I shall endeavor to describe the view."

Geoffrey jumped up beside her.

"There, do you see?" She pointed to a small section of light-colored glass in the stained glass window above the altar.

"Right." Geoffrey nodded agreement as he peered through the window segment. "Even more perfect. We can overpower the coachman of that cab, hurl the footman aside and—"

"Ask him to open the door. That is our carriage," Lucia pointed out. "The Bayles carriage. Those men await our orders. Now we just have to figure out how to open this window and we should be able to climb right down onto the portico roof."

"Stand back!" Geoffrey made ready to smash the glass with his elbow.

Lucia grabbed his arm. "No, wait. This is a chapel. We should not simply smash through the window."

"Especially not a depiction of the Holy Mother." Eugenie crossed herself. Then she began a slow walk around the back of the chapel, her gaze traveling up and down from the wall to the floor as if she were looking for something.

"You really are taking this role rather seriously, are you not?" Lucia asked. "Where did you learn so much about Catholics?"

"Elizabeth Wilfrid." Eugenie kept her gaze on the wall and floor as she spoke. "Do you remember her from school?"

"Yes. I had no idea."

"Her family kept it quiet, but she told me lots of stories. And that's why I think I may know a way out of here." She tapped a section of the floor with her foot.

"What are you doing?" Lucia gave up on her attempt to loosen the window and turned her full attention to Eugenie.

"There may be a secret passage to the outside."

"Of course! Why did I not think of that before?" Geoffrey hopped down from the altar. "The papist priests often devised an avenue to escape royal prosecutors."

"Persecutors, you may as well call them." Eugenie looked up for a brief moment. "They took land, they took money, they took a lot of people's heads."

"Well," Lucia climbed down from the altar, then glanced toward the door at the side of the chapel, "I am afraid someone will have our heads if we do not find a way out soon."

"Redcloak's men." Geoffrey nodded.

As if on cue, the door swung open. "Are ye finished prayin' yet?"

"Ave Maria," Eugenie sang as she grabbed a censer. Waving it slowly to and fro, she turned her walk into a stately procession around the altar. "Agnes Day...Donny Nobeast Pachay. Aaahhhhmen."

Lucia fell in step behind her and urged Geoffrey to do likewise, but he refused.

"Ave Maria," Eugenie began again, even louder this time. "Ave Maaaaarriiiiiiaaaaa!" The door swung shut again. "Perhaps we should consider breaking the window." She held up the censer, wrinkling her nose in distaste. "We could use this. The smell alone should do it."

"There has to be another way. Just as you said." Lucia started toward the back of the chapel.

"A priest's hole?" Geoffrey asked.

"No. Those date back to the days of Elizabeth, and this building is new." Lucia looked out the windows at the back. "We are up rather high, and your ledge would be a challenge, even without the nun garb."

She walked back toward the altar. "You know that hairy man, the one who jumped on the superintendent's table when we first arrived?"

Eugenie gave a little shiver. "Yes, I remember."

"Well, he somehow made an escape from the galleries up here and entered the front of the building. He managed the feat rather frequently, from what I gathered from the superintendent's words." She pulled herself up onto the altar again and peered through the light-colored glass. "I wonder if there might be a way to climb down the front of the building."

"Right." Geoffrey scrambled up alongside her. "I'm sure there must be a ledge we can jump—"

"No, Geoffrey, we will not be jumping at this height." Lucia clamped her lips together in a frown. "And we still have the problem of how to open the window."

"Hmm." Geoffrey looked around thoughtfully. "I wish we knew how they'd opened *that* window. Perhaps it's one of the ones that has not yet been glazed. The keepers say that for the first year, almost none of the windows had—"

"What are you talking about?" Lucia grabbed his arm. "What window?"

"Up there." Geoffrey pointed to a small window in an alcove to their left.

Lucia looked at him in disbelief for a moment before she jumped down from the altar and hurried toward the new avenue of escape. "If you knew this window was open, why did you not say so earlier? I'm sure we can find some article to stand on to reach it."

"That bench, for example?" Geoffrey offered. "Yes, by standing on it, I was able to see out quite well. But we cannot possibly escape through that window."

"Oh." Lucia felt a weight plunge through her chest. "There is no place to step out, I suppose."

"To the contrary, there's quite an easy access to the roof. And that is precisely the problem. Redcloak's men will be expecting us to take just such a route. They will be waiting for us."

Lucia's face split into a smile. "I don't think so, Geoffrey. Not today." She stacked a second bench on top of the one

Geoffrey had used. "Now, I shall climb out and see if I can determine how that hairy man climbed down to the entrance."

"No, no, Lucia, you must let me go." Geoffrey pushed her aside. "This is not suitable for a woman at all."

Lucia bit her lip. The last thing she wanted was Geoffrey's assessment of an escape route. "Perhaps it is not seemly, but these are desperate circumstances. And remember, Redcloak's men are looking for you. They won't be looking for a nun."

"True. I shall hide behind here, just in case."

"Why don't you hide at the end of these benches so you can help hold them steady while I climb?"

"Oh, very well."

With the aid of a third bench, Lucia was able to climb through the small window and out onto the roof. All the galleries of one wing stretched out in front of her, but when she turned, the ground in front and back of the building seemed impossibly far below. Taking a deep breath, she focused her attention on the front and picked her way carefully down to the slanted portico roof outlining the entrance. Creeping to the end of that still left her two stories above the ground. Then she nearly laughed aloud. A line of dirty, smudged handprints pointed the way, tracing a path down the decorative brickwork like a ladder. From the end of the brick "steps," the hairy inmate might have needed gymnastic ability to swing to the ground, but they could simply secure assistance from the coachman.

She crawled back up the portico roof and picked her way over the other decorative half-story roofing until she reached the window again. "Eugenie, Geoffrey! Come out. I've found the way down."

Eugenie paled a bit when she first looked down, but was in fine spirits when she found how remarkably easy it was to traverse. She went first, called for the servants, and giggled as the footman assisted her down from the top of the coach.

"You know," she announced after they all settled inside and she'd reminded the coachman and footman of their vow of secrecy, "that was rather fun, all in all. I should think we might consider offering our services to other families who wish to have a member removed from Bedlam."

Lucia laughed, her sense of elation and relief making everything seem funny. They had freed Geoffrey! She had not felt such lighthearted joy since childhood.

"That is an interesting proposition." Geoffrey pondered as he watched the hospital fade into the distance. "Do you know any families that could use such services?"

"Perhaps Lord Rutherford's family?" Eugenie suggested.

Lucia's laugh stuck in her throat. The thought of him in such a place left a cold ache in her heart. And then there was his mother—in no condition to arrange a removal by them or anyone else.

They'd been able to help Geoffrey but could do nothing to help Lord Rutherford, whom her brother had so grievously injured.

Her carefree sense of elation became a distant memory once more.

* * * * *

They came to Edmund's room late that night. Henry Stansbury, the family solicitor, was accompanied by an older gentleman he did not know and two younger men who could hardly be described as "gentle". Franklin was the last in, and he hovered close to the door as if ready to quit the room at any moment.

They carried candles, the only light in the room save for the red glow of coals banked in the fireplace. His own candles had long since burned down, and his leg injury made it impossible to retrieve others from the candle-box on the mantel. He had tried to sleep, dozing then waking to nondescript sounds in the street or in the garret above.

So it was a relief when someone finally interrupted his solitude.

"Lord Rutherford?" Stansbury looked distinctly uncomfortable addressing a client dressed in his nightshirt. "This is Mr. Groves." He presented the older gentleman.

"How do you—" Edmund started to answer the introduction from sheer force of habit until he reminded himself why Mr. Groves had come to see him. "How did you get in here?" he roared with indignation. "My guard is under instructions to let no one in without my permission."

"But you did give your permission, sir," Mr. Groves answered smoothly. "In the press of business, you perhaps have forgotten. You have so many important matters on your mind."

"You are very understanding." Edmund nodded his imperial thanks. "But I cannot properly address you without my robes of state. Vassal!" He directed a withering gaze at Franklin. "My robes and turban, if you please."

"S-sir, you have no turban." The man retreated backward with mincing steps.

"Who has stolen my turban?" Edmund demanded, wishing he could stand or at least sit up fully without wincing. "Thieves are everywhere," he complained. "Thieves and spies."

"Yes, one never can be too careful," Mr. Groves soothed. He held out Edmund's dressing gown. "Here is your robe, Sire."

"Bring it here, bring it here. I have a grievous injury, you see, and cannot easily move." He leaned in for a conspiratorial whisper when Mr. Groves stepped over to the bed. "One of the rebels attempted to assassinate me."

He nodded. "You know it is not safe for you to remain here. The devil might return for another attempt."

"I'm sure the vermin has had his head separated from his body long since." For a fleeting moment, Edmund wondered what had indeed happened to young Geoffrey. "And the attempt was made at the opera. So if I simply ban composers from the kingdom, I will be safe." Edmund stifled a grin. Mr. Groves was so obviously laying the foundation to lure him away, which was precisely what he wanted. Nevertheless, it was fun to thwart the man just a little.

"I fear not, Sire. Danger lurks in many places."

"Am I so hated in my own kingdom, then?"

"No, no of course not. The devils come from your rival kingdom."

"Which one?"

Mr. Groves paused. "The one that is really ruled by a woman."

"Ruled by a woman?" That was an interesting proposition. "A queen?"

"Not necessarily." Mr. Groves leaned closer. "A man may sit on the seat of power, but there is a woman making every decision he orders."

A most interesting proposition indeed. "What man would allow such usurpation?"

"By a woman? Any number. We all begin our lives under the control of a woman, after all."

"Hmm. You speak the truth there. So which of the neighboring realms is…"

Stansbury stifled a yawn.

"You, there!" Edmund pointed at his mother's solicitor. "No one is to yawn in my presence. Remove his head." This last remark was addressed to Mr. Groves.

"We've no time for it now, I'm afraid." Mr. Groves sighed with what appeared to be almost genuine regret. "We must make our escape now."

"I cannot leave this bed."

"These two men here," Mr. Groves pointed at the two hulking, ungentlemanly men who had accompanied him, "will carry you to your conveyance."

Edmund shook his head. "Absolutely not. No one may touch me who has not been purified in the ritual cleansing process."

"We took care of that downstairs."

"Today? I thought we only offered ritual cleansing on Wednesdays and Saturdays."

"Today is Wednesday, Sire."

"Is it? Well then, off we go. All except for *him*, of course." He pointed to Stansbury. "He is to have his head removed at the earliest convenient opportunity. And him." He pointed to Franklin. "See to it that he is knighted and sent forth to find this mysterious woman who rules my rival kingdom."

Mr. Groves bowed. "As you wish, Sire. Mr. O'Brien, Mr. Stoner, please assist the sultan to his carriage."

"I think I would prefer to travel by camel this evening," Edmund observed as O'Brien and Stoner linked their forearms together to form a makeshift chair. Mr. Groves helped ease him into the human conveyance. "Ouch. Do be careful with the royal leg." Damn, but that boy Geoffrey carried a long blade. Edmund was extremely grateful he was in no danger of actually having to travel by camel.

"Sire, might I offer you a draught to soothe the pain in your leg?" Mr. Groves removed a small bottle of murky, dark liquid from his pocket.

Edmund took the potion, resigning himself to the inevitable headache that must ensue. They wished to drug him to ease his removal to whatever private madhouse they might intend for him.

"Now," Mr. Groves nodded as Edmund returned the bottle to his possession, "as for the camels. Your Eminence, since speed is of the utmost importance, may I suggest your fastest horses instead?"

"Excellent idea. The flying ones, I think. It would be a lovely night for spin through the stars."

"As you wish." Mr. Groves bowed as Edmund was carried past him.

Although he had no idea where they were going, Edmund felt certain he would enjoy the journey.

* * * * *

The next morning, Edmund awoke to the sensation of sunlight piercing his eyelids. Eager to examine his new surroundings, he shook himself awake, pushed up to a sitting position and took stock of his situation.

It was a small room, greater in height than in breadth, with one sizeable window that obviously faced to the east. Outside he could see the dirty brown of dormant fields with no discernible habitation. He had been taken to the country, presumably to an asylum for those devoid of mind but not of ready cash.

Three months of rest here and he would be ready to return to London a new man.

He wished he could get up to explore the rest of the building and grounds, but he was unfortunately at the mercy of others for any movement outside the bed.

At home, his mother might just now be rising. She would know, of course, that he was no longer in the house, because she would have had to have been the one to make the arrangements to have him taken away. He could not blame her for not wanting to view his ignominious departure. In actuality, he was grateful she had not been present—it would have been much less fun playing the fool in front of his mother.

And much, much more difficult.

The clatter of horse and wheels directed his attention to the window again. He could see that some sort of carriage had crested the hill and headed toward his new residence. As the carriage drew closer, however, it passed from his field of vision, since he was so far away from the window.

Suddenly, he wanted very much to see who was arriving. Was his mother coming to visit? Jeanne and her aunt coming to assess his condition? He looked around in vain for a crutch or some other device he could lean on to make his way over to the window. Clenching his teeth to keep from crying out, Edmund turned so that his good leg was closest to the floor, then lowered himself onto that knee. He dragged himself toward the window, wincing every so often, but not as often as he had feared he would. At the foot of the window he paused for a moment to catch his breath and steel himself for the effort to stand. He swayed, clutching the windowsill but taking no notice of the view outside until the dizziness subsided.

When his vision cleared, he began to wonder if his mind were still scrambled. The young man stepping out of the carriage in front of the home appeared to be none other than the ubiquitous Geoffrey. This actually made some sense, however, for unless the young man was a terrific actor, he truly belonged in a place like this one. No one else emerged from the carriage, and after a while, Edmund realized he had been holding his breath. The young ladies who had accompanied Geoffrey to the opera — one, at least, seemed to be his sister — apparently had not accompanied him here.

The door to his room creaked open.

"This cannot be the room, for the bed is unmade and there are — oh my! I am terribly sorry!" With a wide-eyed look expressing complete and total discomfiture in one momentous flash, Geoffrey's sister shut the door as quickly as she had opened it.

"We shall have to take him someplace else!" Her voice was muffled but still clearly audible from the other side of the door.

"Nonsense, I am sure there are other rooms that will suit," another woman's voice answered.

"You don't understand." Then the voices lowered so that he could no longer discern the words. Within moments, their footsteps retreated down the hall, leaving Edmund stunned at how his expectations could be disappointed, gratified and then crushed within the space of a minute.

Chapter Fifteen

ॐ

Lucia wanted to cry as she headed into the massive drawing room where she had left Geoffrey speaking to the proprietor of Shady View. They had come so far, traveling all night, stopping for directions an untold number of times and arguing at length over just how to forge a letter with convincing physicians' signatures.

And then when it finally seemed they had found the perfect place to hide Geoffrey, they learned it was actually an impossible place. Because Lord Rutherford—Geoffrey's "Redcloak"—was here, too. And if Geoffrey saw him again, there was no telling what would happen. "Perhaps the head of this house can give us the name of another," she said wearily.

Eugenie nodded, understanding the situation without a word.

Geoffrey, however, was of different mind entirely. "I am immensely pleased with this place," he announced as they descended the stairs. "With the help of Mr. Groves and the rest of the staff, I am certain to catch Redcloak within a very short time."

Too true, Lucia wanted say. "Geoffrey, listen." She pulled him aside and spoke in a low voice. "I do not believe you should stay here. This place, too, is riddled with Redcloak's spies."

"Nonsense. Mr. Groves has just assured me that I will have his utmost cooperation in capturing the criminal. He has provided a room to use as headquarters for our search initiative, and—"

"Do you not think that it might be a ruse? That Mr. Groves might be working with *him*?"

"No, certainly not," Geoffrey sniffed. "I am an excellent judge of character."

Lucia sighed. "I am sorry, Geoffrey, but we will have to leave. We simply cannot stay here."

"But I've arranged everything!" He stamped his foot. "You cannot make me leave." He ran over and hid behind the gold draperies hanging in a long window nearby.

"Geoffrey, I can if I must," Lucia called out in warning, hoping he would not test her on this score.

"But perhaps you do not need to," Eugenie suggested.

"What?" Lucia wondered if she'd heard her friend correctly.

"Perhaps he can stay here for a while."

"But if he sees Lord Rutherford—"

Eugenie held up her hand. "You've said yourself that Geoffrey's 'professions' never last more than a week or two."

"Yes, but—"

"Well, Lord Rutherford is injured, is he not? He is not likely to be out of his room much, if at all in the near future. So by the time Geoffrey does see him…"

"He will be onto a new occupation. Yes, I see." She looked over at Geoffrey as he stood entwined in the draperies. She could indeed make him leave if she chose, but it might prove extremely difficult. Disastrous, actually. She did not have guardianship over him, and if she attempted to gain guardianship, she would risk alerting authorities who might not approve of his unauthorized "transfer."

He could stay here for a short time. Just until she could arrange to take him back to Hertfordshire.

Only one question nagged at her mind. How would Lord Rutherford feel about the arrangement?

"Eugenie, I do think you are right. But I should speak with Lord Rutherford and ensure that he will not object to confinement in the same home as his attacker."

"I do not think that he will even notice. He seems so far beyond reason."

"Some of the time, yes. And yet..." There was an intelligence in his eye, a sense of understanding that she had never discerned in her brother or sister. Of course, it could simply mean that his disorder was quite different from their own. The truth could only be discovered upon greater acquaintance with the man. "I feel I must speak with him."

Eugenie shrugged. "Very well. Ask Mr. Groves if he can arrange a meeting."

* * * * *

What do you say to a man who's been stabbed by your brother? Lucia paced the floor of the first floor visiting parlor as she awaited the arrival of Lord Rutherford. Located in a corner of the house, the parlor was lit from windows on two sides of the room, creating a cheerful, sunny atmosphere that contrasted sharply with her own gloomy portents of doom.

Eugenie is right. Lord Rutherford will understand. Geoffrey will not see him until he's given over his detective delusions. No harm will come to anyone.

Lucia found that she had stopped pacing and was now chewing one of her fingernails.

She started to pace again, purposefully clasping her hands together behind her back so as to protect her nails from inadvertent carnage. Then she tripped on a small ripple in the carpet, careening into a chair just as she heard the sound of footsteps at the door.

"I am afraid you have me at a disadvantage."

"What?" She whirled around at the sound of the musical voice she remembered from the Adrington soirée.

Lord Rutherford hobbled into the room on a crutch. Each step was hesitant, as if he were unused to using the crutch and forgot that it had to be moved. He bowed his head for a moment. "Forgive me for not showing you proper courtesy."

"Do not think of it." The sight of obvious need brushed all thoughts of propriety from her mind. She rushed over to assist him into a chair, taking his elbow as if he had been one of her dearest friends rather than a stranger. Or perhaps it was *because* he was strange that she felt no shame in her forward action. A proximity that would have frightened her with any other man felt perfectly natural with him.

"Thank you." His smile was a little shyer this time than she remembered. Was he embarrassed at needing assistance? Or was he embarrassed by her touch? He cleared his throat. "I hope you will forgive me for speaking to you without having been properly introduced."

She looked to the door to await the arrival of Shady View's proprietor, but no one else entered the room. When it became obvious that they would remain without a chaperone, she turned back to him. "I thought Mr. Groves would accompany you, introduce us and so forth."

Lord Rutherford shook back an unruly shock of hair. "He seemed to be under the impression that we were already closely acquainted. And I suppose he thought the other young lady — your companion — would accompany you."

"No. I came alone." Lucia felt herself flush — obviously she had come on her own. And now, once again, she found herself in the improper position of being in a room alone with Lord Rutherford. He might begin to think that she was arranging these meetings on purpose. "That is, I thought it best to speak with you in private." Well, no, that would not have been appropriate at all. Her cheeks grew even hotter. "I mean, simply in front of Mr. Groves."

Lord Rutherford nodded toward the doorway. "I suppose, if we leave the door open, no one will think it too improper?"

"And not many of my acquaintance will be likely to see me *here*." With a sigh of relief, Lucia smiled as she seated herself on the settee, then clamped her fingers to her lips as she realized her mistake. Lord Rutherford appeared so absolutely normal that for the moment she had forgotten that he, as well as her brother, was an unfortunate inmate of the institution. "I am sorry. I meant no..." She let her words trail off as she looked down, uncertain what to say to amend her insult.

"Are you truly sorry?" His voice held a note of challenge that was completely unexpected.

"Why, yes." She looked up again.

"Then I want you to prove it." He sat forward slightly, a faint gleam twinkling in his eyes. His smile was no longer shy. In fact, it seemed so much the opposite that she immediately felt she should be on her guard.

Her mouth seemed very dry all of a sudden. She licked her lips. "I beg your pardon?"

"Kiss me." His expression grew reckless, and he would have come across as arrogant if he did not bear so much resemblance to a hopeful puppy.

"What? No!" Lucia turned her eyes to the door, expecting someone to march in to drag her away from this improper discourse. But no one was in sight.

Lord Rutherford cast a quick glance at the door before returning his gaze to her. "'Let them call it mischief: When it is past and prospered 'twill be virtue.'"

She stared at him for a moment, trying to puzzle out why his words sounded so familiar. "You—I've heard those words before."

"So you frequently have gentleman ask to kiss you?" he teased.

"No! Not at all. In fact, I never—"

He sat back and folded his hands. "'The dignity of truth is lost with much protesting.'"

Lucia smacked her palms together. "*Catiline.*"

His eyebrows arched with surprise. "Yes. I am surprised you recognized the quote."

"And at our first meeting, you quoted one of Mr. Jonson's poems. At the Adrington's." She felt her face flush at the memory of his ridiculous behavior there, and her acquiescence in part of it.

"Yes, that was an entertaining evening. As I recall, I found the company most agreeable."

His pointed look left no doubt that he was speaking of her, and while her first inclination was to return the compliment, she did not. Because her second and more proper inclination was to admit his company that evening to have been a mixed blessing at best. Of what use was it to be attracted to a madman? And how flattering could it truly be for such a one to be attracted to her?

He continued to gaze at her, and to her discomfiture, she found herself unable to look away. But the good-natured amusement in his eyes soon removed her sense of unease. "I believe I quoted Mr. Jonson on our second meeting as well. Do you remember?" he challenged. "During the intermission at the opera. Can you guess the source?"

She shook her head, unable to remember anything he had said on that occasion and somewhat amazed that he could speak of the evening's horrible events with such a lighthearted air.

"Ben Jonson is not much in fashion these days, I believe," he continued blithely. "I can't remember the last time I saw one of his plays advertised."

"I have never seen any of his plays," she admitted. "But I've read them many times. We frequently read aloud at home for our entertainment." *And we make up stories.* She looked away again. Who could have foreseen that Geoffrey would take her stories so seriously? And that it would cause so much pain?

She cleared her throat and forced herself to look him in eye. "I *am* sorry, sir, for your injury. My brother has never taken such dangerous action before." Though, if she were honest, she would admit she had lately feared he might do so.

He said nothing for a long moment, but simply gazed back into her eyes as if searching for something. The intense scrutiny should have unnerved her, but strangely enough, it did not. It was exhilarating to stare back into his eyes, crystal blue, as if she could see through their clarity straight into the man's soul. As if she could see and know much more about him than she ever could through words. As if he wanted to know her, as well.

Most men hardly gave her more than a passing glance, and now here was an extremely handsome man giving her his full attention.

"I said before, you have me at a disadvantage." His voice was low and soft.

"Why is that?" She answered as if hypnotized, as though someone else spoke through her lips.

"You know my name. I have heard your brother called 'Geoffrey'. But I do not know your family name."

"Oh." Lucia blinked. The spell was broken. "I am Lucia Wright. My younger brother and sister are Geoffrey and Helen. We live in Hertfordshire."

He bowed his head. "I am pleased to make your acquaintance at last, Miss Wright."

"Thank you, Lord Rutherford. I only wish we met under more pleasant circumstances." Lucia looked meaningfully at his leg.

"I find these circumstances quite pleasant, actually." Lord Rutherford glanced at the sunny windows, the fire crackling in the grate and then at her again.

"Yes, well…" Lucia again found herself growing uncomfortable under his direct gaze. The man must be insane, after all. One day a growling dog, the next a sultan and showing no sign of concern for a mother in a grave state of illness. There was no telling what behavior he might adopt next. She folded her hands together in her lap. "I do have something to ask of you that you may not find pleasant at all."

"Oh? You are going to ask me to dance, I fear." He turned a sad glance at the crutch leaning against the side of his chair.

"N-no. Um…the matter concerns my brother."

"Geoffrey wants to dance with me?"

She giggled despite her apprehension. "No."

"Doesn't *anyone* want to dance with me, then?" He assumed a heartbreakingly sad countenance.

"I do. I mean—I would." She stopped, confused and more than a little embarrassed that she had answered his crazy question at all. "That is, were we at a dance and your leg was well."

"I shall remember that."

She nodded, wondering just how long his memory would last. Did he forget things within the hour? The next day? Or did memories come and go, like the moments of lucid behavior he seemed to have as often as his episodes of insanity? If not more so.

She scolded herself. All this time in conversation and still she had not broached the topic she needed to address. "Lord Rutherford, you may have noticed that my brother, Geoffrey, suffers the delusion that he is some sort of criminal investigator and that you are…are a notorious thief."

"Yes, he managed to get my attention with that assertion."

Lucia smiled weakly. "You see, Geoffrey has a habit of suddenly assuming different occupations, and at the moment he has taken it upon himself to hunt down a particular thief."

"Redsmock or some such?"

"Redcloak."

He pursed his lips. "I must confess I have never heard of this blackguard, so I am not sure how notorious he is, after all."

She felt her face flush. "He is…well known in certain sections of Hertfordshire."

"And I do not even own a red cloak."

"Neither does Redcloak. It is just a name he adopted based on a favorite garment of his sister's. She was hanged for stealing a loaf of bread to feed him when he was quite young."

"How do you know all of this?"

"Err…I believe I read it in the newspaper. Now then, Lord Rutherford, since my brother believes you are Redcloak, if he sees you again, he may do something rash."

"I trust you are not permitting him to go about the place armed?"

"No, of course not. But he could turn anything against you, even his bare hands."

He leaned forward. "And you do not think I would survive such a fight? Is that it?"

"No, I am sure you would acquit yourself most admirably—" Lucia stopped herself again. She had to remember that this man was as unbalanced as Geoffrey and his questions did not have to be answered literally. "I do not want to give Geoffrey another opportunity to harm you."

"Then I suggest you take him home."

Lucia sighed. "I wish I could. The London magistrates have branded Geoffrey a threat. They locked him up in Bedlam. I am hoping that if he remains under supervision here for a time with no further incident, then I can take him home without attracting their ire."

His eyebrows arched in surprise once more. "They let you remove him from Bedlam?"

She twisted her fingers together in her lap. "Not exactly. Now," she untangled her fingers and gripped the edge of her chair, "what I wanted to ask you is if you would be so good as to keep to your room, out of Geoffrey's sight for the next few days."

He grinned. "What do you mean, 'not exactly'?"

"We…arranged to move him here on our own. And Geoffrey is very happy here. It will be hard to convince him to move to another house."

"So you want me to stay hidden away in my room until you take him home?"

She shook her head. "No, no, not that long at all. You see, Geoffrey only keeps up a particular occupation for a week, two at the most. He will have forgotten all about this in a few days. Then you may move about safely."

"I see." He leaned closer. "How did you 'arrange' to move him here?"

"We, uh, oh, look at the sun!" Lucia pointed toward the nearest window. Just touching the tops of the trees on the far edges of the fields, the morning sun cast an orange glow over the gently rolling hills—a show of warmth in the cold winter landscape.

"It's lovely." Lord Rutherford kept his gaze focused inside the room. "How did you arrange for Geoffrey to come here?"

She tried to humor him. "I suppose the same way you arranged to come here yourself. I assume you decided some time in the country was in order and you asked your valet to make suitable accommodations. Is that not so?"

"Err, yes, indeed. A place of my own choosing. Certainly. But what if I do not choose to stay hidden away in my room for the week?"

She bit her lip. "Then I suppose I will somehow arrange to keep Geoffrey in his." Which would probably delay the length of time it took for him to work through his "Bow Street Runner" phase. But it was the most reasonable course. After all, he had been the one to commit the wrong in the first place. She stood. "I am sorry that I even asked this of you. Geoffrey and I are at fault—we should be the ones restricted."

"I fail to see how you are at fault, Miss Wright."

She blinked. "Geoffrey is my responsibility. I failed to control him."

"Do not trouble yourself." He smiled. "I will stay in my room so that he is free to roam and do his bit of investigating. The doctor here has said it is best for me to rest and stay off the leg as much as possible for the time being."

"Thank you." Her words came out as almost a whisper. She backed her way toward the door. "I must let you rest now. Good day, my lord." She dropped a quick curtsy.

"Yes, it has been." He bowed, as much as he could from his position in the chair.

Lucia hurried out of the room, wondering precisely how and why Lord Rutherford had taken up residence in Shady View. She had never met a man more in control—of himself, the conversation...everything. Including her.

Chapter Sixteen

ॐ

She drove him crazy enough to forget that he was supposed to act crazy. At least now he had a name for the dark, serious-eyed young lady who was apparently saddled with the world's most obnoxious set of siblings.

From his position propped up on pillows on the bed, Edmund peered out the window, wondering if she would visit again today. He had no idea how far they were from London, and he assumed she had been staying in town when he met her at the Adrington's.

He could see no reason, really, why she reappeared so frequently in his thoughts. But her evasiveness on the subject of her brother's move from Bedlam intrigued him. He had merely wondered to whom it was she spoke, in case similar arrangements needed to be made on his behalf one day. The look of guilt, so evident on her face, immediately made him suspect she had done more than simply speak to the proper authority. So what *had* she done?

A carriage again appeared right on cue. He smiled. He would have the chance to ask her.

He sat forward to ring for an attendant.

A man, whose abundance of muscle gave the appearance of little room left for brains or any other organs, lumbered into the room. He said nothing, but merely nodded toward the bell pull next to the bed.

"Please notify Mr. Groves that I wish to speak to Miss Wright when she arrives," Edmund said. "It is a matter concerning our conversation yesterday."

The man nodded then left the room as unceremoniously as he had arrived.

Edmund lay back against the pillows, grateful for the chance to relax for a few moments. Walking with a crutch the previous day had been a mistake — the effort left him thoroughly drained of energy and in considerably more pain than he had been before. Staying in his room for the next week would actually not prove much of a hardship.

He fell into an uneasy slumber for a few minutes before the sound of a knock on the door brought him aware. Pushing the pillows around to provide more support, he succeeded in propping himself upright just as the door opened.

The silent man leaned his substantial frame inside, then back outside the door. "'e's awake," he intoned in a flat voice, apparently for the benefit of whomever stood outside.

Which had to be Miss Wright.

"Oh, Edmund, this is all too awful!" Jeanne dashed into the room and fell to her knees at his bedside.

Edmund blinked. How had Miss Wright turned into Jeanne?

"I hate to see you locked up like this."

"I am not locked up. I am free to go at will." He twisted away from her, then grimaced. "Or at least I would be, if I were capable of much movement."

"Brave Edmund." She fluttered her eyelashes at him with great deliberation, though whether the gesture was meant as a flirtation or an attempt to hold back imaginary tears he could not say. She added a sniff. "Always trying to put the best front on things."

"There is nothing brave about being laid up in bed with a leg wound."

Jeanne reached tentatively for his hand. "Does it pain you much?"

Edmund pulled his hand out of her reach. "Yes."

"I am so very sorry. Franklin explained everything to me. But your appearance and behavior are so much improved over what he led me to expect, I am sure you will be out of this dreadful place in no time at all."

Edmund grimaced. He was getting very careless and Jeanne was therefore correct—he would be sent home soon if he did not start acting as though he needed to be kept away. "Get thee to a nunnery!" He turned a look of cold fury on his betrothed.

"Edmund?" She withdrew her hands and drew away from the bed.

"A woman is never to approach my person unless I have given royal permission. In writing," he added for good measure.

Jeanne struggled to her feet. "No, don't. You were not—"

"Get thee away! Dost thou wish to lose thy head?"

She backed toward the door. "You will get better. I can see that you are not always sick. I will visit every day until you are fully recovered. I promise."

Edmund looked for something to throw at her. "I've just ordered you not to visit, wench."

"It is not you who speaks now. Farewell, Edmund. It is my duty to care for you and I will."

The only serviceable projectile item Edmund could reach was one of his pillows. He threw it just as Jeanne reached the door, hitting her on the head.

"Ouch." She felt the top of her head, her expression of concerned tenderness rapidly dissolving into an irritated grimace. "You've made a perfect ruin of my hair. I shall not be able to visit and care for you if you continue to display this sort of behavior." She slammed the door shut. Out in the hallway, he could hear her berate her maid regarding her placement of hairpins.

Edmund felt his face split into a huge grin. His plan was finally beginning to show some promise.

* * * * *

The knock on the door a few minutes later took him by surprise because he had felt certain Jeanne would wait at least until the next day before attempting another visit. "Are you back again, wench?" he called out with a nasty snarl.

"Oh. I thought this was the right room but I might be mistaken." The hesitant voice definitely did not belong to Jeanne. "Um, Lord Rutherford? Mr. Groves told me you wished to speak with me, but if you have changed your mind, then…"

"Come in, come in, Miss Wright. I do indeed wish to speak with you." Edmund winced as he pushed himself upright in the bed, pained both by the movement and by the awareness of his rude greeting.

The door opened at an agonizingly slow pace. After untangling the handle of her reticule from the doorknob, Miss Wright stepped into the room to stand in the space lately vacated by Jeanne. Her plain gown and simple curls made a refreshing contrast to the gaudy finery and ornaments Jeanne had displayed in the same place only a few minutes before.

"Please forgive me the language you first heard on your arrival." He struggled to think of an excuse for the vile words he had uttered. "I, uh, had been…reading a volume of plays with Mr. Groves and thought to try out the lines from one for fun. I believed your knock on the door to be his."

"I'm sorry." She glanced at the door. "Do I keep you from a meeting with Mr. Groves?"

She appeared disappointed with this prospect, and that pleased him more than he would have supposed.

"No, no. No meeting was expected." He smiled and added softly, "Though a certain meeting was indeed hoped for." That was too forward, but then, he was in a position to make improper speeches. Life in Shady View had definite advantages.

She colored and started to inch her way back toward the door.

Ah. Perhaps having the liberty to make untoward statements still did not make such statements a good idea. He sought to change the subject. "What brings you out calling so early today?"

"I needed to deliver some toiletry articles to Geoffrey, and to ensure that he receives...proper assistance and so forth." Her face grew even more flushed. "I am sorry. It seems so awkward to speak of such things. Geoffrey is used to having his valet about, and so I have never given much thought to...shaving and..."

He let her words trail off, enjoying her delightful modesty and obvious embarrassment in speaking of masculine subjects. She dug the toe of her shoe into the soft carpet.

"You'd need not fear for his care on that account, Miss Wright. They've a barber on staff who comes around each morning, usually at an unreasonably early hour, to attend to our needs. I am sure Geoffrey is well cared for."

Her face blossomed into a smile, shy and grateful. "Thank you, my lord. I have not yet spoken with him this morning. He...he said he was not yet ready to receive visitors. Even at home, he would never see anyone before breakfast, with the exception of Nicholas, of course. Nicholas is his valet." She stopped suddenly. "I'm sorry, you really do not need to know all of this."

"Oh, but it is most helpful to know of my neighbor's circumstances. Geoffrey must feel the absence of his assistant and confidant most keenly."

"I believe he does feel a little lost. Nicholas is not the most reliable of men, but his presence has always had a calming effect on my brother. If we may not soon return Geoffrey to Hertfordshire, I hope to bring Nicholas here. Does your valet stay here with you?"

A brief flicker of pain passed through him. "He died last month. I have not yet hired another." It would take a long time to find someone whose service and companionship he valued as much as Mayer's.

"Oh dear, I am sorry. That must be very difficult."

"Not so very. Mayer's illness came on gradually—so gradually I learned to do more on my own. I think now I actually prefer to shave myself," he smiled, "although that has not been an option as of late."

"No, I meant that I was sorry because you must miss him, not his services. As Geoffrey misses Nicholas." Her face twisted into an expression of uncertainty. "Forgive me. It really is no business of mine whether—"

"Miss Wright you must stop. Cease apologizing and desist from asking my forgiveness. You make me feel as though there is something improper in our conversation, and there is not, truly."

She cast a nervous glance around, her gaze soon landing on the door which had apparently swung closed of its own accord. "My goodness, I suppose I had better prop this door to keep it open." Before he could object, she had dashed over and pulled the door so hard that it banged into the wall.

Out in the hallway, a heavy object rolled past before hitting something that clattered out of sight, and a man soon galloped by chortling with glee.

Miss Wright stared after him.

"Ah, that must be Sir Mortimer. I have heard Mr. Groves encouraging him to move his bowls to the lawn, but I believe he prefers the smooth floor of the passage. Are you sure you would rather not close that door again? As you said the last time, no one of your acquaintance will see you here."

"Yes, I did say that, didn't I?" She looked down with obvious embarrassment. "I hope you've forgiven me for that."

"Well, as you recall, I did ask for a token of your repentance." After all, if he begged her for a kiss, it would show him as imbalanced. A gentleman in his right mind would not do such a thing. At least, an honorable gentleman would not.

She looked up, her brow wrinkled in a quizzical expression. "I do not recall such a request."

Then his request for a kiss had not made as great an impression as he'd thought, judging by her shocked expression at the time. Was the demure behavior all for show? She seemed so much more sincere than Jeanne, yet of course, he had not known her nearly so long. Perhaps he should test her. If she responded to untoward advances as willingly as Jeanne had, she would show herself to be of the same stripe.

"Could you come closer?"

She walked a few feet toward him, leaving the door unsecured so that it immediately began to close once more. Not seeming to notice, she focused her gaze at first on his face and then on his leg stretched out on the bed. She reached out her hand as if to touch his knee, well below the bandaged wound.

Jeanne had done much the same, and he had pushed her away.

Miss Wright held her hand just above him, not daring to touch him but seeming mesmerized somehow.

By his knee?

"Miss Wright, would you be so good as to help me with this pillow? I am trying to move it behind my back and just cannot seem to reach…"

She turned her gaze back to his face as she moved to the head of the bed. When she reached toward the pillow he had indicated, he grabbed her arms and stretched forward to kiss her.

She was too fast, pulling herself free with wide-eyed indignation. "What are you about, my lord?"

Edmund shrugged, feigning indifference but greatly pleased that Miss Wright had reacted exactly as Jeanne had not when he attempted a similar ploy with her some time ago. "I don't know." Then a delicious though occurred to him. "I am the sultan. All the women in the kingdom belong to me. If I wish to kiss one of them, I only exercise my God-given right."

Her eyes narrowed. "Oh, God gave you that right, did he? And he gave you all the women in your kingdom?"

"Yes."

"So you owe a duty to protect them and treat them well, do you not?"

He pretended to ponder that for a moment. "I suppose."

"Well, then, you might start by taking a little better care of your own mother."

Edmund sat up straight. "My mother?"

"Yes. The woman you sent into a fit of apoplexy with your wild behavior at the opera."

"Mother?" The word barely squeaked out of his mouth, as if she'd sucked all the air from his lungs. "Suffered a fit?" What had he done?

Miss Wright nodded.

He collapsed back into the pillows. "When?" His voice came out as a choked sob.

"Why, that night, of course. As you, or perhaps after you..." Her voice dropped to a horrified whisper. "You did not know."

He shook his head.

So that was why his mother had not been to see him. That was why she had not been present when they took him away. Who then could have ordered him brought to this place? It must have been the solicitor to whom the letter had been delivered.

He forced himself to breathe. "How is she?"

"I do not know," she said miserably. "We are staying at an inn nearby and have not yet been back to town."

"What was her condition when you left?" he demanded.

"I am afraid we are not of your family's acquaintance and only hear what circulates as rumor."

He waved away her caveat. "News travels as fast that way as any other. What had you heard when you left?"

"Only that she had the attack and had not regained consciousness the next day."

He buried his face in his hands, waves of guilt, pain and anger now flooding over him in a torrent. "I've killed her," he whispered.

"Surely not?"

He forced himself to look her full in the face. "I'm a fool and a coward. And I have killed her." As realization of the consequences of his foolish ruse continued to mount, the burden of guilt coursed through until he really felt he would explode. He turned and smashed the wall with his fist, the pain radiating through his hand and up his arm a welcome relief to the pain of guilt within. He smashed the wall again and again.

"Stop! No! Stop this!" Lucia reached over and took hold of his arm with a surprisingly firm grip. Then she knelt in front of the bed, gently placing her hands over his own as she spoke to him. "You must not blame yourself. You cannot help your behavior." Tears began to glitter in the corners of her eyes. "Please forgive me—I was wrong in implying that you had behaved so on purpose." She looked down, removing her hands to her lap. "I do know better."

He winced, feeling that the tears would be better placed in his own eyes. "You do right to trust your instincts. I *can* control my behavior. And I do not truly belong here. I have made a terrible, terrible mistake."

"I am sure you do the best you can." She gazed up at him, putting on a smile no doubt meant to be encouraging.

He offered only a grim smile in return. "It is good of you to say so, but I am afraid your faith is misplaced. I have not done my best—to the contrary, I affected the worst behavior imaginable."

"If that is the case, and if, as you say, you can control your behavior, then you will soon be home with your mother again." Her smile began to look convincing. "That should improve her condition immensely."

"You are right." He felt the first rays of hope filter into the room, faint but still enough to melt the icy grip of fear that had begun to tighten around his heart. "Thank you." He leaned forward to clasp her hands, but they were out of his reach. Instead, he planted a quick kiss on her lips.

She blinked at him in surprise. But she did not pull away as she had earlier.

Her lips were soft and she smelled faintly of lavender.

He kissed her again. After a moment, she returned his kiss, her lips pressing against his own, warm and sweet. All the pain and worry melted away into a swirl of endless warmth.

"Lucia?" A feminine voice called out as the door banged open. "Are you in here? Since we've sent the carriage back to fetch Geoffrey's clo—"

He felt a sudden rush of air on his lips, harsh and cold. He did not want to admit that the dream had ended. But it had. He opened his eyes to see the young lady with whom Miss Wright had been speaking at the opera.

"Gracious heavens!" The young lady looked from Miss Wright to himself, then back to her again. "What were you doing, Lucia?"

Miss Wright jumped to her feet with an athletic, thoroughly unladylike display of physical prowess. She made no answer, but threw him one fleeting look—regret, dismay…it was hard to read. Then she disappeared through the open door.

The other young lady looked quizzically at him before turning to follow her friend into the hall.

Edmund felt as if his insides had been shredded and reshaped into a new form. Painful thoughts and memories mingled with the unexpected, pleasant sensation of the last few minutes. That sensation faded rapidly, however, when he remembered that he had allowed himself the inappropriate displays of affection to further his claim of insanity. That could never happen again. Because now he had to prove that he was most definitely, positively sane.

Chapter Seventeen

ജ

As her carriage neared Hanover Square, Jeanne attempted to smooth her hair back into place. It was really quite annoying of Edmund to have mussed her hair so when he knew she had such a difficult time getting it arranged. She sighed. He could not help it, of course.

She leaned forward to swat her maid across the forehead with her fan. "Margaret, wake up, you lazy sow. You must do something with my hair."

"Huh?" Margaret blinked and snorted with the effort to return to consciousness.

"My hair. It has come undone on the side here and I have no wish to make a spectacle of myself in the street."

Margaret pushed herself upright and then to her feet to stand in front of her mistress. The carriage lurched, hurling her backward. On her second attempt, she was able to reposition one hairpin before another lurch sent her sprawling on top of her mistress.

Jeanne pushed her off. "You clumsy fool!"

"I'm sorry, miss."

"You *are* sorry. A sorry excuse for a maid. And when I am married, you will be sent to work with the filth in the laundry, where you belong."

"Yes, miss." Margaret reached over to reposition the pins in Jeanne's hair.

"'Tomorrow, you will pin my hair properly the first time, so it will not come all to pieces. This was worse than that horrid episode with the kitten." Margaret's sister Anna had the audacity to allow a stray to play with the stings on Jeanne's best bonnet while they were taking tea with an invalid friend of her aunt's. The little beast had torn the ties and trim to bits so that Jeanne looked a perfect fright on the journey back. "That cost your sister her job."

Margaret nodded, her face grown nearly white. Like her sister, she harbored a weakness for vermin like that vile stray, not seeing the obvious need for such pests to be disposed of.

"Are you finished?" Jeanne demanded.

"Nearly so." Margaret tucked one final strand in place with shaking fingers. "All finished now, miss."

It would be "milady" soon. Come what may, Jeanne would marry Edmund and obtain the title promised all her life. Edmund's illness might delay the wedding, but not for long. As soon as he had spent a respectable amount of time away from the public eye, he could return. After their marriage, people might occasionally look at her with curiosity, even pity. But they would not look down on her with the condescension that was her present lot—the attitude reserved for the *nouveau riche*. Her marriage to Edmund would finally erase that. For twenty years she had waited, but not much longer.

Something pulled on her sleeve and she reached out to swat at the offending article.

"I'm sorry, miss. It's just that, well, the footman has been holding the door open a while but you was looking th'other way and—"

"Yes, I see." Jeanne made her way out of the carriage, accepting the footman's assistance with as much grace as she could muster. She ascended the stairs to the Rutherford home, then waited while Franklin answered the knock.

"Good evening, Miss Newman."

"I am sorry to call so late without sending word."

Franklin bowed. "It is no trouble, miss."

Jeanne had to work to contain a smile. Such polite servants at the Rutherford home! She believed Franklin would have admitted her with complaisance if she had arrived at midnight.

"How does Lady Rutherford this evening?" she inquired after she'd stepped inside.

"Lady Rutherford is no better, I am sorry to say. The physician is with her now."

"I should very much like to speak with him before he leaves. And pay my respects to Lady Rutherford. May I wait in the parlor?"

Franklin bowed once more. "Of course, Miss Newman." He opened the door for her. "Would miss care for a tray of supper to be sent in?"

"Yes, thank you." As soon as the door closed behind the servant, Jeanne sank down into one of the opulent chairs near the window. Soon this would be her parlor. Already the servants treated her as a member of the family — the marriage promise was of long-standing awareness to all and she and her aunt had been frequent visitors since Jeanne came out four years ago. She and Edmund could have wed with propriety at that time, but her mother had wished her to wait until she was closer to her majority. And dying wishes were not to be trifled with, according to Edmund. So they had waited.

Then, last season, Lady Rutherford took ill and all thoughts of a wedding were pushed aside — by Edmund, at least, who would not let anyone speak of it. His devotion to his mother and to her mother's wishes was admirable, but most inconvenient. She far would have preferred to have married that first season. After all, she could not court any other man, nor had she a particular desire to, since Edmund was always one of the most handsome men at any gathering. Of course, his good looks were increasingly offset by his dull, aloof manner.

If the familiarity of marriage did not melt his icy reserve, she had no doubt but that she would find other ways to keep warm.

She rubbed her hands together to bring heat back into her chilled fingers.

* * * * *

Jeanne had just taken a bite of chicken that was too large when a knock sounded on the door to the parlor. She chewed in haste for a moment, then spit the offending mass into her napkin so that she would not appear uncouth to the entrant.

"Dr. Hamilton, miss."

"Thank you, Franklin."

The physician stepped into the room at a brisk pace. He reached for her hand in greeting, then noticed she had removed her gloves. Instead he bowed. "Good evening, Miss Newman. I must say it is a pleasure to see you again, though I had hoped our next meeting might be under more agreeable circumstances."

"Yes," she answered simply, wondering whether circumstances might become more agreeable for them rather sooner than later. The man appraised her with a frank, approving gaze both rare and titillating. It was as if he could envision her without the protection of clothing and liked what the vision portended.

That was the gaze Edmund should have given her, yet never had. His glances in her direction, for they never were much more than glances, were cool and brusque.

"Lady Rutherford recovers even more slowly than last year, I am afraid." He turned his gaze toward the small table near the fire. "I see I have interrupted your supper." He bowed again. "I will not detain you any longer."

"No, please. I have finished." She glanced at an uneaten slice of cake with only a small amount of regret. "I would like to discuss the condition of Lady Rutherford—and her son. Will you not sit down?" She gestured toward the chairs by the window, then immediately wondered at her choice. The two chairs sat so close together that the legs of their occupants would be within an almost intimate proximity. Propriety dictated that she should have instead waved him to the sofa and adjacent chair by the fireplace. Surely her suggested seating arrangement could be attributed to an inclination to avoid the supper dishes and not a desire to sit close to the distinguished physician?

"As you wish." He moved to take the proffered chair.

Jeanne followed, sitting carefully on the edge of her seat, very much aware that her knees practically touched those of the man next to her. "Has Lady Rutherford improved from your first visit?"

"She has, but only to a modest degree. She can take a little nourishment, some broth or juice, and often her eyes follow movement, but of course, she cannot talk and so cannot communicate at all. She sleeps most of the time."

"She was sleeping when I saw her this morning."

The physician nodded. "Her maid says she must go to great lengths to wake her for her small meals. She seems to have no will to do so on her own."

"And what of her son — Lord Rutherford?"

Dr. Hamilton looked surprised. "I have not seen him since the night of the...incident. The surgeon tended his wounds adequately, I suppose. I prescribed some laudanum. And he was taken away soon after."

"You did not order him taken away?"

"No. I believe his removal was a poor decision, if you'll pardon me for saying so. From what I have heard, he would be better off in familiar surroundings. A new setting may only serve to foster the delusion. And his mother might improve more rapidly if she could see him. She may believe him dead, though I have told her otherwise."

"I see." Jeanne nodded, wondering who it was who had Edmund placed in the private asylum. "I will exert whatever influence I have to see that he is brought home." A brief pang of regret followed this last statement. In many ways, Edmund's absence seemed rather more a comfort than not.

"That is good of you." The physician stared at her in silence for a moment, the expression on his face changing from a look of professional authority to the approving gaze he had lavished on her earlier. This time his gaze imparted the uncanny sensation that her clothing was being peeled off one layer at a time.

He stood. "I am afraid I must take my leave. I have two more patients to attend this evening." He bowed. "Until next time."

She cleared her throat. "Yes. Until next time."

At the doorway, he smiled.

The smile sent a searing heat throughout her body, so hot it almost made her cold. She shivered. Then she began to wonder whether Dr. Hamilton would need to visit frequently to monitor Edmund's condition once they were married.

A wicked thought, surely. She should chastise herself for even thinking such a thing.

Instead, she smiled. Her impending marriage might lack passion, but that need not preclude such pleasures from her life entirely.

Another knock on the door made her start, as if the person outside had read her inappropriate thoughts.

Franklin peered around the door.

"Might I have a word with you, Miss Newman?"

"Certainly."

The butler entered the room with precise steps and shut the door carefully. "I hope you will forgive me for troubling you with this matter. I am somewhat at a loss what to do. I cannot ask her ladyship and was ordered not to discuss this with Mr. Stansbury."

"Yes?"

"Since you have always been a close acquaintance of the family and," he coughed, "almost a member of the family, I thought perhaps you might…"

"Of course." She offered her most reassuring smile. "I will be happy to help in whatever way I can."

Franklin bowed. "Thank you. I have a letter — actually, it is little more than a note — written by Lord Rutherford on the night of the…the…"

"I believe I understand. Do go on."

"During the intermission at the opera, he instructed the coachman to deliver the note to me with instructions to take it to a solicitor. Any solicitor. But he specifically stated it should not go to Mr. Stansbury."

"Oh?" Why? Was he trying to keep a secret from his family?

"Well, I could not attend to it at that hour of the evening, of course, so I set it aside. And then, given what followed later that night, I-I was uncertain what to do."

"Should you not follow his instructions and deliver it to a solicitor?"

"Perhaps. But…" Franklin looked around as if he feared the walls might be listening. "What if the note instructs the solicitor to sell off all the family belongings and book passage for India? I am afraid, you see, that the note might contain…something Lord Rutherford might later regret."

"I understand your dilemma. It might be better for you to open the note to see what it contains."

"I cannot open my lord's correspondence." The servant licked his lips nervously. "But I thought, perhaps, you might be able to."

Jeanne felt a bit taken aback. But only for a moment. Then the thought made her want to laugh. She was being treated as head of the family already. They came to her for decisions! "Yes, yes, of course. Have you the note on you?"

"I do, miss." He reached into a jacket pocket and produced a piece of folded, extremely heavy paper. After looking at it for a moment, he handed it to Jeanne.

She read the instructions scrawled on the front, recognizing the lines as a hurried version of Edmund's artistic hand.

The butler waited expectantly, but she waved him away. "Thank you, Franklin. I shall see that the note is passed along to a solicitor, should such action be appropriate."

"V-very good, miss." He bowed, watching her with an uneasy gaze. Then he collected the supper tray, and with one last glance at in her direction, left her to read the note in private.

When she finished the short missive depicting Edmund's deliberate intent to act insane, she collapsed against the back of the chair. Why on earth would he do such a thing? Was his mind perhaps truly unbalanced, to have him make such a statement? She remembered his conduct at their last meeting. He had not appeared insane at all for the first few minutes. His demeanor evinced the aloof, disinterested, polite manner she had come to expect.

Until she had mentioned his return to London. Then he had started to act crazy. Did he not want to return home?

Why?

After reading the note for the third time, Jeanne let it slip from her fingers.

Chapter Eighteen

ಬಂ

"If we send the coachman home tonight," Eugenie explained as they set off in the carriage from Shady View for the Iron Coxcomb Inn, "he will be able to return tomorrow with fresh clothing for us and Geoffrey."

"But that means we might not have the carriage to visit Shady View until late in the morning," Lucia objected.

"We cannot possibly appear out again in the same gowns one more day, Lucia."

"A visit to Shady View hardly constitutes appearing 'out'. No one of our acquaintance will be there, and no one there cares what we look like."

"I dare say Lord Rutherford cares what you look like." Eugenie smirked. "And he is quite handsome himself. But he's as mad as a March hare. Why did you allow him to kiss you?"

"Oh." Lucia cringed. "I had rather hoped you had not seen that. I suppose that now I am ruined."

"Do not be ridiculous. I will not tell a soul, and you know it. But if someone else had come upon you, I cannot say that your reputation would be so safe. Why did you allow it?"

Why indeed? She did not regret the act for a moment. The magical sense of affection mingled with excitement was a thrill she would probably never again experience in her life. But she was surprised that she had allowed herself to take such a chance.

She sighed. "I do not quite understand, Eugenie. Perhaps I felt sorry for him because he is crazy. After all, he is not likely to have the opportunity to court or kiss ladies while locked in his room in an asylum. Perhaps some misguided young lady will similarly take pity on my brother one day if…" She would not finish that thought aloud, or even to herself. Geoffrey would come home—he would not spend the rest of his life in an asylum.

Eugenie leaned forward. "Had you ever kissed a man before?"

"No." Lucia felt her face flush with a slow, creeping sensation running slowly up to her hairline. "Well, once back at school, but that doesn't—no," she affirmed decisively.

"At school? When? Who was it?"

"Never mind. It was—it was not a real kiss. Gerald, the dancing master's son, told me I had to kiss him or he would pour ink down my back."

"Gerald?" Eugenie's horrible grimace left no doubt as to her opinion of the young man's charms.

"You can see why I am not anxious to consider that a real kiss, now, can you not?"

"Yes. But your first real kiss, then, was not much better."

"Oh, yes." Lucia smiled. "It was."

"An inmate in an insane asylum?"

"Now, now," Lucia scolded, doing her best to imitate the artificially dulcet tones of Mr. Groves. "You know we do not refer to the residents as inmates. And Shady View is a special home for those simply in need of a restful environment."

Eugenie giggled. "I am going to tell Mr. Groves that you are not letting Lord Rutherford rest. Who knows what would have happened had I not interrupted you?"

"Nothing would have happened. I do not feel *that* sorry for the man. And besides," she sputtered with a giggle herself, "he is too injured to attempt much."

Eugenie raised her eyebrows. "So it did occur to you, then?"

"No. I just knew it would occur to *you*." But in truth, something, some unknown desire had pricked the back of her mind. A longing for something she could not name. "Are you scandalized?"

"No." Eugenie laughed. "Surprised, yes. Because it is you, Lucia, the girl who always behaved irreproachably, who only ever got in trouble for leaving her books piled too high in our room so that one of us occasionally tripped over them."

"That was rather inconsiderate of me, and dangerous. A blow to the head from a toppling book of epic Greek poems could have proved fatal, you know."

Eugenie wrinkled her nose. "No, that is hardly a fault worth worrying yourself over. The rest of us took advantage of the freedom from our families. We tried what we knew we could not at home. You always acted as if your parents were there watching you every minute."

"Well, they were, weren't they? From up in heaven?"

Eugenie cringed. "Oh dear. Of course, you are right."

"But that was not the reason I behaved 'irreproachably', as you say. I was exercising a freedom, the same as you. But instead of freedom from order and rules, I celebrated a freedom from lawless chaos. An imprudent dalliance with a stable boy or a ploy to steal the housekeeper's keys would scarcely have been noticed at home. I had that sort of freedom all my life. What I enjoyed at school was the freedom to think only of myself, without a worry as to what Helen or Geoffrey might be about."

"I meant for you to have that freedom again on your visit to London. But then you were determined to return to them so soon."

"I know." Lucia smiled. "I suppose Geoffrey and Helen are simply too old now to trust to the care of the servants. When they were younger, we had a wonderful governess—Mrs. Whipplethwait—who kept them well in hand. But she's in her cottage, living in poor health on a small pension these days, and I dared not ask her to look in on the twins."

Eugenie said nothing for a moment, then peered earnestly into Lucia's face. "I am sorry about Geoffrey. That he...and that he has ended up…" Tears rapidly filled the corners of her eyes and began to spill over.

"I know. But you've no need to apologize. You have done nothing to be sorry for. You only tried to fix what is incapable of repair. The attempt was admirable."

"Do you suppose your stepfather might be able to do something for him?"

"As a matter of fact, I wrote to him when we first arrived. I am hopeful that he might help me get Geoffrey home."

Eugenie nodded. Then a particularly severe jolt made her look out the carriage window. "Oh good, here we are at last. I swear, the jostling on these country roads quite wears me to bits. Does it not have the same effect on you?"

"Not really," Lucia admitted. "I find the bumping about rather fun. You know, with Helen's fear of speed, we never hit the ruts with so much force. Sometimes, the jolt even knocks you out of your seat!"

"Yes." Eugenie rubbed her backside. "But then you land."

* * * * *

Jeanne smoothed her gown and hair as Mr. Groves knocked on the door to Edmund's room. She must have been sitting crooked on the long ride out from London, because an ugly crease stretched from midpoint in her gown all the way to the floor. Had she thought to bring another gown, her maid could have worked at straightening this one.

Mr. Groves knocked a second time. "Are you awake, sir? One of your ladies is here to see you."

Jeanne dropped her reticule. "*One* of your ladies?"

Mr. Groves smiled apologetically as he retrieved the reticule from the floor. "A sultan must keep a harem, Miss Newman. I do try to humor my guests whenever possible. I hope I have not offended you?"

"No, of course not." It was a reasonable explanation, surely, but something in his eyes indicated that the man had not shared the entire truth with her.

"You may enter," a voice called imperiously from beyond the door.

Mr. Groves opened the door for Jeanne, then followed her inside. "I see you are without your turban once again, your grace. Shall I fetch it for you?"

"Do." Edmund was not seated on the bed this time but in a chair by the window. He eyed Jeanne impersonally. "Then introduce me to this young lady, for I do not believe I have had the pleasure of her acquaintance."

Jeanne started forward to answer, to throw herself at his feet and beg for him to remember, but the words died in her throat.

This was all an act. Mr. Groves might have been unaware that Edmund feigned this delusion, but she herself was now certain. The eyes glaring at her from under the recently procured turban were those of Edmund in full and complete possession of his faculties.

She still did not know why he pretended to have lost them.

Edmund looked away from her and returned his attention to the book that he held upside-down in his hands.

She addressed her next words to Mr. Groves as if Edmund were not even in the room. "He does indeed know who I am, sir. We have been betrothed for over twenty years. Our wedding date is set for the first of March."

There was a thump and a flutter of pages as the book tumbled to the floor.

"Are you well, my lord?" Mr. Groves asked with a mild display of concern.

"This woman is mad," Edmund declared with savage fury. "I do not marry anyone during the season of…" He struggled to think of an excuse. "I refuse to marry during monsoon season."

"I'm sure Mr. Groves can find an umbrella," Jeanne replied smoothly.

"I will not have a mere woman dictate such matters to me," Edmund huffed. "Take her away."

Mr. Groves offered Jeanne another apologetic smile. "If you would be so good as to accompany me to the drawing room, Miss Newman?"

Jeanne sighed. "Very well. I only came to ask Edmund's opinion on the menu for the wedding breakfast."

A turban sailed past her head, hit the wall and slid down ineffectually.

"Goodbye, my beloved," she called around the door as it closed. She heard some unknown object hit the door as they walked away.

He did not want to marry her! The pieces fit together at last. He was quite content to play the fool here in peace until she made some mention of their wedding. Then he grew furious. That bastard was feigning insanity to put off their marriage contract. He must have hoped his uncouth behavior would cause her to cancel the agreement so he would not look bad to his mother.

She fought the urge to go back to his room and throw something at him, something much heavier than a turban or anything else he could reach.

To smash his dishonorable, scheming brains against the sunny yellow wall.

But that would not help matters at all.

Edmund's title and inheritance would pass to some distant relative, if such existed, or even to the state. She would not see a farthing, despite the promise, despite all the years of waiting.

He planned to make her look petty and leave her without station in society. Then he would miraculously reappear with his fortune and title intact, free to select a bride from any eligible young lady of the *ton*.

"Miss Newman, are you well?"

The sound of Mr. Groves' voice made her realize they had come to the end of the hallway, walking right past the stairs, and she was smashing one fist into the other palm like some sort of prize fighter.

Which is exactly what she was. Edmund's title, if not the man himself, was a prize worth fighting for. And she knew she could fight.

* * * * *

When Jeanne left the room, Edmund jumped to his feet, clenching his fists as if that effort could lessen the searing pain in his leg and the rage of frustration roiling through his head. His attempt to walk ended after two steps, when his weak leg gave way and he staggered toward the bed. He smashed his fist into the headboard. The move made no mark on the hard wood, just as his recent efforts made no headway against the trap he felt closing around him. He needed to appear sane to get out of Shady View to see his mother. Yet when Jeanne arrived, his reason truly did leave him for a moment and all he could think of was how to be rid of her.

And the worst of it, of course, was that the effort had proven fruitless. A wedding date still loomed on the calendar and the days marched relentlessly closer.

Was there nothing he could do to dissuade the woman? He hit the headboard again, this time with such force that it smacked into the wall with a satisfying *whump*. So he hit it again, this time quickly following up with a blow from the other hand. He continued to pummel the headboard in this manner for some minutes, until sweat ran down his forehead, draining away the frustration and rage pent up inside.

But he felt no peace. Only sorrow and a vague sense of fear—fear that he might never see his mother alive again, fear that he had disappointed her fatally by appearing crazy. Tears squeezed out of his eyes, joined the rivulets of sweat for a run to the edge of his chin, then plummeted to the sheets below.

A timid knock sounded at the door.

"Go away," he murmured through his hands. He did not want to face anybody at this moment.

"Lord Rutherford, are you well? I was out in the hallway with Geoffrey and we heard some odd noises coming from this direction."

Even the sweet tones of Miss Wright's voice could not lift his spirits from the black pit in which he'd sunk them. He made no answer, but rolled over so that he lay against the pillows, propped up like a scarecrow and staring at the uneven joint where the wall met the ceiling.

"I could not find an attendant. Lord Rutherford, will you please answer? Just tell us if you are in difficulty? Geoffrey, I think you had better go fetch Mr. Groves, or an attendant if you see one."

"Right, Lu!" Footsteps thundered away down the hall.

"Mind you don't charge into Sir Mortimer as he sets up his pins!"

"I..." Edmund had to clear his throat to get an audible voice. "I am well enough," he called out. "There is no need to send for anyone."

"Geoffrey! You need not—oh, he's gone too far to hear me. Well, I suppose that is good." Miss Wright opened the door and dashed in, nearly breathless. "Then I shall have enough time."

"Enough time for what?" Curiosity started to win out over self-pity.

"Time for this." She flung herself onto the bed, planted an uneven kiss on his lips, then scooted away and was back at the door before he quite knew what had happened.

He touched his lip uncertainly.

"Did I bite you?" All at once, she was timid and uncertain.

Edmund chuckled. "No. Though if you meant to and you'd like to give it another try, I won't object."

"Oh. Was I supposed to bite your lip? I-I've not kissed very many men before."

"Very many?"

"Just you, really. I am not exactly sure what is supposed to happen." A becoming flush spread across her cheeks before she had even finished speaking.

"I think you have a better idea than you realize. Would you care to make another attempt?"

"No, I—that is." She looked toward the door with a twinge of fear, then turned back. "Yes." She made a most unladylike dive toward the bed.

Edmund reached down and drew her up close so that he could smell the lavender in her hair and see the sparkle in her eyes.

She leaned forward to kiss him again, but he stopped her, touching her brow, her nose and her cheek before kissing each place in turn. He moved his lips to her mouth, and she seemed frozen at first, then melted completely, her lips against his, her body relaxing against his own.

Time and space had no chance to recede this time, however, as she broke the embrace after only a few short seconds.

"I must get back outside the room before Geoffrey returns." She slid off the bed. "You must pretend to be asleep or something."

She did like to issue orders, despite her modest demeanor.

He was not entirely sure he enjoyed taking orders from a woman, particularly when they implied fear on his part. "I am not afraid of Geoffrey."

"I know." She smiled. "But I am. Good afternoon, your majesty. Thank you!" She made an impossibly quick curtsy before quitting the room.

Why on earth had *she* thanked *him*?

Chapter Nineteen

෨෨

Outside in the passage, Lucia pressed herself against the wall as she took air in great gulps, willing her heartbeat to slow down.

She had done it. She, good little Lucia, had actually been brazen enough to kiss a man. She recognized a chance that might never come again, and she had not been too fearful to take that chance. The realization and sense of success were exhilarating.

Or was that the kiss itself? Lord Rutherford had a way of making her forget exactly where she was or what she was doing. Sometimes in his presence, she could scarcely remember to breathe, let alone form a coherent thought. At other moments, she felt she could speak to him at endless length on any subject. So which of them should be said to be the one lacking reason?

"There you are, Lu. I did not see you." Geoffrey bustled up to her with Mr. Groves and Sir Mortimer in tow. "We found Mr. Groves on the stairs."

Sir Mortimer held up a bowling pin, apparently to signal his assent to the story.

Mr. Groves offered them both a quick conciliatory smile before turning to Lucia. "Your brother said it was a matter of some urgency concerning another guest?"

"Ah, well…" Lucia wondered if she looked as red as she felt. "We heard unusual noises from this end of the passage, and then Lord Rutherford would not answer our summons."

Mr. Groves glanced at the array of bowling pins scattered at the other end of the hall before he stepped up to the door. "You did the right thing, then, in alerting me."

"He's probably just asleep," she said hopefully. She held her breath as Mr. Groves knocked. No answer.

"Lord Rutherf—your highness?" Mr. Groves knocked again. "Are you well?"

No answer.

"I will go in to check on his lordship. Please excuse me." He opened the door as little as possible to slip himself into the room.

Lucia allowed herself a sigh of relief. Geoffrey could not possibly have seen into the room. Of course, neither then could she now—which was both good and bad. It saved her much embarrassment. But she would have liked one more glimpse of those blue eyes.

Mr. Groves returned after no more than a minute, again keeping the opening of the door as narrow as possible. For the benefit of her modesty, Lucia realized. She almost giggled.

"He appears to be sleeping soundly. Perhaps the noises you heard—and I assume they could not be attributed to bowling—came from another floor?"

"Should we look up or down?" Geoffrey grasped Sir Mortimer's arm, fully prepared to launch the pair of them off to investigate.

Sir Mortimer pointed up with his bowling pin.

"Geoffrey," Lucia reminded her brother, "Miss Bayles is waiting for us in the drawing room downstairs."

"Do you think she might want to join in our search?"

"No. I think she would like to bid you a good morning. Although I suppose it is afternoon now."

"Yes, in that case, it can wait, can it not? If the afternoon has just started, she has many hours yet in which to wish me a good afternoon."

Lucia pondered that for a moment. "I see. But I believe I was mistaken and it is indeed still morning, and there is not much of it left. So we must hurry downstairs at once."

"You're right. At once!" Geoffrey dragged Sir Mortimer several steps down the hall before letting him go. "Oh, I forgot. You've no need to pay your respects to Miss Bayles—she's never even met you. You are at leisure to begin searching upstairs for the source of this mysterious noise." Geoffrey sprinted toward the stairs. "Mr. Groves," he called back, "I shall catch you up presently."

"Very good, Mr. Wright. You will excuse me, Miss Wright?" Mr. Groves bowed.

Lucia nodded. "Of course." She gave one last lingering look at the door to Lord Rutherford's room, then hurried after her brother.

Geoffrey waved wildly in her direction as she entered the drawing room, as if she would have had difficulty catching sight of his tall, spindly, animated frame in the room of short, squat, posed furniture.

"You've a letter come from Papa, Lu. The inn sent it along."

Eugenie held up a compact fold of sealed paper. "This arrived right after you went upstairs to fetch Geoffrey."

Lucia breathed a tremendous sigh of relief. An answer from her stepfather. With his help, she would surely be able to bring Geoffrey home.

"Miss Bayles will not let me open the letter." Geoffrey pouted.

"And right she is, too." Lucia reached over to collect the letter Eugenie held out for her. "Is your name 'Lucia'?"

"Of course not. But he is my Papa as much as yours. Why did he not write to me? He must have meant for both of us to read that letter."

"He writes to me because I first sent him a letter. That is generally how correspondence works, brother dear. You write to someone, they send a reply. If you sat down and—"

"I haven't time for that. Writing is woman's work."

"Hmm. Then perhaps reading must be as well. Now, hush." Lucia marveled that she could banter so casually with her brother while her heart raced. So much depended on her stepfather's reply.

Eugenie offered an encouraging smile.

She broke the seal, then skimmed through the salutation and a recapitulation of the recent hunting season. Then there was unimportant news about some cousins who had come to visit him at Christmas.

Geoffrey tapped his foot with impatience. "What does he say, Lu?"

"Very little of interest so far. They were able to get in three good hunts near Longleat before the weather got too cold. His cousin Sanders has taken a position with the naval supply office. That sort of thing."

"Little of interest? Hunting season and the navy? The very foundations of British life. I shudder to think what must be required to make a letter interesting to you." He shuddered for illustrative purposes.

The letter was not long, but the words she sought were tucked in at the very end. And they were not actually the words she sought. Quite the opposite, in fact.

"Finally, my dear Lucia, I cannot agree with your assertion that Geoffrey must be brought home with utmost expediency. I rather believe that a secluded home such as you've described Shady View to be, that provides discreet security not obvious to society or to Geoffrey himself, is the best place for the boy. I shall endeavor to visit when my health permits. Your most humble and obedient servant, Papa George."

Geoffrey reached for the letter. "From your expression, I daresay he's spoken more of hunting or perhaps shooting and fishing. You look utterly aghast, Lu."

She stepped back closer to Eugenie, keeping the letter as far from Geoffrey as possible. "No, he, ah, spoke of, uh, acting. Yes, the remainder of the missive described a production he'd just seen."

"Lu, Papa George hasn't set foot in a playhouse for as long as I can remember."

"Yes, I believe he mentioned it was part of the village fête. Several children from the manor took part. Would you like to read about it?" She held out the letter, trying to keep her fingers from trembling. If Geoffrey took her up on the offer, he would be devastated by the last few lines of the letter. But if she kept trying to keep the contents from him, he would endeavor to "investigate" his way into the letter somehow. The trick was to make it seem an unchallenging, unappealing target.

He wrinkled his nose, but did not refuse outright. In fact, his hand lifted slowly toward Lucia.

"I believe he said the ladies made decorated cakes to sell at the intermission. And he described the costumes in great detail."

The hand wavered slightly.

"Oh, I believe I hear Mr. Groves heading up to the third floor," Eugenie cut in. "I wonder if he's found the source of the suspicious noise?"

"I promised him I'd be back to help straightaway. Why do I stand here with you two discussing the business of ladies' letters?" He ran toward the stairs. "It was good to see you again, Miss Bayles!" He had reached the first landing before the words even finished echoing off the marble.

"Thank you." Lucia lowered herself into the nearest chair.

Eugenie seated herself opposite. "That letter does not appear to contain good news. Geoffrey was right—you do look aghast."

"My stepfather will not come to help us."

"I am sorry to hear it."

"I actually expected as much. He has traveled no more than a day's ride out of Bath in the last ten years."

Eugenie shook her head in sympathy. "It is still a shame."

"What is the shame, to me, is that he believes Geoffrey belongs in a place such as this. That he should not return home anytime soon." Her voice broke over the last few words. She dropped the letter and closed her eyes, no longer able to bear her friend's kindly, sympathetic gaze.

Eugenie squeezed her hand. "Do not worry. You said yourself that he needed to stay here for a while, until his escapades in London have faded from public memory. By that time, we will have figured out a solution. Perhaps your stepfather might even change his mind. Besides," she added, "I think Geoffrey is rather enjoying himself for the moment, don't you?"

Lucia had to admit she was right.

* * * * *

Several days had passed since Edmund last walked with the crutch, and it was time to try again. Even though he had promised Miss Wright that he would remain in his room, it was now more important that he convince Mr. Groves of his true, sane state of mind. This would be difficult to accomplish in a room absurdly festooned with hanging Eastern draperies and Turkish carpets. So he would have to remove himself from his room and meet with Mr. Groves on more neutral territory, or perhaps even the latter's own office. Once he had proven his sanity, he would extricate himself from the engagement honestly, if not honorably. Make a sizable settlement on Jeanne. Then take his mother someplace warm, far from the damp and gloom of London. And she would recover. She might not forgive him, but she would be well.

But before he could set this chain of events in motion, he would first have to maneuver himself down the stairs with his crutch.

It was only with this goal firmly in mind that he was able to make it the full distance. By the time he reached what he assumed to be Groves' office on the ground floor, he had finally learned to move the crutch without thinking so that walking, though painful, did not take such intent concentration.

At the door, he paused a moment to regain his composure before knocking. He wanted to appear as much the Imposing Lord of the Manor as possible, but it was a posture he seldom assumed, so it did take some effort. He had always found such demeanor unbearably pompous.

But if that's what it took to get him home, so be it. He rapped at the door with sharp, impatient knocks. "Groves, are you in there?" He deepened his voice and assumed a condescending scowl. He knocked again. "I say, Groves, are you within, sir?"

"No, I am not," came a voice from somewhere behind him. "I believe you are knocking on the broom closet."

Edmund grimaced, but forced his composure back into place before he turned around. "Mr. Groves, I have need of a word with you."

Groves approached with an indulgent smile. "Of course, your majesty." He bowed. "I am at your service."

"I would prefer to speak in private."

"Then I think we should return to your private chambers, your majesty."

"No. We will speak in an office or parlor close at hand. And you may discontinue the use of ridiculous superlatives. I am customarily addressed as 'my lord,' or Lord Rutherford. To use any other title is ridiculous and insulting."

"Yes, your maj—my lord. If you so desire, we may speak in the gold room—it is just down here."

"Gold room?" Was Groves humoring his royalty delusion again?

"Decorated in shades of gold and yellow, my lord. Favorite colors of the late mistress of Shady View."

That should have been obvious, since virtually every room in the house was decorated in some shade of yellow. The wonder was not that there was a "gold room" but that a room of such description could be distinguished from any other in the house.

It nonetheless made a better environment than his bedchamber, which Groves had seen fit to adorn with all the trappings of a mélange of Eastern royalty.

He seated himself in a chair with a hard back and seat of a stiff-haired puce substance. "Mr. Groves, this may come as somewhat of a surprise, but I am here to inform you that I am not in the least insane."

"No?"

"No. I have assumed the guise of an insane gentleman for...for my own purposes. But after having heard news of my mother's illness, I believe the time has come to own up to the charade so that I may return home."

"I see." Groves folded his hands into a tent which he opened and closed a few times before replying further. "I am not sure that would be entirely the best course of action at the moment, your maj—my lord."

"What do you mean?" Edmund tried to keep his growing sense of unease out of his voice.

"Perhaps you are not as fully recovered as you assume. I believe your sudden return could perhaps upset the household, worry Lady Rutherford..."

"What you believe is irrelevant." Edmund stamped the floor with his crutch for emphasis. "If I wish to return home, I am certainly within my rights to do so."

Again, Groves offered his indulgent smile. "I am afraid not. You were legally committed into my care by the signature of two physicians under advice and consent from your solicitor acting as your next friend. It is for them to say when you are fit to return."

"Exactly so." Edmund relaxed slightly. His earlier planning, though haphazard, would now serve its purpose. "My solicitor has proof that I am, as you say, 'fully recovered' of my faculties, and he can show this proof to the doctors. However, the solicitor who represents my interests is a different man from the one who has conducted business for my mother. The family solicitor is no doubt the gentleman who signed the papers to convey me here."

"A Mr. Stansbury, I believe?"

"Yes."

"Yet you say that you have engaged a different solicitor to represent your personal interests?"

"Yes."

"And his name would be...?"

Edmund faltered. "I do not know his name." This admission did seem rather ridiculous.

"I see." Groves tented his fingers once more.

"Franklin, our butler, will know him. I ordered him to engage a solicitor on my behalf before I — before I left London."

"I see." Groves contemplated his hands for another moment before collapsing the tent. "I will have to contact Mr. Franklin then, in order to contact your solicitor, who must then contact Mr. Stansbury." He offered a placating smile. "This will take some time, you understand."

Edmund hit the arms of the chair with the heels of his hands as he leaned forward. "I do not have extra time to spend waiting for polite correspondence. My mother is ill, and I need to return to her as soon as possible!"

"Yes, you have made your feelings on the matter quite clear, Lord Rutherford. But as I have indicated, you must remain here until your release is properly authorized. I believe your petition is currently pending in Chancery at the moment, but I shall have to verify the status with Mr. Stansbury."

Edmund stifled the urge to wring the man's conciliatory neck. Such a display of temper would not bolster his claim of sanity, however much better it might make him feel for the moment. He pulled his crutch close to the chair and stood. "Very well. I shall leave you to start making the necessary arrangements. Do remember that speed is of the utmost importance."

Groves stood and bowed. "Of course, your maj—my lord."

Edmund turned and made his way out of the room with as much dignity as he could manage, given the inconvenient crutch and the awkward arrangement of furniture in the room, which had apparently been placed by someone whose chief aspiration lay in the design of steeplechase courses.

At the door he paused, forcing himself to swallow his anger and frustration. He would secure more cooperation with honeyed words than vinegar. "Thank you for your cooperation, Mr. Groves. I realize this must be an unusual request."

"Not at all, not at all," Groves reassured him.

Which was not reassuring in the least.

Chapter Twenty

ജ

After Jeanne had spent the requisite amount of time sitting at Lady Rutherford's bedside watching the old woman breathe and wondering whether the room might be improved with lighter draperies and bed curtains, she decided she was ready to pay a visit to the family solicitor.

As she rose, she smiled at the sleeping woman, noting with some satisfaction that she seemed even more gaunt than yesterday. Lady Rutherford might well recover, and indeed Jeanne hoped she eventually would, for Edmund always behaved more civilly in her presence. But her recovery need not come too soon, nor too easily. She should not recuperate until after Jeanne had secured her own future and punished the scoundrel who had treated her so cruelly. Both he and his mother should suffer for a time, just as she had suffered the disinterest and disrespect of society for so many endless years. But she would be more merciful than they, releasing them after a much shorter span of time.

Closing the door carefully behind her, she made her way toward the stair landing with light steps, turning back to see if her maid followed or if the unreliable girl had wandered off again.

"Good afternoon, Miss Newman."

The smooth, masculine sound of the voice brought a smile to her lips. It was the attractive physician, come to call on Lady Rutherford again. Perhaps she had better stay a while longer yet.

"Good afternoon, Dr. Hamilton."

He bowed. "I am sorry to see that I've missed your visit."

Jeanne smiled. "No, indeed, I only just arrived. But I have need to send my maid on an errand and she has quite deserted me already. Once I've located her, I shall return to wait on Lady Rutherford."

He stepped to the side to allow her to pass, then bowed once more in farewell. His smile, as his gaze traveled slowly up to meet hers once more, indicated he would be pleased with the further acquaintance.

As would she. A great many moments passed before she found herself ready to start down the stairs.

Lady Rutherford would take a great deal of time to recover. Her physician would need to visit often. It would be well for them to develop a close acquaintance.

* * * * *

The doctor had stayed a good deal longer than was necessary, she was certain. And he had enjoyed the visit. Once, he had asked Jeanne to hold a candle close to him in the darkened chamber while he inspected Lady Rutherford's eyes. Keeping her gaze averted from the procedure, which involved a rather revolting prying open of the invalid's eyelids, she stared instead at the doctor's fine profile. When he finished the examination, he turned to her, no more than a breath away. "Thank you for your assistance." Neither moved, each seeming to savor the intimacy and warmth of the other.

Nothing more could come of it, of course. Not for the time being. But now at least she knew that if she could not get this warmth from Edmund, it could indeed be found very close by.

Physicians, however distinguished their university degrees, did not accumulate sufficient wealth from their endeavors. So pecuniary arrangements must be secured first.

She withdrew. "The afternoon grows late and I have an errand of business to attend. So I am afraid I must depart now."

"I hope to see you again, Miss Newman."

"I am sure you shall." She loaded her parting smile with all the desires she could not yet put to voice.

* * * * *

Damnation. It was indeed late in the afternoon — Jeanne had grown careless in her enjoyment of the doctor's mild flirtations and now the solicitor might have left his chambers by the time she reached Lincoln's Inn.

Lamplighters were at work in the streets as they approached, but the presence of lighted candles in the windows of the Inn's chambers indicated that some, at least, still remained at work inside.

As luck would have it, Mr. Stansbury himself remained in his chambers with one lone clerk.

"Ah, Miss Newman. Please, do sit down. I am afraid I do not have much to offer in the way of refreshment, but Wilson could manage a cup of tea, I daresay. May I offer you such?"

Jeanne eyed the young clerk. It would be helpful to have him out of the way without making a pointed demand for privacy. Even though she loathed tea. "Yes, thank you. I would be grateful."

"Now, then," he began after she seated herself, "to what do I owe the pleasure of this unexpected visit?"

She leaned forward and glanced back to make sure the clerk had busied himself at some distance from them. "I have come to speak to you concerning my relationship with Lord Rutherford."

He nodded gravely. "I have been expecting this. Under the circumstances, I think no one could blame you for wishing to end the engagement."

"Oh, no, you misunderstand me, sir. It was my mother's most heartfelt wish that I marry the son of her dearest friend, Lady Rutherford. I intend to fulfill that wish at all costs."

Mr. Stansbury squinted at her through his glasses. "But the gentleman in question has demonstrated a severe...imbalance of personality. Surely your mother would not have consigned you to a life with him, had she but known of it."

"To the contrary, Mr. Stansbury. I believe she would have considered it my duty to marry him and take care of him with quiet discretion. Indeed, my aunt has encouraged me to do so." Admittedly that was before he had been committed to an asylum, but she saw no need to divulge that additional bit of information.

"But it could be some time—a great many years, in fact—before he is well enough to marry."

She cast her gaze down, willing herself to look sad. "Yes, I do realize that." Then she looked straight into the solicitor's eyes. "Which is why I have come to you with a rather unusual request."

"Oh?"

"But first, I should like to know who will decide when Ed-Lord Rutherford is fit to leave the asylum."

"The doctors make such a determination."

"And in the meantime, as his solicitor, do you make decisions on his behalf?"

"Only until such time as the Chancellor rules on the *writ de idiota inquirendo*. If he is declared *non compos mentis*, which declaration is unfortunately expected, then the person and property of Lord Rutherford will be committed to the care of his next friend, called his 'committee'."

Jeanne leaned in closer. "I should like to be made Lord Rutherford's committee."

The solicitor looked askance, his glasses sliding all the way down to the tip of his nose so that when he looked through them, his gaze pointed straight at Jeanne's chest. "That would be most irregular."

"I agree, but then, this is a most irregular circumstance, is it not?" Jeanne leaned forward to give the man a better view. "I assume that such duty would normally fall to his closest relation — is that not true?"

"Y-yes, of course." He pushed the glasses back up into their customary position. "Provided that relation was not his next heir, for that might lead to sinister practices. The law considers it in the heir's best interest that the party should die."

"Oh. That would be dreadful." She hoped her words sounded more convincing to the solicitor than they did to her. The thought of Edmund deceased was actually almost comforting in certain respects. She could well relish the prospect of never having to view the contempt in his eyes or hear the resignation in his voice. But no, he was the one sure path to the title, riches and respect that were her due. She could endure resignation. She could ignore contempt.

"Mr. Stansbury," she assumed her most heartbreakingly sad countenance, "Lord Rutherford's nearest relation is his mother, and she herself lies ill and unable to manage her own affairs, much less those of her son." Clutching her hands together to boost her chest closer to his new line of vision, she put all the pathos she could muster into her words. "And they have no other close relatives living."

"Y-yes, which is why the task has fallen to me." His gaze again dropped to her breasts.

Jeanne smiled. "And I am grateful that you have taken the duty with consciousness and fortitude. But surely you do not wish to be burdened with such a duty all your life? This task takes time away from your other business, does it not?"

The glasses again began to slip down his nose. "Well, the estate will compensate me for my time, of course…"

"But not sufficient to the amount of time and worry expended, I would imagine."

He said nothing for a moment, and she knew she had succeeded with that argument.

She leaned still closer. "So why do you not let me take this burden from you?"

"Miss Newman, forgive my bluntness..." His face colored. "What you say does hold much truth, of course, but you are not a member of the family. And you are a woman."

She sighed and closed her eyes, waiting until she was certain he watched before she focused a heartfelt gaze on him. "Under the law, you are right. I am not yet a member of the family. But in the hearts and minds of all concerned, I have been a member of the family since my infancy. Has not the family always planned for that eventuality?" She willed tears into her eyes and voice. "Lady Rutherford often pointed out certain special family belongings that would one day belong to our children." She covered her face with her hands to make the pretense of crying more believable. "There is a gilt clock in the upstairs passage that plays music on the quarter of each hour. That clock was to go to our first son."

She glanced up to see what effect this had on the solicitor. She had no idea whether Lady Rutherford ever included such provisions in her will or not, but it seemed a good gamble.

And it paid off. The solicitor removed his glasses and rubbed the bridge of his nose with the air of a man confounded and ready to concede defeat. "I shall have to give the matter some thought, perhaps consult with one of my fellows. I am not at all certain that the Chancellor will permit such an appointment."

"I see." She removed her handkerchief from her reticule. "I should tell you that I just spoke with Lady Rutherford's physician."

"Yes?"

"Her condition does not improve and there is no telling which day may be her last."

He looked sorely grieved.

"She cannot speak, of course, but she does sometimes seem to understand what is said. She might be gratified to know that Edmu-Lord Rutherford and I will be together. After all, the marriage has always been her fondest wish as well." She wiped the corners of her eyes with her handkerchief. "It may be her dying wish, as it was my own mother's."

This was plainly too much for the man to withstand. He sighed as he slowly nodded in agreement. "It will not be proper for you to live in the same house as Lord Rutherford while you remain unmarried, you understand. Even if you are made his committee."

"Unfortunately yes, I do understand. I shall reside at Hanover Square, for the time being, to better care for Lady Rutherford. Lord Rutherford will remain under the care of attendants at Shady View." She wiped away another tear. Though the tears were voluntary, it had taken surprisingly little effort to bring them forth. Whether they were tears of sadness or anger, though, she could not say. "I believe Shady View is the best place for him for now. Until he is ready to marry."

The solicitor nodded again, more readily this time. "I believe you are right, much as if grieves me to say it. In the best interests of the family, I will amend the petition to seek a change in committee."

"To me, Mr. Stansbury?"

"To you, Miss Newman."

Chapter Twenty-One

ஒ

When Lucia stepped through the imposing front door of Shady View, she felt a skip in her heartbeat several seconds before her eyes registered the cause of the sensation — the figure of Lord Rutherford standing at the window, looking out over the fields covered with new-fallen snow. Though it was dangerous for him to be out of his room while Geoffrey remained intent on "capturing" him, she had to admit she was pleased to see him.

"I hope they have a great, roaring fire in the drawing room." Eugenie unclasped her cloak and swung it free from her shoulders, releasing a spray of wet snow onto the marble floor. "I believe I'm wet through to my chemise."

"Eugenie!" Lucia giggled at the loud mention of undergarments. She shook the loose snowflakes from her hair, and the exercise dislodged the combs so that wet curls fell about her face in a disorganized heap. She giggled again.

Eugenie joined in her laughter. "I told you that you should let me do your hair this morning. You are all thumbs today. I do not know what has possessed you."

Lucia bent to retrieve the errant combs, casting a covert glance at the figure by the window. He had exchanged his crutch for a cane, which lent a distinguished air to his appearance.

The scowl evident on his face when he turned to look at them, however, though perhaps distinguished, was far less pleasant to behold than his carriage. She turned her gaze back to the floor, feeling around with her hands for the second comb.

"Lucia, dear," Eugenie chuckled, "I imagine they have a servant to wash the floor — you really needn't bother!"

Lucia made a face. "I have lost two combs, yet so far have been able to recover only one. Whatever could have become of the other one?"

"Never mind. We shall make do with just the one. I have some extra hairpins in my reticule, and combs are hopelessly out of fashion in any case. Let's just get to the drawing room fire, shall we?"

Lucia cast one final glance at Lord Rutherford, who had turned back toward the window again. "You are right, of course." She stood, but her gaze dropped to scan the floor again. "I do wish I had found it, though. The set of combs belonged to my mother." She reluctantly followed Eugenie toward the warmth of the drawing room, eyes searching the floor just in case.

"Oh, Mr. Groves, thank you for this lovely fire," Eugenie called as they entered the room. "Such a welcoming sight on a chilly day!"

"Indeed yes, Miss Bayles. I find I have a hard time leaving it to make my visits."

"Or to attend to business," Lord Rutherford muttered from the doorway as he stepped into room behind them.

"What is that? Oh, Lord Rutherford, I am afraid I can do no more than apologize. Our post runner is old and loath to stir on snowy days. Your request will go out tomorrow for certain. Or the next day."

"The snow grieves *me* not in the least," Lord Rutherford replied dryly. "I would be happy to run the post into the village for you."

Mr. Groves laughed with an understanding twinkle in his eye. "Of course you would, my lord, but we cannot allow our guests to put themselves to such trouble."

"No, indeed." Lord Rutherford smiled, but there was a bitter edge to his voice that underscored the tension between them.

"Mr. Groves," Lucia asked quickly, "when you have a moment, would you be so kind as to send someone to tell Geoffrey we've arrived?"

He bowed and immediately took the excuse to leave. "Certainly. I shall deliver the message myself."

Lucia stepped over to the nearest window, trying very hard not to look in Lord Rutherford's direction. Instead, she took note of the room's others occupants. Two men sat at a table opposite one another, engaged in a game of chess that seemed to involve a great deal of gesticulating, nonsense curses and knocking pieces onto the floor. In a corner, an older woman poured tea for herself and three chairs while conducting an animated discourse in different-pitched voices.

"Excuse me, Miss Wright?"

Well, she'd have to look at Lord Rutherford now, since he had moved to stand at her side. "Yes?"

He opened his hand, revealing a hair comb inlaid with mother-of-pearl. "I believe you may have dropped this in the entry?"

"Thank you, my lord." She reached to take it from him, hoping her hand would not shake as she did so. The notion that he had taken extra pains to find the comb on her behalf made her heart skip even faster than it had earlier.

He bowed. "I am grateful to be able to do *something* of use." He glanced toward the window where light snowflakes swirled merrily against the panes. "Curse those foul white flakes."

"Oh." The fluttery sensation in her chest faded as Lucia eased herself away from his unexpected angry outburst. "I find the snow rather lovely, my lord."

"That is not the word I would use for it. Let me just say that it is horridly inconvenient."

"I am sorry to hear that, my lord. It caused us little difficulty on our way from the village."

"Well," he rapped his cane against the floorboards, "you are not trapped in this glorified prison at the mercy of Groves' ancient messengers, are you?"

"No. I am not." Lucia felt sorry for the gentleman, but she saw no need for him to direct his wrath at her. "Perhaps you would prefer to converse with someone more sensible of your situation." She turned away to look for Eugenie.

He grabbed her elbow. "Forgive me, Miss Wright. You, of all people, do not deserve angry words from me."

"I had much the same thought myself."

"Please, do accept my apology." His voice softened, the bitterness replaced with contrition. As he released her arm, he stared into her eyes with an expression of such agony that she felt a wound in her own soul. "I am worried about the news from home — what you told me earlier about my mother. I need to get home to see her as soon as possible, and Mr. Groves will not let me take my leave."

What could she possibly say? She could change nothing. She could not give him hope. All that was in her power to do was sympathize. "Yes. I can understand why that would frustrate you. But perhaps your mother is not quite ready to see you? Ready to see anyone, I mean."

He sighed. "I understand your meaning and can assure you that you have no grounds for concern. I am in full possession of all my faculties and quite capable of returning home."

Would that were true! But Geoffrey would naturally say the same of himself, and she knew how much faith could be put into that assessment. Nevertheless, she agreed with him, hoping to ease some of the pain reflected in his deep blue eyes. "Of course, my lord."

A ghost of a smile flashed across his features. "I am grateful to find one person who believes me." The smile turned to a scowl. "Groves obviously does not, else he would not keep me here against my will."

"He is only following orders."

"Orders?" Lord Rutherford scoffed, filling the air with bitterness once more. "Orders from whom? The man runs this house like a puppeteer with a theater full of puppets."

Lucia's first instinct was to escape Lord Rutherford's angry tirade, to stay away from him until his mood lifted as she would do when Geoffrey became angry and irrational. Yet Lord Rutherford did not seem irrational, and something told her that he should not be humored like an irate schoolboy.

She decided to rebuff the outburst, rather than evade it. "Every person is accountable to someone for his actions," she countered. "Mr. Groves must answer to a board of trustees, and he is responsible to the families of patients. He cannot just let his charges leave at will."

"Well, if he were responsible to *my* family, he would let me go home to see my mother. Or at least deliver the promised message to my solicitor."

She began to concede that perhaps his bitterness might be justified after all. "He will not even let you send a message! That is dreadful."

"Well, it is not that he will not let me. He insists that his courier will not carry it through the snow."

"Oh." It was not so painful for her to look into his eyes now. The sorrow and bitterness was now tempered in some way. "And since your mother is ill, it grieves you to wait?"

"Yes."

"Perhaps," she began timidly, looking away, "I might deliver the letter to your solicitor for you?"

"Oh, no, I could not ask that of you." He leaned forward to catch her gaze. "Would you really?"

Lucia chuckled. "Yes. I cannot leave before tomorrow, mind you, but at least you will not have to wait for the post. Will I find your solicitor at Lincoln's Inn?"

"Err, no. That is, I do not know. But my butler will know, so if you simply deliver the message to him, all will be well." He smiled.

The flash of even white teeth and blue eyes filled with hope would have given her the fortitude to undertake the journey to London and back twelve times in one day, if necessary.

"But I must ask you," his smile faded into an earnest expression even more boyish than the grin, "why you would offer to undergo such hardship for a virtual stranger."

She shrugged, then immediately regretted the unladylike gesture and tried to act as though she had been tossing her hair back from her face. This move succeeded in sending the loose pieces of hair cascading back into her eyes.

"You need to visit a hairdresser?"

"No." Lucia looked down while she tried to tuck unruly strands back into place. "I suppose I feel a bit guilty about your condition, since my brother was the cause."

"Nonsense. The action was of my own choosing entirely."

"You would choose to stab yourself in the leg?"

"What? Oh, the, uh." He glanced down at his leg. "No, I meant, well, never mind what I meant. You've no need to assume any guilt or responsibility."

"Nevertheless," she smiled, "I would feel better knowing I have been of some help to your family."

"Then it is my duty to let you feel better. If you will excuse me, I will write the message straightaway." He bowed before hurrying over to a small desk along the far wall.

Lucia moved over to join Eugenie by the fire. "I hope you do not object, but I've offered to deliver a letter for someone tomorrow."

"For someone, eh?" Eugenie looked meaningfully at the figure of Lord Rutherford extracting sheets of paper from the desk.

Lucia felt intense heat in her cheeks. "I feel sorry for the poor man, after what Geoffrey did to him. I decided it was the least I could do."

"Do we take this letter to the village, then?"

"No. To London."

"London!" Eugenie gaped at her for a moment. "But do you not remember? Since Father kept the carriage in London, we've only the pony trap we rented from the inn. You cannot travel all the way to London in that. What if it should snow again? Did you not mark how wet we became during the short trip from the village?"

"What's this? You went for a drive in the snow? That sounds enchanting." Geoffrey burst into the room in one of his extraordinarily exuberant moods.

"Enchanting was hardly the word for it, dear," Eugenie informed him. "It was simply wet."

Geoffrey stared down his nose at her. "I see you have suffered no ill effects."

"Well, we are a little better now, after sufficient time before the fire. But the fur trim on my cloak will be all stiff now. And look at your sister's hair. A disgraceful mess."

"Thank you for that assessment." Lucia grinned. "I thought you were going to help me repair it?"

"So I was."

"I shall go ask Sir Mortimer to join us," Geoffrey announced as he bounded toward the door.

"Um, yes. That would be splendid." Lucia watched his exit with no small amount of relief. At every moment, she expected him to notice Lord Rutherford at the desk. Now, however, she and Eugenie were free to make their way to the retiring room on the ground floor where ladies might have undertaken similar repairs to coiffure and dress back during the days when Shady View entertained guests for a less permanent duration.

Soon after they returned to the drawing room, which was really so large that Lucia decided it must have been a ballroom at one time, Geoffrey entered wearing an old greatcoat that appeared to have been made for a man with substantially less height and length to his arms.

"Are we having a fancy dress party, now? Eugenie wrinkled her nose. "Wherever did you get that coat?"

"And why do you wear it indoors?" Lucia added. She noted with discomfiture that Lord Rutherford still remained in the room, though with his back toward them his presence was not obvious.

Geoffrey pointed out the window. "Look at that snow! It is splendid weather for a drive. I heard Eugenie say you came in a trap—just the thing to enjoy the open air."

Lucia rested her hand on his arm lightly. "I really do not think we should go for a drive at the moment."

"Who says you have to go, then?" Geoffrey waved toward the door. "Eugenie will come with me, will you not?"

"Heavens, no. I have no wish to go back out until it's time to leave."

"Then let me drive you back to the inn."

"Geoffrey, we cannot do that." Lucia tried to keep the tone of her objection light, fearing possible rebellion if she came across as overbearing. "For one thing, the trap was hired under the Bayles name and—"

"Are you saying I am not a good enough driver to be trusted—"

"No, no, just simply that the vehicle should remain with Miss Bayles."

"Then I shall stay at the inn tonight." Geoffrey crossed his arms against his chest. "I begin to tire of this place in any event. Perhaps it is time for us to return to London."

"Well," Lucia glanced nervously at Eugenie, "not today, surely. We've not made any preparations, and the weather is so—"

"The weather is splendid for a journey. It will be quite bracing."

"Do you not have further inspection work to undertake here, Geoffrey?" Eugenie put in hopefully.

He pursed his lips and shook his head. "I believe they can carry on here without me. I've done the difficult bit, you know. All that is left are a few details."

"Ah, so you've found Redcloak, then?" Eugenie asked.

Lucia shook her head in alarm, forcing herself not to look in Lord Rutherford's direction.

"He has escaped to the continent." Geoffrey sighed. "I am certain of it. So, you see, I can do nothing more here. Perhaps from London I might put together an expedition for France."

"Eugenie, do you think you could ask Mr. Groves to join us?" Lucia beckoned her friend to lean in closer. "I have a question for him." In a lower voice, she added, "I do not like the way this conversation turns. Let us see if Mr. Groves can find the means to make Geoffrey want to stay."

"He does seem to have a way with them, doesn't he?" she whispered back. "I shall fetch him quick as a hare." She smiled at Geoffrey and exited with all due haste.

"I really do not understand why you seem so intent on discouraging me from taking a drive in the snow. Back at home, you always encouraged me to take a drive with Nicholas in the afternoon."

"That's just it. Nicholas is not yet here with us, and it might be dangerous for you to drive alone. Perhaps when Nicholas arrives..."

Geoffrey frowned. "In any case, I am not some weak, fainting young lady who must be nursed and accompanied at all times. I am a grown man, Lucia, and I do wish you would treat me as such."

Lucia reached out to squeeze his hand. "I am sorry. I suppose I shall always think of you as my little brother." She smiled.

"Yes, well, you can stop that now, as I am a good deal stronger and heavier than you," he announced matter-of-factly. "And I am going for a drive *now*."

Lucia moved in front of him to block his path toward the door. "No, please don't."

"You cannot stop me, Lu." He pushed her aside.

"Why don't you wait for Mr. Groves? He-he might want to join you."

Geoffrey stopped to consider that for a moment, then shook his head. "No, I am done with his company for the moment. I really wish to be by myself for a time." In a few paces, he had made his way to the drawing room door.

"You could return to your chamber upstairs." Lucia hurried after him. "No one will interrupt your privacy there if you so choose."

"I am sick to death of that chamber and never wish to see it again." Geoffrey marched into the hall on a path straight for the front door. "I am leaving it and all of this place behind now. You may have my things sent along whenever it is convenient."

Lucia quickened her pace to a run, finally catching up with Geoffrey at the door. "You cannot simply leave like this."

"Yes, I can. I am a gentleman. A gentleman may do what he pleases, within reason. And when one has come to visit in the country, it is certainly within reason to leave when the visit is over." He opened the front door.

"Your visit tain't over, sir." A dark, heavyset man appeared from out of nowhere. He closed the door and favored them both with an unpleasant grin.

"What? How dare you, you unmannered rogue." Geoffrey wrenched the door open again. "It is not for you to tell *me* when my visit is over."

Still grinning, the man shut the door, more firmly this time, nearly slamming Geoffrey's fingers in the process. "Mr. Groves don't like his guests to leave early."

"How rude! My sister will make my farewells for me. I am leaving *now*." Geoffrey took a deep breath and heaved the door open with all his might, in the same motion hurling himself out into the snowy afternoon.

He was yanked back inside just as quickly as he had left.

"Perhaps the gennelman misunderstood me." The heavyset man grasped Geoffrey by the collar and pulled his face down toward his own. "Mr. Groves likes having you here. He's not ready for you to leave." He pushed Geoffrey back into the center of the hall.

"You won't let me leave? You won't let me leave!" Geoffrey waved his arms with the frantic energy of a caged animal. "I insist. I will leave."

The heavyset man planted himself firmly in front of the door, arms crossed in a pose of mute defiance.

"Geoffrey, please," Lucia begged, "let us go find Mr. Groves. I'm sure he can—"

"I will leave, I tell you!" Geoffrey looked at Lucia only for a moment. "I will." He turned and bolted back into the drawing room.

As Lucia followed, she heard heavy footsteps behind her, indicating that the man who had previously blocked the door now trailed behind them at a slow, steady pace.

In the drawing room, Geoffrey headed for the windows at the far end of the room. He fumbled with the latch, his breath coming in frantic gasps. "Help me, please, someone. I am being held here against my will." He tried the latch again, to no avail. "You, sir." He turned toward the writing desk. "I beg you..." The words died away as he recognized the figure of the man seated there. "You! It is you who have kept me prisoner all this time." He began to advance toward him.

Lord Rutherford looked up from his work in surprise, then pulled himself up to a standing position.

Lucia screamed, "Geoffrey, no! You mustn't!" Her feet moved so slowly she could never reach him in time. Lord Rutherford would come to grievous harm again and once more she would fail to help him.

Geoffrey looked around as if for a weapon, then simply flung himself headlong at Lord Rutherford, sending the chair over with a resounding crash. He reached to grasp him by the neck. "You planned this! All of this! Made me look the fool!"

Lord Rutherford brought his arms up to break Geoffrey's grip. He rolled away from him and stood, grimacing horribly when he placed weight on his left leg.

Geoffrey kicked him in the leg, causing it to collapse. As Lord Rutherford went down, he grabbed Geoffrey's legs and pulled him down as well, knocking the wind out of him. Within seconds, the heavyset man from the entry had reached them, secured Geoffrey's arms behind him and hauled him to his feet.

"It's time for a little rest upstairs now, sir."

"I'm not going back!" Geoffrey screamed. "I'll not stay in this house of deceit!"

Another man equally rough in appearance joined Geoffrey's captor. Together the two of them propelled Geoffrey quickly from the room despite his screams of protest.

"Mr. Wright, please do calm yourself." They heard Mr. Groves' implacable voice in the hallway.

"Redcloak is here!" Geoffrey's voice grew hoarse in his frenzy. "You…he is keeping me here."

"No, no, sir, I shall explain everything to you upstairs," Mr. Groves soothed. "That man is one of ours. A disguise, you see? We had to test you, and I am pleased to see you passed the test in fine form…"

The protests died out and murmurs of ordinary conversation floated away down the hallway.

"How on earth does he do that?" Lord Rutherford shook his head in disbelief.

"Oh, I am so sorry!" Lucia knelt down to assist him. "Geoffrey thinks you are—"

"No," he corrected, "I understand your brother, at least as much as I suspect anyone does. But that Mr. Groves, he does have a remarkable way about him, does he not?" He winced only slightly as he regained his footing.

Eugenie brought over his cane.

"Thank you, ladies." He turned to Lucia. "And thank you especially for your kind offer to deliver the message to my butler tomorrow."

"When the snow stops," Eugenie interjected.

"Oh, of course. Please do not undertake the journey until it is safe to do so."

Eugenie looked out the window, watching snow fall in large, lazy flakes that fluttered from the sky like feathers shaken from an enormous gray pillow in the heavens. "I think we had best return to the inn before the snow collects any deeper."

"But..." Lucia looked down the hall where Geoffrey disappeared. She tried to think clearly, to quell the trembling, nervous sensation in her belly. "I need to make sure that Geoffrey is—"

Eugenie grabbed her arm to steer her to the front door. "Geoffrey will be fine. You need to ensure that you remain whole."

"*Au revoir*, ladies." Lord Rutherford bowed, losing his balance just a little. He grinned. "Or perhaps you'd better stay to help me up if I take another fall."

"I do not think you will." Lucia offered what she hoped was a reassuring smile. Her face felt a little crooked, as though she might laugh and cry at the same time.

Eugenie looked from Lord Rutherford to Lucia and back as she practically pushed Lucia out the door. "I think you very well might. Both of you. And you had better not."

Chapter Twenty-Two

ᔥ

He must have overslept. An insistent pounding on the door woke him to a dark room where he lay undressed, unshaven and in no condition to accept visitors. Especially those of the fairer persuasion.

Anticipating that Miss Wright would be by to collect the message this morning, he had left instructions to be awakened early and to have warm water for shaving. Someone had neglected those instructions, so now he would have to ask Miss Wright to wait downstairs.

He pushed himself up. "I'm sorry. I am just now awake. Can you wait in the drawing room for a few minutes? They can probably get you some tea or something."

The door opened.

Edmund reached for his trousers. "No, wait, I am not—"

"I despise tea. After all these years, I thought you might have the decency to remember that much about me."

"Jeanne?" He sank back into the pillows, thankful that the darkness in the room would hide his expression of disgust as she made her way into the room.

"Whom else were you expecting, Edmund?" She stepped close to the bed to lean over him. "I believe you *were* expecting someone else. You are plainly not happy to see me."

"No, not at all. It's just that, uh…" Edmund stopped himself before he could make any polite excuse. He still wanted to drive her away after all, even though he now had to appear sane. He made no further effort to suppress a frown. "I am not dressed."

"Then stay in the bed." There was a hard edge to Jeanne's voice that he had not remembered before.

"If you will wait downstairs for a —"

"I will not wait downstairs with an insipid cup of tea while you shave and select the proper waistcoat for the morning. You have wasted enough of my time, Edmund. I will not allow the practice to continue." She marched over to the window to yank open the shutters.

Edmund stared at her, numbed with disbelief. It was as if an incompetent, harmless old hunting dog had suddenly gone mad.

She stalked back to the bed and stood over him, her hands planted on her hips. "You needn't speak, either, because I have enough to say and any words from you will be an unnecessary interruption." She began to count off on her fingers. "First, I know why you are here, and I know that you are sane, or at least as sane as you ever were. Second, I know that you planned your little retreat here and that you planned to stay only three months before resuming your comfortable life in town."

Edmund felt as though she had sucked the air from his lungs, leaving him dazed and helpless. "What? How —"

"You spelled it all out on paper, so your intent is plain as day. Of course," she leaned in toward him with a smirk, "you did not give the reason for this planned escapade, but you have no face for cards, Edmund. No face for deception." By this time, she nearly spat the words into his face. "You created this whole elaborate ruse simply to end our engagement."

"Well," he shifted away from her, "it was not that elaborate. I only wanted to discourage —"

"I told you not to interrupt." She stood erect again, walked two paces from the bed, then whirled to face him. "Now, not only did you plan to end our engagement, but you would make me be the one to break the contract. I would be the one to appear the callous, unfeeling —"

"No! I had no intention of making you look —"

"Stop interrupting!" She picked up a papier-mâché elephant figurine that Mr. Groves had procured from someplace and threw it toward the foot of the bed. With no weight, it flew only a few feet toward its target before falling harmlessly to the floor. Her lip curled into an ugly sneer. "This is unpleasant enough without having to listen to your excuses."

"Very well." Edmund crossed his arms in front of his chest.

"Now, I have come—"

"I will not interrupt."

"To tell you that—"

"I promise."

"Stop that!" Jeanne looked around, presumably for another figurine to throw.

Edmund decided he had better hear her out before she found something heavy enough to cause actual damage.

"Now," she continued sternly, "you will not...absolutely will not...will not..." She faltered as if unnerved that he was no longer interrupting her.

"Not what?" Edmund stifled a smile. This ill-tempered shrew was the woman he expected to find in her all along. And because she was so very angry with him now, there was no way she would want to—

"You will not treat me in this manner. You will marry me and give me the status that I have been promised all my life."

It took a moment for Edmund to remember how to speak. "You still want to marry me?"

"Yes." Jeanne's haughty demeanor evaporated. She sat on the corner of the bed. "It was a great deal easier when I believed you wanted to marry me too. Not that you've ever been very enthusiastic about the idea, I must admit. But at least I thought you'd do your duty. Now I see to what lengths you will go to avoid it."

Edmund sighed. "I wanted to save you from an unhappy marriage as much as myself."

"That is a lie," she scoffed. "You do not care about me and you never have. I suppose you've had another in mind all this time, just waiting until you could find a means to rid yourself of me."

"No, that is most definitely not true. I simply never believed that we could be happy together." Though he had to admit that now he was starting to think there was another.

"I have no reason to believe you anymore." She leaned back, examining him with narrowed, suspicious eyes. "Even if you promise you will marry me, I have no reason to believe you. But I will tell you this—if you do not marry me, you will never leave this house of fools."

The supreme confidence with which she uttered the words was unnerving, even though he knew they could not be true.

"That's utter nonsense." He sat up straighter. "I will be leaving, and quite soon, as a matter of fact. I can prove my sanity. I had proof sent to my solicitor so that he can inform the physicians—"

Jeanne smiled. "I have your precious proof, dear boy. I now possess the note you intended to go to the solicitor."

A weight settled on his chest. "Do you mean that he never..."

"Yes." Her smile widened. "Franklin was so concerned about your health that he never approached a solicitor. Later he was uncertain what to do, whether you were in your right mind when you wrote the note, whether it might direct a solicitor to take rash action. So he showed it to me."

Edmund nodded. It made sense. Horrible, rational sense. "So that is how you knew of my intent."

"Of course." She laughed. "And I am the *only* one who knows."

"Jeanne, don't be melodramatic. Mr. Groves can still contact Stansbury, who I understand will be made my committee in Chancery—"

"He *was* to be your committee. But that role has been assigned to someone else." Her grin left little doubt as to whom that power was now entrusted.

"Oh dear God." The weight on his chest grew heavier, his breath more shallow.

"Blame Him, if you like." Jeanne stood and smoothed her skirt. "But the fault lies only with you."

"You cannot keep me here." He leaned toward her. "I will tell the truth. I intended to anyway, so that I could get home—"

"Tell the truth. Ha! No one will believe it. I will say that it is just the madness inside you, making you say crazy, unbelievable things."

She was right. He cursed himself for his lack of planning. "No one knew," he admitted softly.

"What's that?" She came closer to more fully enjoy her opportunity to gloat. "You never told anyone you did not want to marry me, did you? You did not have the nerve to disappoint your mother, did you?"

"No." He sighed. "I never did tell. But that was not for my mother's benefit but for yours. I did not want to hurt—"

"I don't believe you," she turned away from him and walked over to the door. Then she turned and methodically began to adjust the fit of her gloves, one finger at a time. "I do not believe a word you say to me anymore. So it is of no use trying to explain. I will not listen. Now," she smoothed the front of her gown, "I will come back with a minister. You can marry me then. Or you can stay here and rot." She opened the door and walked out calmly, as if she had just bid him a good morning rather than threatened him with an ultimatum of truly nasty proportions.

He had to force himself to breathe for the next minute or so. It was certainly a good thing no one had asked him to lead an army against Napoleon, for if he executed all plans as poorly as this one, they'd have raised the tricolor over Westminster within a week of his appointment.

Had he so mismanaged all things in his life? He'd actually had very few opportunities to manage anything. This did not bode well. It was not an auspicious beginning.

He could not know when Jeanne would return, but if she went back to London, presumably she would not return to Shady View before the next morning.

What could he do to stop her?

And why did he have the nagging sensation that there was someone else he needed to stop?

He rolled out of bed, landed on his bad leg and crumpled to the floor in an undignified heap. Where the devil were his trousers? Now he remembered — he had to stop Miss Wright from undertaking the journey to London.

But she would have to come up to him to get the note before she could leave. So he had no reason to hurry.

He scooted across the floor to where his stockings and shoes lay in the corner.

There was no need for him to hurry to see Miss Wright. But he wanted to hurry. He wanted to explain the whole sorry mess and he wanted to engage her help in extricating himself from the attachment to Jeanne. And perhaps he wanted to attach himself to her instead.

* * * * *

Lucia was surprised to see Lord Rutherford waiting when she stepped through the front door.

He scowled with impatience. "Thank God you're finally here."

"Good day to you, too, Lord Rutherford," Eugenie said as she stepped in behind Lucia.

What right had he to be annoyed with them? They were, after all, here to do him a favor. "I am sorry if our arrival is not early enough for you," Lucia added frostily.

He waved away their words. "Forgive my haste. Miss Wright, I need to speak with you alone. Would you come with me to the side parlor?"

"No she will not," Eugenie objected. "That would not be at all appropriate." She glared at him. "And I don't think I can trust you to keep your communication purely verbal."

"Yes." Edmund fixed a withering gaze on her. "You can." He turned to Lucia. "Now hurry. This is important."

Lucia planted her feet firmly in place. Though she had to admit she had come to value Lord Rutherford's attentions a great deal, she still would not allow him to keep her from her duty. "I will need to see Geoffrey before I start off to London to conduct your business."

"There isn't time for that." Edmund took her elbow to steer her down the hall.

"What?" She pulled away. "How dare you—"

"You will not be traveling to London, in any case." He took her elbow again.

"But I still…" She looked toward the stairs.

"Geoffrey is fine." He turned her back toward the passage.

"What does that—"

"He is sleeping." They took a step down the hall.

"How do—"

"I checked." They took another step.

"Why would—"

"Come on!" He pulled her several more steps away.

"I cannot just leave Eugenie in the entry!"

"She is a grown woman. She can make her way to the drawing room by herself."

"Why can she not listen to whatever it is you must tell me?"

He stopped. "This is difficult enough to admit to one person, and I have chosen you. Now, if you do not want to help me, I shall find someone else."

He wanted her help. He wanted to confide in her. He perhaps had no one else to turn to. Or perhaps he had many in whom he could confide, and of those he had chosen her. How could she refuse?

"I do want to help you," she said softly. "But Eugenie might be of help, as well."

"Possibly," Lord Rutherford admitted. "But I am not prepared to confess my sins before an ensemble."

Lucia continued her progress down the passage with reluctant steps. What on earth was he going to confess? Why was he so insistent that they speak alone? Would he try to take advantage of her, as Eugenie feared? She did not think she would put up much resistance, which was troubling. Lives were ruined by small meetings such as this.

But once inside the narrow side parlor, her fears were instantly put to rest. Lord Rutherford sank into a chair and urged her to take a seat on the sofa opposite. Away from him. Not the posture of a gentleman bent on seducing her. More like a brother, in fact. Instead of relief, however, she felt a small sense of loss. This man, like all others, saw her as a friend or a sister. Nothing more. He did not even look at her as he began to speak.

"The night I met you at the Adrington's, I had decided to pretend I had gone mad. I jumped about in the ballroom, doing whatever came to mind, then ran off to hide to see what would happen." He looked up at her for a moment. "I did not expect to find you hiding in the room with me, of course." Then he looked down again. "In any event, it was all quite deliberate, my behavior. I have been in full possession of my faculties, from then until now."

A lightness gradually filled her as he spoke. She had not merely imagined him to be sane—he truly was. Not at all like Geoffrey. She was not falling in love with a—

Falling in love? One serious look at Lord Rutherford's grave demeanor quelled her elation. If he had feelings for her as she did for him, he would not appear so grim.

She felt herself sink into the sofa as she nodded slowly. "That makes some sense. How you could appear so…reasonable at times, then turn completely delusional."

He looked up. "You believe me? You can believe this all to have been an act?"

"Yes." She peered closely into his eyes. "But why?" Her elation now gone, a growing sense of anger rose in its place and her words began to tumble out faster than her thoughts. "Why would you do such a thing deliberately? Do you know what kind of torture this inflicts on your family and friends?"

Lord Rutherford turned away from her gaze. "I am beginning to have some idea."

"It ruins the complexion of a family. It makes the soul ache with sadness to think of a life that must now go unfulfilled. And it becomes a constant work, a constant worry. 'What has he done now? What will he do next?' No one may rest easy. And everyone begins to…question the state of their own minds."

"I am sorry." Indeed, he did look truly sorry and more than a little surprised.

But now she felt no compassion for him. "I cannot think of any inducement in the world worthy of adopting such a pretense."

"Perhaps there is none."

"Then why did you do it?"

Edmund sighed. "To break an engagement."

"You cannot be serious." He was engaged? And he concocted this elaborate ruse merely as a trick to end it?

"Yes." He folded his hands together and considered them for a moment as if they could somehow provide words to explain his horrid behavior. "I have been engaged to marry Jeanne Newman since I was seven years old. For twenty years, the obligation hung like a black cloud over my head. This was the only means I could think of to end it."

If she had any hopes of a good explanation, they were gone now. She could scarcely conceal her disgust. "Why do you tell me all this?"

"Because Jeanne has discovered my plan. Somehow she has managed to convince Mr. Stansbury to have her named as my committee, able to make decisions on my behalf. And now she insists I must either marry her or remain locked in this house for the remainder of my days."

"And so? What does this matter have to do with me?"

"I want you to help me find a way to escape so I can get home."

She sniffed. "You must think me a fool." *And so I am. To think that I valued this man's confidence!*

"Heavens, no. I think you are quite clever." His sudden smile caught her off guard. "And I know you to be very loyal. That is why I sought your help."

"Help?" She gaped at him in disbelief. "You ask me to help you avoid an obligation of twenty years' standing? Certainly not."

"But…" His blue eyes pleaded with more eloquence than words could ever muster. "If you only knew her. I cannot marry a woman so grasping, so deceitful. And she is crazy."

"Perhaps she was merely putting on an act." Lucia loaded her words with sarcastic bite. She would not allow those eyes to sway her. Lord Rutherford was a coward, and nothing he could say and no amount of silent pleading could change that fact, though her heart ached at the sudden loss.

"No, no," he continued, "she was truly acting beyond all reason. She insists that we marry even if we shall both be unhappy in the union."

Lucia stood in preparation to quit the room. "I believe, Lord Rutherford, that once again it is you who act beyond all reason. You've tried to trick your betrothed into ending an engagement on which she has no doubt centered her whole life. You would disappoint family and friends who arranged the match, not through outright defiance, but through cowardly deceit. And now you ask me to help? The answer is no. Some of us believe that responsibilities are to be borne, not evaded."

She turned and fled before he could answer. She did not want to hear his answer. Somehow, perhaps simply through the power of his mesmerizing blue eyes, he might convince her that what he had done was right. And she knew in her heart it was not.

Chapter Twenty-Three

ഇ

"We are leaving, Eugenie," Lucia announced as she strode into the drawing room.

"Perhaps you may wish to reconsider that verdict, Lucia. Do you see who has come to visit?" Eugenie inclined her head toward the fire.

Lucia's gaze followed the gesture to the form of a tall, gaunt man bent over to warm his hands. "Sir, it is good to see you again." She hurried over to greet her stepfather.

"A pleasure too seldom indulged in, my dear." His hands shook as he took hers into his own. "I have been too long away from you all." He cast his gaze to the floor. "Much, much too long. Can you forgive me?"

She squeezed his trembling fingers. "There is nothing to forgive, sir."

"There is much to forgive, my dear." He looked at her with eyes watery from the cold, or perhaps the effort to hold back emotion. "I only hope you will listen to my feeble reasons before you harden your heart against me."

She smiled. "I could never harden my heart against you, Papa George."

He returned her smile, then began to cough.

"Are you ill, sir?"

"No, no just the effects of the long ride. Too much fresh air."

She nodded. "Indeed, much more than you prefer, I know. Perhaps you had better take some rest?"

"I will. But I wish to see my son first. Mr. Groves went to wake him."

Lucia glanced out the windows at the bright sky. "It is rather late for him to be sleeping."

"I imagine the doctor has prescribed a dose to calm his nerves — my physician often does for me, you know. These medicines cause excessive sleep."

"I see." Lucia smiled again. Then she could think of nothing else to say. She gazed into the fire, watching as hungry licks of flame circled the bark of a fresh log, slowly eating away at the edges until gradually the whole was consumed and joined the inferno.

"Lu, they said you were down here." Geoffrey rushed in at a frantic pace. "You've got to get me out of here, Lu. They said-"

Her stepfather turned away from the fire. "Good afternoon, Geoffrey, my boy."

"Papa George! This is — this is simply wonderful, sir." He clasped his stepfather's hand and pumped it up and down numerous times. "I had no idea. When they said I had another visitor, I thought they meant old Eugenie, there."

"Excuse me?" Eugenie called from the writing desk.

Lucia grinned.

"This is simply so wonderful!" Geoffrey continued to clasp his stepfather's hand, waving it about with enthusiasm as he spoke. "To have you here with us! Mr. Groves! Have a chair brought to the fire for my papa, will you? Sit yourself down, sir. Take your ease. We can have some refreshments brought in here, of course, but we shall have to step down the hall to smoke, I am afraid."

Lucia moved over to the desk where Eugenie sat writing a letter. "To Sophie?"

She nodded.

"You miss her, do you not?"

"I do, strange as it sounds. Perhaps it is only my jealousy—Sophie has told me of all the entertainments she and Helen have enjoyed in London while we are out here." She grinned. "Mother would never believe that I miss my sister's company."

Lucia smiled, but remained serious. "I would imagine you miss your mother too."

"Yes."

Lucia placed her hand on her friend's shoulder. "Thank you for staying with me, Eugenie. Now that my stepfather is here, we should be able to take Geoffrey home soon. In fact, now that he has arrived, I have someone to stay with at the inn. You may return home anytime you wish. Helen writes me to say that she has a host of new discoveries to share."

Eugenie set down her pen, pressed her lips together and nodded. "But you won't be coming back with me, will you?"

"No. I must go directly home to take—"

"I know." Eugenie finished her sentence for her. "You must take care of Geoffrey."

Lucia smiled at her understanding, unwilling though it was. "I know where my duty lies. There is a certain comfort in that."

Eugenie looked hard at her. "You are throwing your life away, Lucia."

"Hardly." Lucia propped up her smile and tried to force a joy into her voice that she did not feel. "I am putting my life to good use—the best. Caring for those who cannot care for themselves. No one understands Geoffrey and Helen as I do." She pushed aside the worry that even she could not always control Geoffrey so well as she used to when he was younger.

Eugenie sighed and looked down. "It sounds so noble the way you describe it, and I feel a perfect fiend for wanting to urge you to come back with me to enjoy a round of parties and dinners." She clapped her palms together in frustration. "I just cannot think but there must be another way."

Lucia placed her hands over Eugenie's in a gesture meant to be comforting. "This is the best way. The three of us have always relied upon each other. We always shall." Lucia quickly removed her hands from her friend's when she realized that they were shaking.

* * * * *

Edmund felt somewhat dishonest listening in on the conversations in the drawing room, but he found he could not help himself. And frankly, he had not the energy to get up and leave or even close the door.

Miss Wright had described him perfectly—a coward. A deceitful coward. That behavior, more than any feigned insanity, should have made Jeanne reluctant to marry him.

And yet she still chose to honor the obligation. He could do no less himself.

Though it would tie him for the rest of his life to a woman he despised, it was no more than he deserved. At least in his loveless union he could content himself with the resolve that he would not sink to the level of dishonor evinced by his neighbor—ridiculing his wife in public, openly flaunting his mistresses, frequently voicing doubt as to the paternity and worthiness of his own heir. He would even try to remain faithful to Jeanne, so long as she remained faithful to him.

The sense of resignation weighed him down so that he had no desire to even attempt to rise from his chair. But he heaved himself to his feet, nevertheless. When Jeanne returned, she would not find him unshaven, sitting like a lump in wrinkled, dirty clothes. He must make all the proper preparations of a groom approaching his wedding day.

* * * * *

Jeanne breathed a small sigh of relief when the carriage pulled up to Shady View. Long shadows stretching across the lawn indicated that the hour was well before midday, and so the wedding could take place this morning.

Only three days had had passed since her fateful interview with Edmund—she hoped that the interval had not given him sufficient time to find a way to avoid her ultimatum.

"Wake up, Vicar!" she called tersely. "We have arrived. Margaret, is my hat on straight?"

"Yes, miss."

"Very good. Now, I do not know which of the rooms we shall use for the ceremony, but I imagine it will be one of the rooms on the first floor, probably the drawing room. So when we get—"

"Excuse me, Miss Newman." The old vicar rubbed his eyes. "Did you say you planned to use one of the rooms in this house for the ceremony?"

"Yes. We purchased a license, so we may be married anywhere in the parish, may we not?"

He shook his head. "You must be married in a church. Any proper church or chapel, that is. Nothing dedicated for the papists or dissenters, of course."

"I want to be married in the house."

He scratched his head. "Well, that simply is not possible. You must be married in a church. I imagine there is a country church in the nearest village, and that'll do. Assuming we can arrange for someone to open it for us."

Jeanne felt a prickle of fear down her neck. If they left the house before the wedding, Edmund would try to escape. She could no more trust him than the pickpockets and confidence men roaming the streets of London. He would do anything to avoid this marriage—he had proven that plain enough.

"Why must it be in the church?" she demanded. "If we have a license—"

"An ordinary license is only valid in the church where one of the parties has lived for, I believe, at least four weeks. You do not live here, obviously. I assume Lord Rutherford has resided here for the required length of time?" He peered down his nose at her.

"Yes, yes, of course," she lied. It was obvious that the while the vicar might not be particular about verifying residency, he would insist on the ceremony being held in a church. "Very well, take the carriage and make arrangements in the village. But do hurry. My aunt earnestly wishes us to be married today."

"Why is your aunt not here with us?" He removed a silver snuff box from his coat.

"A small illness prevents her from traveling. She will host a celebration when we return to London." At least, Jeanne hoped she would. Her aunt would disapprove of a wedding ceremony performed while Lady Rutherford remained in such precarious health. But as Jeanne had reached the age of majority, her aunt's approval was not necessary.

"Ah, I am grieved to hear it." The minister took a pinch of snuff into each nostril, following with a series of deep snorts.

Jeanne rapped on the carriage window. "Open up now, please!"

She hurried through the entrance to the house, removing wraps and greeting Mr. Groves inattentively while pondering the problem of how to keep Edmund from escaping during the ride to the church. But she realized she needed to acquaint Mr. Groves with the situation.

"I come on a happy errand today, Mr. Groves. Lord Rutherford and I are to be married this morning."

"Married?" The man looked so taken aback that he actually took a step backward. "Well that's...do you think it...he will...he will need..." He pursed his lips. "This is most unusual, you understand. He will need approval from his committee, and I am not yet aware that the procedure has been formalized. As a matter of fact, he was trying to contact his solicitor concerning the matter only—"

"That has all been arranged." Jeanne smiled. "The committee has approved the wedding, and a license has been obtained." She was grateful that the document itself bore no evidence of the copious amounts of flattery, flirtation and funds needed to obtain it on such short notice.

Mr. Groves folded his hands and nodded. "Can I assume, then, that Lord Rutherford will be leaving us after the ceremony? Once the physicians have approved it, of course."

"Well," Jeanne twisted a loose strand of hair at the nape of her neck, "the committee has not yet actually approved the move. But such approval will be forthcoming, I have no doubt, when Ed-Lord Rutherford displays appropriate behavior."

"Err, yes." Mr. Groves looked down and straightened his waistcoat, shifting slightly from side to side as he did so. Then he looked up again. "This really is most unusual. Are you…? But then, it is not my position to—"

"No." Jeanne smiled sweetly. "It is not. Would you be so good as to tell Lord Rutherford of my arrival and the splendid news about our wedding? I shall wait for him in the drawing room."

Inside by herself, she sat down and took a deep breath. If Mr. Groves were to accompany them in the carriage to the church, or if he would permit two of those muscled men who always seemed to lurk in the corners to accompany them, then they could catch Edmund if he tried to jump out along the way. They would all remain with him from house to church, so he would have no opportunity to trick someone into letting him go free. This ceremony would probably be carried off.

But even afterward, Edmund could not be trusted, could he? He might yet escape and broadcast embarrassing stories of a forced marriage from the asylum. Or he might try to obtain an annulment or divorce.

Jeanne felt her hands shaking as she gripped the edge of her chair. This would never end. This nightmare of worry and deceit would never end. She would live every hour of every day wondering how Edmund was going to try to get away from her.

Her solitude was soon interrupted by the arrival of a tall, skinny young man accompanied by one of those heavy muscled men of the staff. The latter helped the former get settled at the writing desk before moving to a post outside the door.

Jeanne turned her attention to the fire several feet away, willing the warmth to soothe her frayed nerves and shaking fingers. She stood, walked closer to the fire, then turned so that she could see the young man at the desk.

He looked familiar.

She rubbed her hands, then spread them over the flames.

He was the young man who had attacked Edmund at the opera.

She looked back at him again, but it was difficult to tell from this distance, so she moved closer. And closer.

And suddenly, she thought of a means to make all her worries disappear.

Chapter Twenty-Four

ॐ

Lucia had been watching for Lord Rutherford from the moment their trap pulled to a stop in front of Shady View. For three days now, from the outside of the building, from the inside of every room, at the sound of every footfall, every door opening, she braced herself to turn away so she would not have to meet his gaze. And it was necessary to brace herself, because she wanted to see him despite the dishonor he had confessed.

He had sought her help. He did value her "cleverness and loyalty". And perhaps his reasons for feigning insanity...

She actually stamped her foot to stop this unfruitful line of thought before it could go any further. She wanted desperately to recapture the anger that had so consumed her when she first learned of the deception. All that seemed to remain now, however, was an aching sense of loss.

She paced with restless abandon back and forth down the passage from the entrance, hoping that her exercise did not disturb the gentleman in the side parlor playing chess with a stuffed dog. The dog appeared to have captured the majority of pieces. Lucia tripped on a throw rug and staggered into the nearest chair, grasping it clumsily to steady herself.

And then Lord Rutherford appeared in the passage, dressed in a dark formal suit with a greatcoat draped over his arm and a hat tucked under it. Two heavyset employees of the house accompanied him. If he had observed her uncouth athletic display, he gave no sign, greeting her with an implacable cheery smile. He bowed. "Good morning, Miss Wright." Then his forehead creased with concern. "Have you injured your hand?" He stepped closer.

She could no more turn away from him than she could fly to the ceiling by flapping her arms. She wanted to see him again. He was all she had thought of for three days and nights. If the woman to whom he was affianced was truly unprincipled, then he wasn't really wrong in seeking to avoid attachment to her. Though the means by which he sought to end the engagement had been poorly chosen, she could forgive him that, for he truly had not understood the pain he had caused. "G-good morning, Lord Rutherford."

"Your hand—may I see it?" He reached out to her with genuine concern.

"My hand?" She looked down at her fingers clasped together and realized that she had been rubbing a sore spot on the side of one hand where she hit the chair with greatest force. Immediately she dropped her hands to her sides. "It is nothing, my lord." She wanted to remain formal, to keep her distance, to erase the familiarity that had grown between them during the time of their acquaintance. She would do nothing that might encourage him to take her hand.

But each of these resolves required more effort than she would have believed possible only a few minutes before. She suddenly realized the significance of the coat and hat. "D-do you leave today?"

"For a brief excursion, yes." His smile radiated more warmth than any fire.

"Oh." She could feel her cheeks flush. But she told herself that he was probably only being so attentive so that she would agree to help with his wretched plan. "I-I was not aware that Mr. Groves permitted excursions."

"This is a special case, I believe. We, Miss Newman and myself, accompanied by various and sundry persons," he glanced at the heavyset men, "are taking a trip to the village church to be married."

A large chunk of stone settled in the bottom of Lucia's chest. She simply stared at him for a moment.

If he bore any continued objection to the wedding plan that had so distressed him earlier, he evinced none of it. His face and voice radiated cheerful good humor.

"And-and then you shall return home," she said finally. With *her*. Whoever she was. The unfortunate, damnably lucky lady.

"Oh, eventually I shall, if I am good. But not today, I believe."

"Oh." The weight in her chest lifted just enough to allow one more breath of air. "Then perhaps I will see you...sometime after."

"Yes." The aura of bright cheer faded from his face and voice, and it became obvious that his high spirits had been the result of a determined effort rather than a true sense of happiness. "I should like to see you again," he added softly.

"Goodbye, Lord Rutherford." Her voice sounded gravelly and choked, and she didn't want to even imagine how she must look.

"Goodbye, Miss Wright." He took her hand as if to shake farewell, then put it to his lips. "Thank you," he murmured.

Why would he thank her? "What do you —"

"There you are, Edmund. I've been searching all over this house." A tall, elegant young lady swept down the passage toward them, her face flushed and gray eyes glittering.

"As your humble and obedient servant, I wait here by the door, as I believe you ordered me to do."

"Yes, well, perhaps you wait a little *too* close to the door." She glanced at Lucia. "Saying goodbye to the servants, are you?"

"Jeanne, you may dispense with manners when speaking with me, but I will not permit such rude behavior to others. Apologize to Miss Wright."

Lucia began to back away. "No, please don't —"

"Oh, she is not one of the servants, then?"

"Jeanne." Edmund's voice took on a low, menacing tone that Lucia had never heard before.

"Do forgive me," Jeanne extended her hand, "Miss Wright. That shade of *brown* really is rather becoming on you, you know."

"Th-thank you," Lucia stammered, uncertain how to reply to an insult when framed as a nominal compliment.

"There, see?" Jeanne smiled. "All is forgiven. Now I do hope you will excuse—"

"If all is forgiven, the credit goes entirely to Miss Wright for her display of mannered restraint," Lord Rutherford interrupted. "I am not sure you can count on as much from *me*."

"Restraint, like any other virtue, can be cultivated, Edmund dear." Jeanne smiled with a hint of a glance at the heavyset men. "Now we really must keep our appointment with the vicar. You will excuse us, Miss Wright?"

"Of course," Lucia murmured with the sensation that she was fading to smaller and smaller proportions into the shadows. "I wish you both the greatest happiness." She turned and fled the room so that her wish for happiness would not be undermined with a show of tears.

* * * * *

Edmund stared past the golden gleam of Jeanne's hair out the window of the carriage as they started to move. He and Jeanne had been permitted to ride alone in the Rutherford carriage, but Mr. Groves had placed an attendant with the coachman and he rode in a separate carriage following closely behind, leaving Edward no chance of escape even if he intended to make one.

Jeanne leaned forward to catch his gaze. "Can you not at least pretend to be happy or at least *willing* to participate in your own wedding?"

Edmund sighed. "I tried, Jeanne. I really tried to be cheerful for your sake. But the scene in the entry at Shady View made it difficult to maintain the illusion."

"Was that woman your mistress? I saw you kiss her hand."

"No, she is a young lady of my acquaintance. A friend. And a quick kiss of her gloved hand is hardly a gesture worth working yourself into a jealous rage over."

"You have never done as much for me."

"What? I am sure I've kissed your hand scores of times in the years we've been together."

"But in all those years, you've never *looked* at me that way."

Was his regard for Miss Wright so obvious to everyone? "What do you mean? You imagine—"

"That look of adoration, of longing, of sadness—"

"I said, you imagine what you want. I was saying goodbye to a friend whom I shall very likely never see again. Was I a bit sad? Perhaps. Is it worth an argument? No." Edmund sat back as far as the padded seatback would allow.

"I still believe that woman was your mistress."

"Do not be ridiculous, Jeanne. Miss Wright is obviously a lady of good character. Not likely to be any man's mistress." Which was a damned shame, because if she were, he might have a chance at some happiness in his marriage. Of course, if she were, she would not be herself, and then she would not be half so appealing.

He sighed again and turned his gaze back to the window as with each clop of horses' hooves, the house faded further from view.

* * * * *

"Good morning, Geoffrey." Lucia reached down to the settee to give her brother an unaccustomed hug, needing the closeness, the reassurance of family warmth.

He did not return the embrace, however.

231

"You seem troubled. What is the matter?"

"Where is Papa George?" He looked around dispassionately. "I need to speak with him."

"He…does not like to stir about until afternoon." She sat down next to her brother. "I sent the trap back to the inn to fetch him, and he will be along very soon." At least, she hoped he would. His routine for each morning apparently allowed for no deviation, even while traveling. His valet said he would not stir abroad before one o'clock save on hunting days. She, on the other hand, was anxious to be out. So she had come alone, despite her stepfather's entreaties that she join him for a morning reading from Priestley's sermons and a half hour of what he called exercise, which usually consisted of standing on one leg for long intervals of time.

Geoffrey stood and paced several steps away from her. "Papa will join us soon, you said?"

"Well, yes, I believe so."

"Very well." Geoffrey sighed, his forehead creased with worry. Which was very unusual, now she thought of it. He often caused *her* a great deal of worry, but seldom if ever could she remember him displaying worry himself.

She stepped toward him. "Could you perhaps speak to me? About whatever it is that troubles you?"

"I suppose." But he did not say any more.

"What is it, then?"

"I do not like this place, Lu."

Lucia worked to suppress a grin—this was hardly a startling revelation on her brother's part.

"Layers of deceit. I do not know whom I can trust." He looked at her. "I do not even know if I can trust you, for you insist that I stay here."

"Actually, Geoffrey, I would like very much to take you home. I only had to wait for the proper time. And now that Papa George has arrived, that time may be here."

A relieved smile lit his features. "Wonderful. May we leave today?"

"Probably not." She would have to find at least one physician who could be convinced to sign release papers so that they would not have to forge them again. "But perhaps we may leave as early as tomorrow or the day after."

He shook his head. "That is too late. She told me to do it tomorrow, in the morning. And I want to be gone so that she will not know if I do not."

"Know what? Who is *she*?" Lucia felt her face settle into a frown. What was he onto now?

"I do not know whether to trust her. She said Mr. Groves lied to me." Geoffrey stared down, seeming to speak more to himself than to her.

"That he lied to you about what?"

"So if he lied, that would mean I have been right all this time. Does Mr. Groves lie?" Geoffrey looked up at last.

Lucia rather wished he hadn't. His look of utter, wretched confusion made her ache for him. "S-sometimes I believe Mr. Groves may stretch the truth a bit, but I am not sure I would go so far as to—"

"She said I was right." Geoffrey paced away from her again. "And that he lied. So if he lies, and she tells the truth," Geoffrey spun around to face her, "then I must kill him."

"What?" The room swam out of focus for a moment before Lucia steadied herself on the arm of the settee. Then she rushed to her brother and clasped his hands in her own. "You must not kill anybody, ever. Who told you to do this?" She searched her memory, trying to remember if her Redcloak stories ever involved a villainess of such evil propensities.

"She wore a purple cloak."

In vain she waited for him to elaborate. "Is that all?" She squeezed his hands as if she could wring the information through his skin. "Do you not know her name? Is she a resident of this house?" Lucia glanced around, but no one else was in the room. "When did she tell you this?"

Geoffrey took a deep breath. "She said my enemy would strike tomorrow, and that I must strike first."

"I don't understand." Lucia flung down his hands in frustration. "What enemy?" Then a wave of nausea coursed through her as she realized of whom he was speaking. "Dear God, you do not mean…"

"Redcloak, of course." Geoffrey sighed impatiently. "I still see him about the house. Mr. Groves told me 'twas not him at all but another in disguise, but *she* said —"

"What do you mean? Who is this 'she'?"

"I think," Geoffrey leaned in close to whisper. "I think that she is one of his sisters. That is how she knows so much about him."

"His sister?" The sisters in her stories were sweet, vapid creatures who could scarcely stand the thought of killing the rats in the pantry, let alone a human being.

"Yes. His sister comes to visit him, just as you come to visit me. And they left together not long ago." Geoffrey nodded toward the front of the house.

She grabbed his arm. "And it was *she* who told you to kill him?"

"Yes."

"Are you absolutely sure it was she? The lady who just left with Lord Rutherford?" The woman he was to marry? That was plainly ridiculous. Geoffrey's grasp of reality seemed to grow more tenuous by the day.

"Yes. It is my business to remember others' countenances. And I do wish you would stop squeezing my arm so." He twisted away from her. "You are worse than Helen."

Lucia took a deep breath, trying to keep calm. Her stepfather would likely be able to persuade Geoffrey to give up this dangerous notion, even if she could not. Or they could keep

Geoffrey locked in his room. She dared not tell Mr. Groves, for then he would be far less likely to allow Geoffrey to leave. But together, she and her stepfather could keep Lord Rutherford safe.

From Geoffrey.

If Lord Rutherford's intended bride really did propose his death, however, could she not find another means?

But that was simply too much to believe. She could not possibly have asked such a thing. Geoffrey must have misunderstood, if not imagined the entire episode outright.

"Geoffrey," Lucia licked her lips and tried to swallow through an impossibly dry mouth, "did this lady tell you...how to kill Lord — Redcloak?"

"Certainly not. I would never accept instruction on such from a lady."

"So-so were you planning to hit him with something, or — "

"She gave me this." Geoffrey pulled a long awl out of his boot. "From the stables. Not a gentleman's weapon of choice, naturally, but they do not allow much freedom in that regard here." He glanced around. "And if it catches a vital organ, it will do the job just as — "

Lucia gestured for him to stop before the waves of panic and nausea completely overwhelmed her. Inmates at Shady View were never allowed more than a spoon. Geoffrey could not have such an instrument unless someone from outside had brought it in secret.

Would Lord Rutherford's intended wife really do such a thing? It seemed preposterous to make such an accusation. Yet if Lucia did not, if she did not warn him, he could be in danger for the rest of his life. Which might be unnaturally brief.

Better to risk appearing the fool than to chance that Geoffrey might actually speak the truth, however crazy it sounded.

She pulled her brother toward the door. "Do you know how to saddle a horse?"

"Of course. Why do you ask?"

"We're going to ride to the village to see this lady and the man you believe to be Redcloak." With two of the three burly Shady Groves attendants accompanying Mr. Groves, she should be able to help Geoffrey manage a temporary escape.

His face split into a wide grin. "Wonderful."

"You had better give me that." She pointed to the awl.

He shrugged. "If you insist."

Chapter Twenty-Five

ဆာ

"As ye will answer at the dreadful day of judgment when the secrets of all hearts shall be disclosed, that if either of you know any impediment why ye may not be lawfully joined together in Matrimony, ye do now confess it. For be ye well assured, that so many as are coupled together otherwise than God's Word doth allow are not joined together by God — neither is their Matrimony lawful."

Heavy silence hung in the still air of the old stone church. The vicar took the opportunity to push his spectacles up the bridge of his nose.

Edmund knew plenty of reasons why they should not marry, but as he had vowed to go through with the pledge, he obviously could not voice any of those reasons now. He certainly wished someone else would, though.

But there was hardly anyone in attendance. Mr. Groves and two of his ubiquitous well-muscled assistants stood near the back of the church, along with Jeanne's maid. They remained silent.

The vicar cleared his throat as he turned to fix Edmund squarely in his gaze. "Wilt thou have this woman to thy wedded wife, to live together after God's ordinance in the holy estate of Matrimony? Wilt thou love her, comfort her, honor and keep her in sickness and in health, and, forsaking all others, keep thee only unto her, so long as ye both shall live?"

He had to answer. It was his duty to answer in the affirmative. But to promise to love, comfort and above all honor a woman for whom he held such little regard would require fortitude such as he had never been required to display in his whole life. Nevertheless, he had promised. "I will."

The priest turned to Jeanne, whose countenance bore a look of beatific reverence. "Wilt thou have this man to thy wedded husband, to live together after God's ordinance in the holy estate of Matrimony? Wilt thou obey him, and serve him, love, honor and keep him in sickness and in health, and, forsaking all others, keep thee only unto him, so long as ye—"

"Wait, please."

It was small voice in the back of the church, angelic and so quiet that Edmund thought at first he had only imagined it.

But Jeanne turned her head. She, too, had heard the interruption. And her saintly expression dissolved into an irritated scowl.

"Please, wait." Miss Wright rushed breathlessly down the aisle. "I-I—There's something I think you must know, Lord Rutherford. A reason why you should not marry this lady."

"Miss!" the vicar hissed at her. "This is a holy ceremony and you've missed your time to speak your objection. Hold your peace."

"No, let her speak." Edmund turned to her, wishing he could reach out to soothe her trembling hands. "What is it, Miss Wright?"

Despite his efforts to speak gently, he feared his words must have come out in an overwhelming rush, for she looked to the floor and remained silent, as if she had lost her nerve entirely. "Please, tell me," he encouraged.

"She…" Miss Wright looked up at Jeanne for a moment and then to him. "I must confess I do not remember the lady's name. She…asked my brother to kill you."

The last words came out so faint that they could scarcely be heard. And if hard to hear, they were even more difficult to believe.

"What?" Edmund shook his head. "I am not certain that I heard you corr—"

"You lying strumpet!" Jeanne turned on her with a gaze of cold fury. "How dare you interrupt my wedding? Will someone please remove this woman from the church?"

Edmund held up his hand. "No." He stared at Jeanne for a moment, nearly awed by the unreasoned hatred emanating from her eyes. She really might be capable of such a feat. It was easy enough to believe she could wish him dead.

Then he looked at Miss Wright, who now trembled less, as if she drew strength from Jeanne's malevolent stance. "I think perhaps I did hear you correctly." He turned to Jeanne. "I think *you* heard her correctly. But the vicar did not. Please repeat yourself, Miss Wright."

Unshed tears sparkled in her eyes as everyone in the church leaned closer to hear her words. "This lady asked my brother to kill you."

"Edmund!" Jeanne grabbed his shoulder and turned him toward her. "I cannot believe you would listen to such an accusation."

Edmund shook her off.

Jeanne fumed. "She *is* your mistress then. If you would listen to her and not me—"

He waved her to be quiet. "Enough, Jeanne. Now, Miss Wright, this is grave accusation you make and you must admit, your brother is not always…"

"I know. It is difficult to believe. But he had this." Miss Wright held up an object encased in fabric. She unrolled it to reveal a leatherworker's awl. Not a traditional weapon, certainly, but capable of some harm if wielded for deadly purposes.

Miss Wright cleared her throat. "He said she gave it to him. And he would have no means of getting such on his own."

Edmund nodded. Flames from the altar candles reflected dully along the metal shaft of the impaling tool. "No, indeed."

"You brought it to him," Jeanne hissed. "You want to discredit me so Edmund will marry you instead. Well, that will not happen."

"You are right as to the last," Miss Wright replied, more firmly this time. "I do not intend to trick Lord Rutherford into marrying me. But I also have no desire to see him marry someone who would have him killed."

"This is insane." Jeanne turned away from her. "She is as crazy as her brother. You cannot believe any of this."

The vicar shook his head as if he did not know who to believe.

Mr. Groves had come forward — he now reached out to take Miss Wright's hand. "Why don't you come back here and tell me all about it?"

Miss Wright shook her hand free. "I needed to tell Lord Rutherford. He is the one in danger."

"Well, you've taken the weapon you say she provided Geoffrey. So he is in no danger now." Mr. Groves offered a condescending smile. Miss Wright allowed herself to be led away.

"I still have this one, though," Geoffrey called from the back of the church. He produced a second awl from the lining of his coat. "You were right," he said to Jeanne. "They did find one of them. So it was quite cleaver of you to bring me an extra."

"You fool!" Jeanne exclaimed. "I told you to wait until…" She stopped as she realized her mistake, her hands shaking, her face a mask of intense rage.

Mr. Groves turned away from Miss Wright to face Jeanne, a frown of suspicion wrinkling his forehead.

The vicar nervously fingered the cross hanging from his neck as if he considered holding it up like a talisman to fend off Jeanne's wrath.

In the back of the room, one of the Shady View assistants stepped up to Geoffrey to remove the makeshift weapon from his hands.

Jeanne looked at each one of them in turn with a snarl etched deeply into her features. "You are all insane. This village is insane. This whole part of the world is insane. And if you choose to listen to them, Edmund, then you prove yourself insane." She flung down her bouquet and stormed out of the church.

The vicar hurried out in her wake and after a moment of uncertainty, Mr. Groves followed, motioning for his assistants to bring Geoffrey.

For some moments, all Edmund could do was stare after them. Perhaps Jeanne was right about this part of the world having gone mad, for her own behavior now ranked as thoroughly crazy. She had arranged to have him killed? Well, then she would have his title and money which, he gathered from her previous rant, had been the primary attraction of the match. And he had to admit he had given her little reason to anticipate much else from the marriage.

After remaining motionless, like him, for some moments, Miss Wright eventually sank to her knees, her eyes closed. Her body soon shook with sobs.

Edmund stepped over and, leaning heavily on his cane, kneeled at her side, tucking his arms around her. "Do not fear. All is well now."

"He c-could have killed you."

"No." He squeezed her arm. "It would have been Jeanne's doing, Jeanne's fault."

"It does not matter. The idea was his at first, remember? I could not stop him." Her voice fell to a mere whisper. "I could not stop him." The tears flowed with renewed vigor.

"But you did stop him, don't you see?"

She shook her head, but took some time to catch her breath before she could speak. "S-so close. He came so close this time. What will happen the next time? Or the next?"

"We shall find a way, do not worry. We will make sure Geoffrey is taken care of." He hugged her close and kissed the

241

top of her head, loving the way loose strands tickled his nose. Always with the faint smell of lavender. "Thank you," he murmured gratefully.

They would take care of Geoffrey. And he would take care of her. For so long, he could see that she must have devoted all her energies attending to the needs of her brother and sister. Now the time had come for someone to care for her.

And he wanted to do that more than anything in the world. He hugged her closer, and she at last relaxed against him, her sobs reduced to quiet hiccups.

"Miss Wright, this is hardly the proper time or place for me to say this, but in the days of our acquaintance, I believe there's been no appropriate time for anything. So I shall speak now. When you came into the church, I hoped it was as Jeanne said— that you wished to stop our wedding because you wanted to marry me yourself. Because that was what I wanted, though I was not brave enough to confess it. Will you forgive me that?"

She nodded against his chest. "But there is nothing to confess. You were bound by honor to marry her."

"Not any longer." Now that she has disgraced herself so thoroughly before witnesses, Jeanne would have to relinquish her position as his committee, and Edward would soon be free. He leaned closer and lowered his voice so that only Miss Wright would be able to hear his declaration. "I want to marry you." He leaned in to kiss her. His lips grazed hers for a brief second before she shrank away from him.

"Oh, no." She struggled to her feet. "You cannot marry me. I cannot…" She staggered backward for a few steps before turning to run from the church, following the same footsteps Jeanne had trod only a few minutes before.

* * * * *

Lucia slipped on the crusted, icy snow as she made her way out of the churchyard. It was ridiculous to run away like this, as if she were a child trying to leave home over an imagined slight.

But by racing, struggling for breath, keeping her focus on the treacherous ground, she kept her unwanted thoughts at bay.

For a while.

There was one thought she wished to remember.

She slowed her pace to a walk.

He wanted her. He cared for her. In his embrace, she felt a peace, a strength—a hope she had never experienced before. There was a chance for something more.

But, of course, there wasn't.

Because she could not be with him. She could not marry him or anyone else. She would have to find that hope in the life she had always planned, secure within the needs of her own family. Geoffrey and Helen needed her. They had no one else who could care for them. She understood them better than anyone because she was one of them. They needed to stay together. Together and unmarried. The family "peculiarity," the madness, would not extend to the next generation.

Lucia realized her steps had slowed to the point that she barely traveled forward at all. Indeed, she took rambling odd steps from one dry patch of ground to the next without any thought as to where the steps might lead.

"Miss Wright."

She felt a warmth descend over her as Lord Rutherford placed his coat over her shoulders.

"You cannot run away from what troubles you. That is one lesson I hope I have learned from all this." He reached out to steady her as she slipped on a small piece of ice.

"I know." She sighed. "But it was too awful. I simply could not stay another minute."

"Jeanne's conduct, you mean? Or was it the nearness of me?" He leaned in closer, his blue eyes sparkling.

She smiled, wishing she had the strength to look away. "Neither. Your presence made me want to stay, in fact. And that is why it became so awful."

He shook his head. "I am afraid you've lost me."

"I don't make any sense, do I?" She took a deep breath, searching for words to explain the paradox. "Lord Rutherford," she began.

"Edmund, please. And I will call you Lucia whether you let me or no."

"Very well." She folded her hands together and stared at them for a moment, as if they could impart the strength to face him. She bit her lip and looked up. "Edmund, I will confess that I am very fond of you."

"And that's what's awful, is it?"

"Yes." She had started to nod in agreement before fully understanding his words. "I mean, no." Her face twitched with the beginnings of a laugh. "Well, in a way yes." She smiled at him in wonder for a moment and he waited patiently for her to continue, eager to listen. Had any man so obviously cared to hear what she had to say before? It was almost as though their souls were attached by an unseen line. "I think I loved you the moment I first set eyes on you—the hunted fool—at the Adrington's soirée."

He nodded. "I begin to understand why you see this as something awful."

Her face twitched again, but this time it was not laughter that threatened to erupt. "The awful part," she turned and began to move away, not daring to continue until she had put some distance between them, "is that I think you return my affection."

Even walking unevenly without his cane, he followed her steps so quickly that he soon stood even closer than before. "I believe I should be insulted by that."

She put a finger to his lips to shush him. "It is awful because we cannot be together."

"Now this you will have to explain. Why can we not be together?" He took both of her hands in his own, peering closely into her eyes. "Are you married to someone else?"

"No." She tried to twist her hands free, but he held them fast. "I cannot be married to anyone."

"Why not?"

"I have a duty to stay with Geoffrey and Helen. To care for them always. I promised my mother on her deathbed—"

He dropped her hands with a loud sigh. "Somehow I knew this would involve a deathbed promise. I want *you* to promise *me* that you will never allow me to require such a promise of anyone. They bring nothing but trouble."

Lucia took a step back. "You jest, Edmund, when I speak of something very important."

"I was not in jest, Lucia." Again, he stepped forward to follow her. "When I am old and dying, I want you to ensure that I don't require our children to do something that will ruin their lives."

"You have not heard me, have you? I will not be with you when you are old. I will be with Geoffrey and Helen."

"Why can you not be with all of us?" He took her hands once more.

"What?" Before the question had escaped her lips, she already understood his meaning. But it would never work. Geoffrey and Helen were her responsibility.

"I can help you take care of Helen—and Geoffrey, once we've convinced him that I do not now, nor never have, owned a red cloak."

"That is very good of you." She swallowed over the lump rising in her throat. He really believed he could help her, and his willingness was truly touching. But he did not know the half of what he was proposing. "I could not ask you to share a life that—"

"I *want* you to ask me to share that life. Any life." He kissed her fingers. "As long as we share it together."

She looked away, fighting against the tingling, joyous sensation spreading from her hands out to the rest of her body. "You are making this very difficult."

He caressed her hands. "If you mean that I am making it difficult for you to say 'no', then I would hope so. I want you to marry me."

"But I cannot." She pulled free from his embrace and folded her arms across her chest.

"You can." He moved until he could catch her gaze again. "I've told you, Geoffrey and Helen will be our responsibility—together. You will keep your promise."

And again she turned away from him, this time keeping her eyes focused on the rocks cropping out from under the snow. She had never imagined divulging this misgiving to anyone before, but he left her no choice. "That is not the only reason."

He leaned down so he could look up into her face. "You said you are not married."

"I am not. And I can never marry because of…the family. The peculiarity in the family. Someday I will probably…and I might have children who would…" She shook her head. "I cannot allow that. I could not burden anyone with such a trial." The stones on the ground melted into a teary blur.

"Yes, you could. You could and you should." He tilted her chin up as he stood to his full height, then placed his hands on her shoulders. "I am asking you to."

She knew she should look away again, because if she continued to avoid his searching, earnest gaze, she could still keep him at bay and keep him from sacrificing his life. But this time, she could not turn away. "You do not know what you ask."

"Listen." He very nearly laughed. "You said you think you loved me at the Adringtons'—when you thought I was crazy. And you did not even know me. Will you not allow that I, after knowing and admiring all your fine qualities, might be able to love you even if your behavior were to turn a bit odd on occasion? Do you believe me less capable of love than you?"

"No." Her objection did sound mean, when he phrased it in those terms. But still… "You really have no idea what you might have to endure in a future with me."

"No, I must admit you are right, that none of us knows what the future holds." He pried her arm loose so he could wrap it in his own. Then he started the two them walking back toward the church, leaning on each other as they traversed the uneven ground. "I do know that for most of my life, I imagined a future without someone like you, without your sweetness, and loyalty and gr—"

She stumbled over a collection of rocks, but he caught her before she could fall. She smiled. "I believe you were going to endow me with the virtue of grace, were you not? It is fortunate I was able to correct you in time."

"Now it is you who jest when I am trying to be most serious."

"I am sorry." For a fleeting moment, she wondered whether she could keep the conversation light until they reached the church and thereby dissuade him from making his point.

But she did not want to.

"All that I endeavored to say is that I had never before dared to dream that I might enjoy a life with the company of such an agreeable woman. And the prospect makes me want to explode with happiness."

She nodded. "You anticipated an unpleasant marriage." She sighed. Did she really want to bring up this point? She had to. "But now that encumbrance is gone. I daresay you might have your choice of a great many agreeable young ladies."

"You forget, I've spent enough seasons in London to have met a fair sample of ladies who consider themselves agreeable. Only I have not found any to be truly so. Or I had not, until the Adrington's party."

"It is you who are acting so very agreeable. To voluntarily take on the burden of caring for a family of no small difficulty. I feel I should not accept such kindness."

"Ah, you have been listening." He stopped and kissed her hands. "Will you please trust me, then? It is a great deal to ask, I know, as I have not given anyone much reason to trust in me."

"There is no need for a reason." She leaned in and gave way completely to the sincere, sparkling blue eyes. "I do trust you."

Chapter Twenty-Six

ജ

Edmund suppressed a grimace as he peered into the drawing room at Shady View. Lucia's stepfather was indeed present among others in the room, as he had hoped, but he was engrossed in conversation with Geoffrey, which situation he had feared to find. If Geoffrey should make some untoward move, then Lucia might well have second thoughts about the prospects for their harmonious future together. But any reticence on his own part could be equally discouraging to her. So he decided to forge ahead and pray for the best.

He turned back to Lucia, who had just finished handing her cloak to one of the attendants. "Your stepfather and brother are in there. Let's join them, shall we?" He grinned. "I have a particular question I wish to put to your stepfather."

She bit her lip. "Are you certain?"

"More than I have ever been before." He placed a hand on her back as he bent to brush a quick kiss against the indented lip. "You should not abuse your lips so," he whispered.

She shivered lightly, then giggled once as she looked up at him.

He should have taken her arm for the short walk to the drawing room.

Instead, he leaned down to kiss her again, heedless of the ubiquitous attendant, the possibility of others entering the passage or the fact that her stepfather and brother might even see them if they happened to glance out the door.

None of it mattered for several long and wonderful moments.

"Ahem."

The surroundings abruptly returned. Mr. Groves stood just behind Lucia, but in order to speak with him, Edmund first had to disentangle his fingers from her hair and the lace on the back of her gown.

"Lord Rutherford, your committee has agreed to sign papers permitting your return to London as soon we have procured the necessary physicians' signatures, which we will do shortly."

"Thank you. Did my committee require any...encouragement?"

"Only a quick reminder, my lord." He stepped closer and lowered his voice. "I am prepared to serve as witness should you—"

"Thank you, but I don't believe that will be necessary. I believe she poses a negligible danger now, and I intend to arrange sufficient settlement to discourage any future discontent."

The man raised an eyebrow, but replied with a perfunctory, "Very good, my lord. Shall I have your belongings prepared for departure?"

"Yes, thank you. And see if you can arrange some sort of hired conveyance to take us to London. I assume Miss Newman returned to London with the vicar in the Rutherford carriage."

"Unfortunately, yes, my lord."

He smiled. "No matter. It is well to let her use it one last time."

Mr. Groves bowed and departed.

"Hmm." Edmund sighed. "I suppose I should mention that circumstance to your stepfather."

"Which?" Lucia asked.

"I have decided to settle a substantial portion on Jeanne. I objected to sharing my future with her, but I really have no objection to sharing the money." He shrugged. "Perhaps in that way I can fulfill some of the promise, at least. But I must tell you, and your father, that the settlement will reduce our living somewhat, at least for a time Since I cannot give her the title, I shall give her more money than she needs." With his money added to her own fortune, she would no doubt find a title for sale somewhere in the *ton*.

"I am exceedingly glad of it, that you will help that poor young lady."

"Poor young lady? Did you see the parting look she gave you? She'd have had you sliced and toasted for breakfast soon as not."

Lucia giggled. "You had better stop being so silly if you are going to speak to Papa George."

"I will not have to address him by that appellation, will I?"

She giggled again. "I expect he shall want you to call him 'sir'."

"Then I had better not disappoint him."

They swept into the room at a good pace, so that they had almost reached her stepfather and Geoffrey before the two, deeply engrossed in conversation, noticed their arrival.

"Lord Rutherford, it is good to see you again." Geoffrey reached out to shake Edmund's hand. "You seem to be getting around much better these days. Leg well healed, I daresay? May I present my stepfather, Mr. Lewis? Papa, this is Lord Rutherford. We just concluded work together on a criminal investigation. Captured the notorious Redcloak. Who'd have ever guessed the thief would turn out to be a woman, eh? The red cloak, though, should have been a dead giveaway. Because only women wear red cloaks! Is that not prodigiously funny? Here we thought 'he' was being so clever, disguised in a woman's cloak, when it was really a woman all along."

Edmund nodded. "Very amusing, yes."

Mr. Lewis cast a suspicious glance at his stepson before turning to address Edmund. "I am glad to hear that Geoffrey has been of…service in the investigation."

"Oh, yes. He did a splendid job." Edmund took a breath, hoping he was about to make the right move. "And I trust, Mr. Wright, that we can count on your help in future investigations in town?"

"Ah, no, I am sorry to say that I've decided to retire from investigations," Geoffrey replied. "In fact, I've decided to retire permanently to the country."

The collective sigh of relief was nearly audible as Lucia, her stepfather and Edmund glanced at one another.

"I will manage my stepfather's estate," Geoffrey announced with obvious pride. "I imagine that will take the better part of my time. And, of course, I shall need to see to his health and so forth, now that he is getting on in years."

"Of course."

Lucia looked confused. "But Papa George may not—"

"It is all arranged, Lucia," her stepfather assured her. "I asked for Geoffrey's help, and he graciously agreed to give it."

"But…" Lucia glanced at Geoffrey.

"Geoffrey," Mr. Lewis urged, "perhaps you had better go see to your things so that we can be on our way as soon as the physician signs your release."

"Excellent idea, sir. If you will excuse me, Lord Rutherford, Lu?" Geoffrey bowed and turned all in one motion, exiting the room with great, bounding steps.

"Sir, I have a request." Edmund spoke in haste, the words tumbling out of his mouth before he was even aware of them. "Would you do me the honor of granting your daughter's hand in marriage?"

"I would be most pleased to do so, but it is not mine to give. Lucia is of age and it is for her alone to make such a decision. Although I gather from her appearance here that she does not object."

"Indeed I do not, Papa." Lucia smiled, but only for a moment before a frown darkened her face. "I do, however, have some concerns about Geoffrey and Helen. I promised Mama that I would always take care of them, and I mean to keep my promise. If you'll forgive me for saying so, you have spent little time with them these last years and you may not realize what — "

"I do realize." Mr. Lewis sighed. "And that is why I have kept my distance. It became so difficult to watch, you see. I only hope some day you can forgive me. That they can forgive me."

"We've never seen a need to forgive, sir. Your marriage to Mama came late in our lives, and since we are not your children, we had no reason to expect your close involvement after her death."

Mr. Lewis shook his head. "You had every reason. A man who marries a woman with children should ensure their happiness after her passing."

"You always managed our affairs for us." Lucia offered a smile of reassurance. "We could have no complaints."

"You should have." Mr. Lewis rubbed his fingers together as if they had gone numb. "I fear it is only your goodness that has kept you from thinking ill of me."

Lucia took his hands in her own. "I am only pleased now that we are to see more of you."

Edmund shifted impatiently. As wonderful as it was to see Lucia settle differences with her stepfather, he could not help but feel that the scope of conversation now left him out entirely, when all he wanted was an answer to the marriage question so that he could get back to London to see to his mother's health. "Yes, well, now that you've settled everything, and if you have no objection to our marriage, sir, then — "

"We've not settled everything," Lucia objected. "It is my responsibility to keep watch over Geoffrey, and if he moves to my stepfather's estate — "

Mr. Lewis held up his hand. "Geoffrey is not your entire responsibility. It is I who should exercise care over him."

Edmund suppressed a groan — this could go on for some time.

"But, sir," Lucia protested, "we have never expected you to exercise care over children not your own. I am their own flesh and blood."

"They are as much mine, Lucia, as yours."

"Yes, I understand what you mean, but—"

"No, I don't think you do." Mr. Lewis spoke in a hushed voice so fused with meaning that Lucia let her objections fade into the air. "Geoffrey and Helen are my children, Lucia. I am their natural father. Not yours, but theirs."

"I-I do not understand." The blood drained from Lucia's face and Edmund reached out to steady her. "You and Mother did not marry until we were—until I was…"

"No," Mr. Lewis sighed, "we were not married. That is why I've said nothing of it all these years. But you needed to know, or at least, I felt I needed to tell you."

"But Father was still…"

"Still alive, yes. He had been very ill for over a year when we—"

"Mama! How could she?" Lucia was growing limp in Edmund's arms.

"You must not think any less of your mother, Lucia. It was my fault entirely. I had—had always cared for your mother so much, I…took advantage of an opportunity when I should not have. Then, when…I thought that she would surely marry me, when your father passed on."

Lucia now looked at the floor. "But she did not."

"No. She made me wait twelve years. It wasn't until she feared her own health was failing that she let me step in and care for her."

"I cannot believe all this. And yet …" She turned her gaze back up to her stepfather. "I see Geoffrey in you, or I guess it must be you I see in Geoffrey. I do not remember what Father looked like."

"I fear the facial resemblance is not the only trait we share. There is a certain…want of reason in members of my family. My brother Fitzwilliam particularly. When I saw signs of it in Geoffrey and Helen, I-I could not bear it. And so I moved out."

"Your family. You said this…malady runs to members of *your* family? So perhaps I am not…"

"You are as reasoned a creature as I ever beheld, Lucia. I felt quite confident leaving Geoffrey and Helen under your guidance. But that was too great a burden for you. I see that now. I do hope someday you will forgive me."

"I do not know what to say." Lucia grasped Edmund's arm. "I feel as if the carpet, or the whole floor has been pulled out from under me."

Edmund quickly led her to a chair, though despite her assertion, she seemed much stronger and steadier now than she had a few minutes earlier. "I do not think you need to say anything, except to answer my question. Will you accompany me to London to meet my mother? I hope you'll forgive my haste, but with her delicate health I am most anxious to see her as quickly as—"

"Have I mished the wedding?" a woman's voice croaked from the doorway.

"Possible. Good heavens! Mother!" Edmund raced to the door, where his mother stood with her weight supported by her maid, Susan, on one side and Franklin on the other. "This is…this is a miracle! Should you be out?" He glanced accusingly at the accompanying servants.

"No, sir, she should not," Franklin agreed with the unspoken accusation. "Dr. Hamilton would be horrified."

"He would be thrilled," Susan objected, "to see her up and taking an interest like this."

Edmund peered at his mother's pale face with concern. "Well, she should not be up any longer than necessary. Let's move her to that sofa, quickly!" He helped them carry his mother's frail body to a sofa near the fire, then kneeled beside her.

When they had her settled and removed her cloak and mittens, she stretched forth one hand to touch her son's cheek. "I am so pleashed," she murmured.

"Oh, Mother, it is I who am pleased. To see you awake, and speaking, when I had heard you lay as if dead."

"She did that, sir, long enough." Her maid nodded. "Until Miss Newman told her you were to be married at last, sir. Miss Newman left in all haste, but my lady tried to call after her. She moved her lips like to speak, but no sound came out. After a time, she could make some sounds, only I was the only one as could understand her. We've been together so long, you see." She smiled at her mistress. "She thought you were dead, and I think she didn't want to go on living herself. Then when Miss Newman said you would be married—"

"She thought I was dead?" Edmund could not believe his ears. "Did you not tell her I was here, that I could not come to see her because I was here?"

His angry reaction obviously intimidated Susan because she was some moments in responding, and even then her words came out cowed and apologetic. "Miss Newman said it might upset her, sir. To know you was...you know..."

He leaned in close to his mother's face. "So you thought I had died?"

She nodded, tears shining in the corners of her eyes.

He stretched his arms around her thin shoulders. "To think what I have put you through. Oh, Mother, I am so sorry." He choked on the last words and felt the sting of tears in his own eyes.

"You," his mother licked her lips, her voice growing stronger as she continued, "you should not be shorry. Sorry," she repeated with greater clarity. "All is well now that you are married."

How on earth could he admit that he was not? He could not begin to explain what had happened. But neither could he hide the truth from his mother any longer. "I did not marry Jeanne," he admitted softly.

"Tomorrow, then? The wedding is tomorrow? I shall get to see it?" Hope radiated from his mother's eyes.

"Look how well she is speaking now!" her maid interjected excitedly before Franklin silenced her with a stern look.

"No, the wedding is not tomorrow. There will be no wedding — at least, not between me and Jeanne."

The light faded from his mother's face. "No wedding? Again?"

"I do not want to marry Jeanne, Mother."

"Your hand was promised." A stern frown creased his mother's forehead. "We cannot break that promise."

"It was you who promised Jeanne's mother that I would marry her and care for her. And I will still care for her — she and her aunt will be given additional resources. But I cannot enter into a marriage with no love or respect."

"Jeanne loves you."

"She loves my title and position in society. And my money. And I suppose she might have loved me, if I had given her a chance. But I never did." *Probably because you never gave me a choice*, he added to himself.

Tears trailed down the creases of his mother's face. "I so wanted to see you married and happy."

"I will be married — and very happy." Edmund took out a handkerchief and blotted her tears.

"Well, I must say you don't look very happy," Geoffrey appraised dubiously as he suddenly approached. He stretched forth his hand. "Congratulations. I hear you are to marry Lucia."

"What?" his mother struggled to sit up. "You are to marry whom?"

Edmund cleared his throat. "Well, I suppose I had better make some introductions. Mother, may I present Miss Lucia Wright and Mr. Geoffrey Wright and their stepfather, Mr. Lewis."

Geoffrey and Mr. Lewis bowed while Lucia curtsied very prettily. "Pleased to make your acquaintance, Lady Rutherford."

Edmund's mother sat up further. "You are Lucia? The one he is to marry?"

Lucia bowed her head. "Yes, my lady."

She frowned. "This is a disappointment." She turned to Edmund. "She will never fit into the gown we picked out."

"Gown?" Edmund asked.

"Katherine and I designed the gown for the wedding years ago."

"Perhaps the gown can be altered?"

"Ah no." She peered at Lucia. "Come here, Miss Wright, let me see you. No, the color is all wrong. I suppose Jeanne will have to wear it on her own wedding day." She sighed. "If she ever has one."

"She will." Edmund patted her hand. "Jeanne is a beautiful girl and will have a handsome fortune. She will choose someone to please her."

"I always thought that someone would be you. Oh well. I suppose I will have to make the best of it." His mother pursed her lips. "I think a rose color, not too pale, would be lovely."

Edmund looked at her blankly. "For?"

"For Miss Wright's gown, of course. I came all this way to see a wedding, and I'll not be disappointed."

Edmund leaned in to whisper to her. "So you do not object to the change in bride, then?"

"I knew you did not like Jeanne," she whispered back. "I never liked her much, either. I just never could see any way to break the engagement promise. However did you manage it?"

"It's a long story, Mother. One best saved until you are a little stronger and all of us are fortified with a good meal and copious quantities of drink."

"Edmund!" His mother struggled to make her expression stern rather than amused.

"I am not sure you'll believe the tale, Mother. In fact, I am not sure I do myself." He took Lucia's hand and kissed it affectionately. "But there are certain ways to remind myself of my good fortune."

Lucia smiled up at him.

"Do you still feel as though the floor has been swept out from under you?" he asked her softly.

She nodded.

"I think I feel that sensation a bit myself."

"It has intensified, actually," she confessed, "so that now instead of feeling merely like I'm tumbling aimlessly about the room, I feel as if we've all been swept out there." She pointed out the window to the darkening sky. "Like we're tumbling among the stars." She shook her head. "It makes no sense at all."

"No sense whatsoever," he agreed. "But there are times when no sense is exactly what we need."

Enjoy an excerpt from:
CAPTAIN'S LADY

"Perhaps I'm waiting for a shining knight on a white horse to sweep me off my feet," Alice told the laundry tub one day shortly after noon as she scrubbed at the baby's dirty linen. "Sir Lancelot. No, Sir Galahad. He would be better. Sir Lancelot turned out to be sadly loose in his morals." She wiped her upper arm across her forehead, trying to push away the strands of hair that fell into her eyes as she scrubbed. She paused for a moment to look around the dingy scullery where she worked. Was this it? Her lot in life from now on? A skivvy? Dear lord, surely not.

"Sir Galahad! Come and rescue me."

Almost before she'd finished her absurd cry for help a bell pealed on the board in the servants' hall.

"Someone's at the front door, Miss Alice," Cora called.

Giggling at the absurdity of Sir Galahad ringing the doorbell like a morning caller, Alice dried her hands and hurried to button her cuffs before straightening her hair as best she could without a mirror. Barlow would answer the door, but no doubt she'd be called on to deal with the debt collector, or worse still, that maggot, Scripps.

But no, it wasn't Scripps. A stranger stood there. He'd just handed Barlow his cocked hat and was in the process of extricating himself from the folds of an ankle-length boat-cloak. Alice didn't need to see the blue and white of the naval uniform to guess who he was. Not Sir Galahad, this, but the new owner of The Priory and the master of all their destinies. Sir Edward Masterman had arrived.

Still unobserved, she paused to inspect the newcomer. What a man! Her heart skipped. Two gold epaulettes graced his shoulders. No longer a lieutenant then, but a captain and a post-captain at that. He was tall, taller than Sir Gregory had been by far and infinitely slimmer than his brother's self-indulgent corpulence. His dark hair was cropped in a businesslike style, while his countenance was deeply tanned, much as she expected. There was menace here, barely concealed. A man ready for action, was Sir Edward.

Perhaps aware of the scrutiny he turned to face her. The impact of brilliant blue eyes contrasted markedly with his complexion, but Alice was more struck by the depth of his expression. He looked tired beyond mere weariness and yes, even a little bewildered. In an instant the look was gone as an impassive mask hid any hint of his emotions.

The butler introduced them. "Master Edward, this is Miss Carstairs. She's governess to Miss Penelope." Barlow shuffled off with the captain's cloak and hat after he made the introduction, leaving them alone for a few moments. Alice sank into a curtsey and then held out her hand.

"Welcome back to your home, Sir Edward. I trust your journey wasn't too frightful. Traveling the highways in February is never a pleasant thing. Won't you please come into the book room?"

He took her hand very briefly and she became aware of a piercing scrutiny. She colored a little under his direct gaze. Of course he wasn't to know that she'd been engaged in scrubbing linen. She must present a very odd appearance to one used to naval discipline and order. Her nose and cheeks were red from the cold and from exertion and her hands were rough and chapped. Her old gray gown was clean, but that was all that could be said for it.

His own appearance was immaculate, even after his long journey. She'd been judged and found wanting. Confused and embarrassed, she turned away.

"Unfortunately we have no fire, but the sun strikes through the windows here. Barlow will have gone to fetch you some refreshment and as soon as you're comfortable I'll inform Lady Masterman of your arrival. I regret she is as yet too unwell to leave her bed…"

Her speech withered under his continued scrutiny. Stop babbling, she told herself harshly.

"Thank you, Miss Carstairs. I'm sure you've duties to attend to."

His voice sounded pleasant, the cultured tones of a gentleman, but the dismissal was as curt as it was final. Unbelievably mortified, Alice bit her lip. Without venturing on another word she curtsied briefly and almost ran from the room. Even in her anguished state she noticed that he made no move to open the door for her. She was merely another servant as far as he was concerned. Less than nothing.

In a dismal mood Alice set about her tasks, all the while struggling to banish the impact made by those harsh blue eyes. He knew nothing about her. Oh, horrors! What if he thought her red nose and cheeks was a result of drink, not the bitter cold? His old nurse had been a drunkard, according to Barlow.

After tending to Lavinia and informing her of her brother-in-law's arrival she prepared the master bedchamber as best she could and then returned to her laundry. The problem of what to serve for dinner occupied her thoughts as she completed the mundane duties. There was no help for it. They would have to sacrifice one of their three remaining chickens. She'd been hoping to save them for the eggs. They had potatoes still and cabbages. There were always turnips. Alice never wanted to see another turnip in her life. Perhaps she could prepare some soup followed by the roast bird. It would have to do. She couldn't work miracles, or turn a sow's ear into a silk purse, even though a sow's ear would have been a most welcome addition to the menu if it had magically appeared just then.

Penelope wasn't in the kitchen when she went to look for her. She'd left her to practice her handwriting, but the slate and copybook were abandoned on the table. Cora had no idea of when she'd left. Alice sighed. She was probably whining to her mother again. Hurriedly she set off to find her before she could cause trouble.

Penelope wasn't with her mother. Alice's stomach churned. Penelope had insinuated herself into the book room and was pouring out her tale of woe to her Uncle Edward. Alice was just in time to catch the end of her complaint.

"And she makes me sit for hours and hours in the kitchen. Last night, all I had for supper was bread."

Which was more than I had, Alice thought as she hurried to Penelope's side.

"Here you are. I've been searching for you, Penelope." She risked a glance at Sir Edward, but quailed at the look of burning anger in his eyes. What had the little madam been telling him?

"Penelope, would you please return to the schoolroom for a few moments while I speak to Miss Carstairs? She'll not be long in coming to you."

"I don't have to go back to the kitchen, Uncle Edward, do I?"

He looked down at her with grave understanding. "No, child, you do not ever have to return to the kitchen."

Penelope fled, her eyes alight with triumph as she smirked up at Alice before closing the door.

Why an electronic book?

We live in the Information Age—an exciting time in the history of human civilization, in which technology rules supreme and continues to progress in leaps and bounds every minute of every day. For a multitude of reasons, more and more avid literary fans are opting to purchase e-books instead of paper books. The question from those not yet initiated into the world of electronic reading is simply: *Why?*

1. **Price.** An electronic title at Ellora's Cave Publishing and Cerridwen Press runs anywhere from 40% to 75% less than the cover price of the exact same title in paperback format. Why? Basic mathematics and cost. It is less expensive to publish an e-book (no paper and printing, no warehousing and shipping) than it is to publish a paperback, so the savings are passed along to the consumer.

2. **Space.** Running out of room in your house for your books? That is one worry you will never have with electronic books. For a low one-time cost, you can purchase a handheld device specifically designed for e-reading. Many e-readers have large, convenient screens for viewing. Better yet, hundreds of titles can be stored within your new library—on a single microchip. There are a variety of e-readers from different manufacturers. You can also read e-books on your PC or laptop computer. (Please note that Ellora's

Cave does not endorse any specific brands. You can check our websites at www.ellorascave.com or www.cerridwenpress.com for information we make available to new consumers.)

3. *Mobility*. Because your new e-library consists of only a microchip within a small, easily transportable e-reader, your entire cache of books can be taken with you wherever you go.

4. ***Personal Viewing Preferences.*** Are the words you are currently reading too small? Too large? Too... ANNOYING? Paperback books cannot be modified according to personal preferences, but e-books can.

5. ***Instant Gratification.*** Is it the middle of the night and all the bookstores near you are closed? Are you tired of waiting days, sometimes weeks, for bookstores to ship the novels you bought? Ellora's Cave Publishing sells instantaneous downloads twenty-four hours a day, seven days a week, every day of the year. Our webstore is never closed. Our e-book delivery system is 100% automated, meaning your order is filled as soon as you pay for it.

Those are a few of the top reasons why electronic books are replacing paperbacks for many avid readers.

As always, Ellora's Cave and Cerridwen Press welcome your questions and comments. We invite you to email us at Comments@ellorascave.com or write to us directly at Ellora's Cave Publishing Inc., 1056 Home Avenue, Akron, OH 44310-3502.

Cerridwen Cotillion

The Golden Swan
Phylis Warady

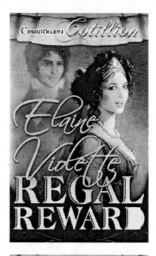

Elaine Violette's
REGAL REWARD

Kate Dolan
A Certain Want of Reason

CAPTAIN'S LADY
Sharon Milburn

Cerrídwen Press

Monthly Newsletter

News
Author Appearances
Book Signings
New Releases
Contests
Author Profiles
Feature Articles

Available online at
www.CerridwenPress.com

Cerridwen Press

Cerridwen, the Celtic goddess of wisdom, was the muse who brought inspiration to storytellers and those in the creative arts.

Cerridwen Press encompasses the best and most innovative stories in all genres of today's fiction.

Visit our website and discover the newest titles by talented authors who still get inspired — much like the ancient storytellers did…

once upon a time.

www.cerridwenpress.com

Printed in the United States
77969LV00001B/25